ABOUT THE AUTHOR

Brian Cunningham is 56 years old and lives in Norfolk with his wife Pauline. They have been happily married for thirty-eight years. He is a father and grandfather, and is known to the grandchildren as Bapou. After a long and unfulfilling career in industry, he now does a little of many things; reading, writing, history, politics, chess, travel, and tries to enjoy himself as if each day were his last.

ISBN-13: 978-1522752691

ISBN-10: 1522752692

ERPINGHAM

Hero of Norfolk

By

Brian Cunningham

DEDICATION

This book is dedicated to the memory of my mother,

Margaret Mary Cunningham,

who died on 7 June 2015.

ACKNOWLEDGMENTS

I am indebted to my good friend Andrew Sangster for his help and guidance on how to get started, and what worked and what didn't. The book would not have seen the light of day without him. For reference, I owe particular thanks to the various works of Philip Ziegler, Marie Louise Bruce, Anne Curry and Juliet Barker, whose knowledge of the subject far exceeds my own.

PREFACE

Who is Norfolk's greatest hero? Horatio Nelson, of course, would be high on any shortlist. There are other names too; Boudicca, Queen of the Iceni; Robert Kett, leader of the 1549 agricultural revolt; Jem Mace, the Victorian champion bare-knuckle boxer; World War One heroine Edith Cavell; Egyptologist Howard Carter, the discoverer of Tutankhamen; four-time Olympic gold medalist rowing champion Sir Matthew Pinsent CBE.

None did more to achieve the accolade than the controversial and enigmatic medieval knight Sir Thomas Erpingham. Born in the troubled and war-torn reign of Edward III, Erpingham's England was decimated by repeated epidemics of plague, where life for all was organised by a feudal system of serfdom and hierarchical obligation, and of religious beliefs and superstitions which would seem alien to most people in our modern, 'enlightened' age. It was an era when the English were rarely at peace with their neighbours, or amongst themselves. When the King was not attempting to suppress rebellion in Scotland, Wales, and Ireland or even among his own English nobility, he was either at war with France, or engaging in complex negotiations and alliances to avoid such a war.

Erpingham's military career spanned five decades, culminating in leading the English archers at Agincourt. He risked the status and prosperity of his family and his own life in choosing exile abroad, invasion of his homeland and in helping a friend usurp the English throne. He was the close confidant of two kings, yet kidnapped and was quite possibly complicit in the murder of a third. He directed the affairs of state, yet never lost focus on his home county of Norfolk and could be considered the founding father of the medieval city of Norwich. He was a pilgrim to the Holy Land and a chivalrous champion at tournaments of arms. He was arbiter in local disputes over the theft of sheep; and negotiator in the surrender of besieged cities, and the betrothal of princesses to kings.

Later in life he bestowed enormous wealth on the county of Norfolk, and particularly the city of Norwich, where his legacy can still be seen everywhere today. If you should visit that fine city, stand at the northern end of the ancient Viking marketplace known as Tombland and look to the east where you will see him still, in effigy, kneeling in prayer with his sword hanging by his side, in the niche above the Cathedral gate which he had built and which bears his name. On that same gate, and in many other historic buildings in Norfolk, you will come across the word 'Yenk', which is said to have been Erpingham's motto. Though its meaning and origin has been lost, it is thought to mean ‘Think’ or ‘Remember’.

Now walk west along Princes Street until you come to Suckling House, a fine old merchant residence, now a cinema and restaurant, and gaze north at the great St. Andrew’s Hall which was rebuilt twice at Erpingham’s expense. You will see his coat of arms repeated between each of the clerestory windows. Look around you at any of the many early 15th century flint-walled churches in the vicinity and you will see the result of the largesse of Sir Thomas Erpingham, and his contemporaries.

Much is known about his life and he features in many histories of the medieval period, of the battle of Agincourt and even in Shakespeare, where we meet him in Henry V, on the eve of that most famous historical battle:

‘Good morrow, old Sir Thomas Erpingham. A good soft pillow for that good white head were better than a churlish turf of France,’ (Henry V, Act IV, Scene 1) whereupon he lends his cloak to the King, so that he may pass unknown amongst the troops, and gauge their morale for the battle to come.

We know much of Erpingham’s deeds and a little about the man himself, but there are gaps in his story. This book sets out to fill those gaps, and to capture his life and times, so that we may ‘Yenk’ this great hero of a bygone age.

PROLOGUE

Jacob ran wild with all the other street children around the marketplaces of Norwich. His gang fought pitched battles with the others up on Mousehold Heath, and he often returned home bruised and bloodied. One day, his mother noticed that a graze on the side of Jacob's nose had failed to heal properly and was suppurating and inflamed. He said that he could not feel it as his face was numb. Over the next few weeks the inflammation spread and Jacob complained of blurred vision and weakness in his muscles. Another wound, long-healed, reopened on his thigh. His mother and father confined him to the barn at the back of the smithy which was his father's business, and the family's livelihood. They brought him food and water but kept their distance and seemed afraid.

One evening, two men appeared at the barn door, both red faced and smelling strongly of beer. They carried long poles with which they motioned that Jacob should precede them out onto the street. He caught the briefest glimpse of his mother, kneeling in the dirt of the smithy and crying while his father stood strong and resolute at the forge, avoiding eye contact with his wife. The men used the stout Ash poles to prod

Jacob along, several paces in front of them. They did not inflict any unnecessary hurt and seemed to want to just keep their distance from the boy. Jacob sobbed quietly, hard bitter tears.

He did not speak and nor did the two city wardens as they walked up Magdalen Street and through the city gate. They kept walking north for several hundred yards, their way lit by flaming tar torches carried by the two men.

On the right, and set back from the road loomed the flint walls and round-arched doorway of Magdalen House. Jacob was pushed one last time toward the doorway where his arm was taken by a hooded figure who also carried a flickering torch. Beneath the hood he saw the face of a middle-aged woman, grossly disfigured, yet kindly and welcoming to the child. A heavy wooden door closed behind him as Jacob entered the house of the lepers.

***

CHAPTER 1

(In which we meet our hero as a child, and join him on an eventful journey to Norwich with the harvest)

Before we begin, let me ask you a question. How will you know if the account that follows is true; that it bears accurate testament to the man that was Sir Thomas Erpingham? He is dead now and cannot answer, and I will no doubt shortly join him. I assert that I am as reliable a narrator as you will find, though I did not know him for much of his life, and rely for this manuscript almost entirely on the testament of others. If he was an evil man; roasted the children of his enemies on the spit for fun, and nobody reported such crimes to me, then for the sake of posterity they may as well not have happened. Likewise, if he glided through his days like an angel upon a cloud, dispensing wealth and succour to all in need, and none thought it apt to tell me, then those kindly deeds will be known only to God. I am content to record whatever testimony I am offered.

Now I sit here in the shack that I have called home for countless years, drinking myself stupid on the mead that I brew with honey from my own hives, and occasionally I am joined by old friends and acquaintances, until recently Sir Thomas himself among them, who drink away the hours and reminisce, while I scribble. It is a pleasant enough occupation for an old man.

Rufus Long is with me now, recounting a story that his own father had told him, of a time when Sir Thomas was a mere child. I pour from the jug and settle to my pen while he looks out over the pasture to the low hills beyond, recalling days before he himself was even born.

***

Several babies had been delivered dead and just one had breathed for a short time; a scrawny purple whelp, before Anne of Erpingham was eventually blessed by the grace of God with a fine strong son. Her prayers had been fervent; that the boy should stay close by her as he grew, to watch over all that was theirs and not follow his father abroad to die like a dog in some foreign ditch. The Erpinghams had held their manor and hundred by right of blood for generations, and answered only to the old Duchess and her to none but the King, and him only to God. Anne used to say that if theirs was a house that allowed blasphemies and heresies, which it did not, then they could be said to work their land but three steps from heaven.

At that time, everyone in the manor worked, including the lady of the house. All the wives and children and old men bent to the task, while Sir John led his troop of local muscle to serve in foreign lands. Good family men away for months or years at a time, laden down with bow, mallet, pike and stave, to lay siege to castles and rout hordes of painted savages and make waste of other people's lands. Meanwhile, those that remained at home sowed and nurtured and reaped and stored, lest the crops wilt and blacken in the fields for want of the labour to harvest them.

It had been early springtime when the King's messenger brought the summons. Sir John's obligation, this time, had been to provide and finance six men at arms and twenty archers, plus equipment, horses and servants. They were to join with the King's second son, Lionel of Antwerp, on a punitive expedition to Ireland to put down the rebellious aspirations of a group of Irish lords, by force if negotiation failed. They had cantered away from Norwich to cheers of adulation from a drunken and bloodthirsty crowd; nearly sixty young men in total, noblemen and serfs, full of pride and barely concealed excitement, and deeply hidden fear. It was Whitsun, and the late cherry blossom still clung to the trees in the Cathedral gardens.

Then autumn came with the crop heavy in the fields. Thomas grew strong and straight and healthy as befitted the future lord of the manor. He swung the scythe and fork like a peasant and in the evenings wrote his French and Latin, under the eye of Brother Anselmo, staying at the manor as tutor for the boy at Sir John's bidding, from the Abbey out in the wetland at St. Benet Holme.

One evening in late September, everyone at the manor house was tired, having worked a full day at what remained of the harvest; the dirt of the fields still jammed hard under their finger-nails. Thomas picked constantly at a thorn splinter wedged in the meat of his thumb. His mother told him to soak it in vinegar to keep it from festering. Even Anselmo, who nominally helped alongside everyone else, but more often skulked in the hedgerows, was tetchy and ready for his straw and pallet. He whacked the boy irritably on the knuckles with a hazel switch when he failed to concentrate on his letters. Thomas stared at him defiantly and earned another blow. Anne thought that if the monk were not her husband's creature she would have him thrown outside with the pigs where he belonged. Tallow candles flickered and smoked in the evening breeze which came down from the north, bringing with it the faint kelpy salt flavour of the sea. The household readied themselves for sleep.

As Thomas settled in his corner, the maidservant from the village sang a local song, part ballad part lullaby, to herself mainly, as the boy was evidently not listening. He checked carefully in the small wooden box at the foot of his bed to ensure the stag beetle he had found that morning in the hedge was still alive, and checked beneath his straw pillow for his collection of treasures; a flint arrowhead from antiquity, the rock-like impression of an ancient fish trapped inside a stone, a crystal of quartz and one of pyrite, a small paring knife in the sheath of a dagger which he did not know that his mother knew he had stolen from the kitchens. It was just one of several items which had mysteriously disappeared in recent weeks.

The monk approached the mistress of the house; head bowed and sat at the window ledge looking out over the home farm to the fields beyond in the gathering darkness. He did not speak at first but she knew there was something on his mind and she sensed some vague ill purpose, without being able to put her finger on the reason why. She did not easily forgive the malicious striking of her son and did not acknowledge his presence, but continued reading the list of produce they would be taking to market the next day, prepared with great care and precision by the family's oldest and most trustworthy servant, William Long.

At length Brother Anselmo coughed quietly and turned to face her, voicing three questions and a statement, without preamble.

'Is the decision made, mistress? Do we travel tomorrow? By which route? There's plague in Aylsham.' The thing they feared most, more than war, more than famine, they feared a return of the great pestilence more than the devil's visit, or the damnation of a priest.

'Then we'll give the town a wide margin. We leave tomorrow and will close the house here for the winter. I am heartily sick of scraping mud from my boots.'

'And the fruits of our labours? To market yes, in Norwich, but think too of my brothers at the Abbey; do they not labour at God's work? A cart-load, no more, as right and just tithe?' It seemed that every utterance from him took the form of a question.

'My husband will settle all dues with your Abbot when he returns.' She stared hard at Anselmo and he met her gaze for a moment, then looked downwards and turned his head away. She thought she detected a smirk and felt, not for the first time, that she would be glad to see the back of this one. She knew he was right though, to query their intended route; to travel south by way of Aylsham would be dangerous; the plague was no respecter of quality and would take a Lord's woman and her son as readily as a man of the cloth. Yet there was no other route that would get them and their harvest goods to market in no more than two days. Norwich was twenty miles south via the only good road and with their herds and flock setting the pace, the hours would pass quicker than the miles.

Dawn came early still at that time of the year, with a light mist trailing over the newly stripped fields upon which the pigs were already turned out and rooting up whatever remained of the turnip and parsnip main-crops. Up there, close by the coast, it was never the usual sounds of a country dawn that woke the household; cows lowing to be milked or roosters making their dawn racket, but sea-gulls shrieking as they dived among the scavenging pigs to snatch whatever they could. Already, Anne found herself longing for the more civilised dawn sounds of the family house in Norwich, snug and safe in the lee of the castle keep, the bells of fifty churches competing, the rush and gurgle of the Wensum in autumn spate. Yet she knew that before the spring she would be yearning again for their ancestral home, the manor house in leafy Erpingham, quiet and remote, but the centre of her world.

The maidservant stirred milk and honey into a pot of crushed oats which was bubbling on the hot bricks around the hearth, the big fire still smoky from the green and damp kindling she had used to reignite last evening's faintly glowing embers. The smell of the sweet porridge roused Thomas from his slumber, though Anselmo snored on loudly from beneath his pile of blankets and furs. None chose to wake him.

William Long approached as they were finishing breakfast and took a seat opposite Anne at the oak trestle table. He was a small man, barely five feet tall in his boots, and his name had always been a thorn in his side, yet he commanded the greatest respect among the farm workers and local villagers, who did his bidding without question. He spoke confidently and with familiarity; the family had never encouraged formality in their trusted retainers and William was a friend as much as a paid servant.

'The reckoning is checked Ma'am, and checked again. It will have been a modest year at best and that only if we get everything into market while the prices still hold. Still, we'll none of us starve this winter coming.' The maid passed him a steaming bowl of porridge and he blew on it reflectively while continuing to peruse the account document. The complexity of the harvest arrangements always astounded Anne, the wages owed, the loans repaid, the local storehouses to be filled, the tithes to Church and Abbey, the donations to the lepers at Magdalen House, the commissions for replacement equipment for the following season. She wondered there was anything left for market, yet still there would be a train of more than thirty carts that day, among the herds of sheep and cattle driven to Norwich. She thought they should be thankful for the recent rains dampening down the dry earth, lest the train raise a cloud of dirt around them so thick they would miss the city altogether.

As William ate his breakfast a succession of local men entered the hall and approached the table, each one bowing and tipping their soft felt caps toward Anne, but speaking directly to the seated man. She was reminded again that they were all either too old for the task at hand or too young or in some way infirm, not one of them in his prime; all such men were away cleaving skulls and whoring and running about the countryside like madmen with her husband. William gave quick confident orders, and the men were fast away about their business. They needed to be on the road before the sun was much above the church bell-tower if they were to make camp a safe distance south of Aylsham that night, and enter Norwich before nightfall the following day.

Though much of the preparation for departure had been accomplished in the previous days, and some of the men had been up and working through most of the night, there was still much to do. Anne heard the thump and clash of hooves on hard mud and flint, and the shouts and curses and jostling for position as chaos unfolded in the courtyard below. A variety of carts and wagons, already loaded with produce, were being hitched to horses and bullocks as a caravan of sorts began to take shape. Pigs squealed in terror as they were forced onto a caged wagon, each pig wedged in tight between his neighbours. The cattle and sheep were mustered in the fields behind the home farm, herdsmen and shepherds with their dogs forming a loose perimeter. They would set off first, setting the pace for the whole convoy, but only once sufficient armed outriders had been dispatched to deter the various brigands and thieves who would doubtless track the convey all the way to the very outskirts of Norwich, picking off whatever they could like carrion.

Anselmo had risen and gone outside to his ablutions while William and Anne were talking. They rose from the table and, together with the boy Thomas, made their way across the busy great hallway and out into the courtyard. It was just beginning to get fully light. Some semblance of order was beginning to take shape and several of the old men and boys who made up the household retinue were already mounted on horses, ponies or donkeys while others were seated on heavily laden carts. They were arguing about how much they ought to be paid for this work. It seemed to Anne that she had heard little else from their kind in the last twenty years, since the great pestilence had put most of their ilk in the ground and created a great competition among those who laboured for their daily bread.

William would ride a small horse, not much bigger than a child's pony and was to be dispatched ahead to check the road, keep an eye out for trouble and fetch help if it was needed. The monk would ride his own mule, a cantankerous beast who was not unlike its master in that respect, with a mind of its own, but which seemed to have formed a bond with the man of God. He looked ridiculous riding with his feet almost touching the ground and his dark cloak dragging in the dirt, but seemed unaware of the mirth his progress generated among the peasants. Anne and Thomas would travel in a part-covered wagon, in a recess behind the driver which had been lined with furs and blankets, and would carry with them their more portable wealth in coin, jewels and gold, secreted in a compartment beneath their feet. They could have travelled ahead by fast horse and been in Norwich that night, but there was much danger on the roads for a woman and child travelling light, and Anne judged that safety in numbers was their better option.

While Anne and William surveyed progress for departure out in the courtyard, Anselmo had thrown some water on his face and, stepping outside the rear door of the house, had urinated copiously against the wall of the building, spraying from side to side and aiming as high as he could reach. With a satisfied sigh he had returned to the great hall and helped himself to a breakfast of bread and porridge, washed down with weak beer. With his belly full, the monk sat in contemplation for several minutes then went back outside and squatted over a bucket that had been left by the rear door for that purpose. He cleaned himself with some dock leaves, which grew in profusion around the fence of the nearby pig-sty, and then returned indoors, leaving the contents of the bucket to be disposed of later by the maidservant.

He checked that nobody was about and then ascended the stairway which led to Anne's bedchamber. He could see that the corridor had been recently swept and thought it unlikely that he would be disturbed by any of the servants. Anselmo entered the room and looked about for likely plunder. His eye fell on a pair of finely wrought candlestick holders on the windowsill and he deftly slipped them into a large pocket concealed within the voluminous folds of his cloak. Before making his exit, the monk looked around the room again and hesitated; the absence of the pieces looked obvious and there were dust marks showing where they had stood. He carefully replaced them on the window ledge and chose instead a small silver tray from amongst the jumble of items on a dressing table, which Anselmo thought would not be immediately missed. As he turned to leave the room, the monk's fingers played across the fine embroidered material of the bedcovering. He picked up the pillow and held it to his face, inhaling the aroma of the lavender pouches inside the linen cover, mixed with the gentle scent of Anne's nocturnal perspiration. He stood for several seconds, lost in a world of frustration and covetousness. Replacing all as he had found it,

Anselmo returned to the great hall and then went outside again by the rear door, walking briskly along a pathway through the home gardens in order not to miss a pre-arranged appointment up at the manor gates.

Unaware of the invasion of her privacy and the theft of her property, Anne's eyes traversed the great courtyard to see if all seemed well, and she noticed Brother Anselmo up by the main gates talking to a man on horse-back. As the rider wheeled round and cantered off southwards she noticed that his mount was a piebald with unusual and distinctive markings. She wondered momentarily what message he had brought for the priest; news of further cases of plague spread from the outbreak at Aylsham perhaps, or tidings from his Abbot, or news of prices in the market at Norwich, but quickly her attention was taken with organising their departure and she thought no more of the matter. Anne spoke a few words to the housemaid and several others who were staying behind to close down the big house for the winter. She and Thomas mounted the sturdy old cart, which was harnessed to a pair of fine plough-horses, getting a hand up from the driver who was a huge old farmhand with a grip so strong she feared he would break the bones in their hands. They settled themselves in, Thomas with his treasures in a pouch at his side, so excited at the prospect of the journey that he looked as though he might burst. At a signal from William the great convoy began to move out through the main gates towards the southerly road, and the harvest caravan was on its way.

Progress was slow and frustrating as both cattle and sheep seemed determined to head north toward the coast and there was much shouting, whistling and cursing from men and much lowing, bleating and bellowing from beasts before they were all heading south on the well-travelled roadway. The road surface was already in poor condition, rutted and pot-holed as the Felbrigg herds had passed through a few days earlier in pouring rain and the mud surface had dried in hard lumps, hillocks and water-filled depressions. They bounced around in their wagon like two peas in a dried pod.

Of their first day's journey there was little enough to tell. They ran the gauntlet of the usual roadside beggars, entertainers, musicians, whores, beer-sellers and quack doctors along the way; each having staked out his, or her, own stretch of the road in anticipation of their coming, their patch defended with fierce aggression against interlopers. Occasionally, the convoy passed timbered buildings, no more than sheds really, rough inns where travellers were lured into an overnight stay and often robbed or worse before the dawn broke. A beggar priest approached their wagon offering phials of the true Christ's blood and the teeth and finger-bones of a variety of saints. He was given short shrift by Anselmo, who made it clear there was room for one man of God only on the road that day.

As the convoy approached the outskirts of Aylsham they saw the warning skull and bones chalked on walls and out-buildings, a clear message to stay away. Anne and Thomas held their posies up hard against their mouths and noses, the lavender scent strong and heady mixed with the sharp fragrant lemon balm, the two in combination a deterrent and even a possible cure for the plague, depending on whether you believed Jonas the Healer in Erpingham, or Father John the parish priest who took the view that ardent prayer alone was sufficient.

There was no sign of anyone about, but in the distance behind the church they saw a vast pit had been dug, the mound of earth clearly visible against the green backdrop of the fields and woods behind. From close by the pit a great fire was raging and thick white smoke was rising sluggishly in the still air. There was a faint, sweet cloying odour. A thin layer of greyish ash coated the leaves of the trees and the tops of the walls in the lane leading into the town. Anne's eye was drawn to a clump of ash against the lee of a barn wall which had seemed to flicker and shift momentarily. The mound moved and resolved itself into a pale and filthy little girl of perhaps seven or eight years, no older than the boy Thomas. She had been sitting a long time; there was no disturbance in the layer of ash coating the road around her. She stared at them as the cart passed and mouthed something which Anne could not hear. As the girl tried to speak, blood and pus seeped from sores on her tongue and lips. She had been crying and watery blood and mucus had cut pink rivulets through the caked dirt on her face. There was no one to help her, not even to fetch water to drink. She would be dead by morning, if she was lucky and God willing.

They left the town in their wake and continued south as the afternoon drew on. There was more smoke in the air as the wheat stubble in the surrounding fields was burnt off before the plough and team were set to work. Flocks of pigeons and crows wheeled above them, settling on newly dug fields and rooting for grubs and worms in the freshly turned soil. The sun was low in the sky when William rode back to their cart to report that field and lodging had been found for the night with a gentleman farmer who was in debt to Sir John. A convoy such as theirs which took plenty of getting going was equally difficult to stop and there was, not for the first time that day, much cursing and swearing. Eventually, with herd and flock safe and other livestock temporarily penned, a guard was posted and they sought their beds. Anne declined the proffered hospitality of their farmer host, and she and Thomas shared a modest but comfortable bed in which they both slept soundly until dawn.

They were awake early and after a standing breakfast of milk and hard, flat scones, the chaos commenced anew. The morning had dawned misty and cold, even the faint trace of an early frost in the grass of the meadow. Anne watched as a buzzard circled above a stand of oak and elm trees at the far end of the field, being harried by a pair of crows who objected to the raptor encroaching on their territory. Eventually, Thomas came to find her to say that all was ready to commence their journey. She felt confident that they would be in Norwich by late afternoon, certainly before dark.

As the morning wore on to early afternoon, she became aware that several mounted men were following alongside the train using a series of pathways away to the west of their road. They were always in view but never close enough to identify. There had been no attempts to steal any of the herd or produce yet and she wondered if the gang would try to isolate a few cows or sheep on the edge of their convoy and make off with them. Anne confided her concerns to William and they agreed that he would ride on ahead to Norwich, which was now only five miles distant, and return with a company of city men to give them a strong guard and deterrent for the final few miles. She and Thomas watched him disappear into the distance, so small on his pony that he seemed no more than a child.

An hour or so later they crested the brow of a hill in a forest of ash trees and Anne could instantly see turmoil ahead. The progress of the herd had been blocked by fallen trees and the log-jam effect had horse and bullock teams running into the back of the cart in front, and people and horses and sheep and cows milling around and pushing off to the sides of the road and into the fields beyond. As both man and beast fought to regain direction and control, Anne looked away to her right and saw the group of mounted followers wheel their horses left and approach the column across a wheat-stubble field. They made straight for the covered wagon in which she was travelling and as they got nearer she noticed the distinctive black and white piebald markings she had seen on the strange rider's mount the previous morning.

By this time the column was stationary as the train of beasts and wagons backed up ahead. The leading rider spurred his mount up the embankment to the road and she saw that he was no messenger boy, but a full grown man in a cloak with a hood obscuring his face. Anselmo and his mule were between them and Anne was certain that a word or gesture passed between them, and then the mounted man was at their cart.

'What do you need from us? How can we help you?' she asked, not yet fully convinced that his purpose was ill. The rider threw back his hood and Anne was momentarily taken aback at the deformity of his face. His upper lip and palate were cleft badly so that his lower jaw appeared to abut the base of his nose. The bone and cartilage of his nose seemed to have collapsed, leaving just the dark cave of what had once been two distinct nostrils. She found it difficult to tell if these facial abnormalities were the result of a birth defect, disease or from a blow from axe or sword. When he spoke it was with a lisping whisper and he did so without opening his mouth more than a fraction, as if he was self-conscious about his appearance and wished to disguise the ruin of his face.

'I will take what you carry, there beneath your feet.' He pointed downwards to the furs that lined the floor of the cart and the hidden compartment therein. Anne noticed that the finger he pointed with was an ugly deformed knob, and she wondered if in fact he was a leper, or even one of the few who survived that disease and lived the rest of their days with the marks of leprosy upon them.

Their driver, to his credit, told the robber to be on his way, but was quickly dragged from his seat by several of the other riders who compelled his silence at sword-point. Anne tried to speak and looked around desperately for help, but in truth she was terrified and had already resolved to hand over their valuables. One or two of the older men were close by, but they looked away in fear and she did not blame them for that; to intervene on her behalf would mean certain death.

While she sat in panic, pale and unable to speak coherently, Anne became aware that Thomas had moved round to stand in front of her. She could see that he had the little paring knife concealed in his right hand. The mounted thief swung down off his horse, jumping up onto the bed of the cart and raising his arm as if to strike her son. Rather than shy away, Thomas took a step closer, and his mother could see that the man's exposed knee and calf was now within the boy's striking range. The thief tried to land a blow but Thomas was too quick, ducking under the flailing fist and his assailant temporarily lost his balance, grabbing onto the driver's seat to prevent himself from falling. Anne tried to clutch at her son, to hold him close and shield him from danger, but he pulled away from her with the strength of one twice his size. As the robber lunged to grab her, Thomas darted in again and swung his arm in a half circle, thumping the small blade into the tendon and sinew behind the man's knee. The robber screamed and swatted Thomas aside with his forearm, grasping at the wound in his leg, more engrossed in his injury for the moment than in his prize.

Suddenly, there was the sound of commotion ahead and both Anne and her attacker looked and saw a troop of twenty or so Norwich men on horseback pushing though the crowded flock of sheep on the roadway towards them. At their head rode their own William Long, sword drawn and a fierce expression on his face. The thief limped down off the cart, clutching at his leg which was welling blood and, with evident pain, mounted his horse again. At a signal from him the gang galloped off across the field and into the woodland beyond. Anne caught Anselmo's eye and he looked back at her in panic, then toward the approaching rescue party, and then back to his mistress again. Suddenly, decision made, he kicked the mule hard in the ribs and trotted away after the departing gang. As the troop of Norwich men finally reached them she saw him disappear into the tree-line and the forest beyond. Anne swore silent vengeance on the viper Anselmo, one who had shared her family's home and food, then sold them to rogues, who would rob and murder them all.

William approached and quickly ascertained that Anne was unhurt then picked the boy up who had been knocked to the floor. Thomas grinned at them both and dabbed cautiously at the blood coming from his nose with the sleeve of his cloak. His mother held him close to her breast and felt his young heart pounding in his chest. He was a frightened child, but only the two of them knew.

As the convey finally began again on the last leg to Norwich, so the story of what had happened started to spread through the ranks of their people, and in that way the legend of Thomas Erpingham was begun.

***

For the first few days Jacob sat in a dark corner, terrified of the inhabitants of this place. Gradually, though, he became accustomed to seeing deformity and ugliness and noticed that nobody seemed to want to hurt him, that in fact they ignored him entirely. He found clean water to quench his thirst from a rain water trough behind the building, but by the third day he was very hungry. He set off to explore and found that there were several outbuildings linked to the main house by pathways. In one of these he found a refectory with roughly hewn wooden trestle tables and benches and at the far end of the room a vast iron pot suspended by a heavy chain over a fireplace. The woman who had greeted him at the doorway on his first night was tending the pot, cutting up carrots and stirring them into the stew. She beckoned him to come forward and filled a wooden bowl with thick vegetable broth. Jacob had no spoon and raised the bowl to his lips, slurping down the food noisily, oblivious to its scalding heat. The woman stayed his hand.

'You must be careful now. Your skin may be numbed to the heat but it will still burn you and when you blister it may

not heal as it once did. The slightest injury sustained here could mean your death.'

Jacob asked the woman what she was called, but she told him that she preferred to forget her given name because it linked her to a past which had ceased to exist.

'Most people here call me Mother.'

When Jacob had filled his stomach, Mother gave him a wicker basket and sent him outside. Up by the ditch that ran alongside the Wroxham road, he found a great pile of half-rotted vegetables, heaped up where they had been dumped by well-meaning townsfolk. He began to sift through the pile, picking out the best and cutting away rotten ends and roots with a knife he had found in the basket. With each loaded basket he returned to the refectory where Mother eyed what he had brought and selected the best only for the pot.

'There'll be time enough to eat poor stuff this winter, for now we'll pick and choose as if we are buying in the marketplace.'

Jacob worked hard all day and Mother asked him if he wished to help her on a regular basis. He slept that night on good straw and could feel the warmth of the embers of the cooking fire. He did not mention to Mother that he had nicked the tip of his left index finger with the paring knife.

***

CHAPTER 2

(In which the captain of a troop of English archers teaches young Thomas when to stand and fight, and when to run away)

I tend my hives, oblivious to the bee stings; I have been stung so many times that the poison no longer affects me. The old archer is here this evening; he has walked the short distance from the village along the lane to my shack, keen to taste the latest batch. He sets his penny down on the table and swats ineffectually with his one good arm at the bees which circle his head. I advise him to be still and we share news and talk of mundane matters. He seems in a melancholy and nostalgic mood and I pour a mug of mead and ask him to tell me a story of his youth. The old warrior sits on the bench and rests his feet on a stool, smiling as he remembers.

***

The captain thought that the august sun might burn them all black, there on the Biscay coast of France. It was not the sun he knew of the hills around Shrewsbury, which rarely appeared from behind the clouds for long and, when it did, just singed you a little, raising freckles and reddening noses. This sun burned with a fierce intensity, day after blistering day, and his lads were all starting to look like Moors. They had been out in it for weeks on end with little shade, and nothing much to occupy them. What do you do with a troop of longbow-men, when the sun is shining and there is nothing to shoot at?

Still, they had drawn easy enough duties that day. Some of the other men had been detailed to dig latrines outside the perimeter of the camp. That was hot, sweaty work in the heat and dust and flies. He thought that if their lordships would get on and agree who ruled this piece of land, then they might all be able to sleep in comfortable beds inside the city walls, rather than in tents out there on the plain, like gypsies.

His orders were to look after the son of one of Prince Edward's retinue of noblemen, Sir John Erpingham of Norfolk, who was with the negotiating party. He was to give this boy a gentle introduction to military life over the course of a few days, ensuring that he was not exposed to risk or danger. This education was to continue while his father helped set out the case for unity of the kingdoms of Aquitaine and England, a subject about which, frankly, the captain cared little so long as he and his men were paid what they were owed. The boy, Thomas, was with them today for the first time, a likeable lad who was not yet a man but no longer a child, already tall and with a shock of unkempt straw coloured hair, and the faint beginnings of a wispy, adolescent beard. He had a degree of confidence, as you might expect from a nobleman's son, but his youth made him a little bashful, and quick to blush. He asked the captain to introduce him to the men of the troop.

'That filthy looking bag of offal sitting on the log is Maggot. Let your breakfast settle before you ask him to explain why we call him by that name.' he pointed toward a grubby looking man of twenty odd years with long, dirty and matted hair, tied in a loose pony-tail at the back. He was bare-chested, like the other members of the troop, and just wore short trousers and leather sandals. His shirt, helmet, leather jerkin, boots and leggings, along with his bow, quiver, mallet and other archer's paraphernalia, were piled up in the lee of a derelict farm building on the edge of their section of the camp. He had the sharp, pointy features of a ferret, and grinned back at the boy, exposing a mouthful of crooked and rotting teeth, then went back to whittling the initials of his real name, S H for Silas Holm, with his dagger on the bark of the felled tree.

'The big lump over by the water trough is Koenig. I found him in a tavern in Shrewsbury, blind drunk and wanting to fight all comers. God knows what he was doing there, probably came to England as a mercenary and got left behind after some battle or other. He only speaks something that sounds a bit like the German tongue, so don't expect much by way of conversation.' The giant blond warrior poured a jug of cold water over his head, and shook himself like a wet dog. He gave their young guest a half wave; half salute, then thumped his chest and howled like a wolf. Thomas looked at the captain quizzically, but he just shrugged. They had all become used to the strange mannerisms of this foreigner, and learned to communicate effectively with him in various non-verbal ways. He was strong and loyal and could shoot straight, and that was enough.

Next, the captain introduced their visitor to The Pope, so named because, when not firing a murderous rain of iron tipped arrows on an enemy, he was constantly worrying his rosary beads, mouthing the Hail Marys and Our Fathers, in an endless litany. The Pope nodded a greeting, and continued with his prayers. Finally, Thomas shook hands with Pretty Boy Jones, the troop's youngest archer. Boyishly handsome and barely even shaving yet, he was only a few years older than Thomas. Jones was the butt of many of their jokes, but was a superb archer and held in high regard by all.

The captain was struck by the thought that this was all that remained of his troop from those that had set out from Shrewsbury, several months before. Finch and Jack Miller had both died on the road south from Calais, marching in gut-wrenching agony as watery excrement dribbled down the backs of their legs, victims of the bloody flux which had decimated their numbers that summer. He had buried them both at the roadside, with little ceremony. Fat Duncan, who had been more suited to the life of a public house landlord than that of an archer, had been lost in the harbour at Dover even before they sailed; toppled overboard when drunk and got himself crushed between their boat and the jetty.

'Me, they call Stretch. Good name for a bowman, eh? John Stretch, I'm the captain of this little band of Shropshire's finest.'

As Stretch showed Thomas where he was to stow his gear, the boy drew the captain aside and addressed him quietly, with a look of embarrassment and consternation.

'My father Sir John, and Grandfather Sir Robert before him, both commanded men such as these in battle. I am told that I must too, when I'm a little older. But how? I don't even know what to say to them.'

Stretch answered as best he could. 'Don't tell them son, show them!'

They were off to shoot some practice arrows, to keep their hand in just in case Prince Edward got tired of talking, and decided to break a few heads. The men gathered up their gear and headed off towards the sand dunes to the south of the city walls, at the mouth of a small river. Young Thomas walked among them asking relentless excited questions about their equipment. He offered to carry The Pope's longbow, and ended up lugging kit for everyone. The boy could not stop staring at Koenig, who looked like a small mountain on legs. All of the regular archers had built huge strength in their right arms, and around the right side of their torsos. The muscles of their left side were also strong and well developed, but looked puny in comparison, except for Maggot, who shot lefty, and so was built up the opposite way to the rest of the troop. It was said that a longbow-man looked deformed, almost like a hunchback, but they wore the body build of their trade with pride.

Their route led them around the city wall and past the southern gate. They crossed the roadway and found themselves among rough lodging houses and taverns, built of timber and tied in to the walls of the city itself. A large gang of local men were leaning on a rail outside one of the inns, drinking wine from skin bags. The troop were subjected to jeers and whistles, English soldiers had a well-deserved reputation for taking what did not belong to them, and they were less than popular with the locals. They gave the gang the old two fingers, gesture of an archer's derision since the French had introduced the infamous practice of lopping off the right-hand index and middle fingers of captured English longbow-men so they could no longer draw a bow-string. The troop moved on into the dunes, aware that they were obliged to avoid trouble with their noble young visitor in their care. Thomas was still full of questions.

'Stretch, why do you all carry the blackened arrow scar on your shoulder?' He was referring to the badge of belonging of their small company, the image of an ascending arrow, cut into the flesh of the right shoulder with a hot knife, then a mix of tar and black linen dye rubbed into the open wound to permanently blacken the scar tissue.

'That's a thing you earn the right to wear. Other troops have their own mark, this one is ours.' Stretch touched the slightly raised scar with the fingers of his left hand and smiled discretely when saw Thomas flex his biceps to make his own shoulder look more muscular. He slipped an arrow out of his quiver and gave it to the boy to look at, then explained some important facts.

'Everybody thinks it's all about the bow. This cut of Yew, that length, this grip, that weight, this type of gut for binding. None of that is true. The only important thing about your bow is that you always use the same one. It becomes part of your body, and your muscles learn its ways, and it gets so that the bow fits you, and you fit the bow. If I borrowed The Pope's bow, I couldn't hit a damn thing with it. Remember that, and don't ever let your own bow out of your sight.'

Thomas pressed the hard iron tip of the arrow with his thumb and ran his hand along the yard-long length of the arrow's wooden shaft and through the goose feather quills of the flight.

'The arrow is the key. It has to be well made, so it stays true in flight. Take my advice, find yourself a decent fletcher, and keep on the right side of him. More important, the arrows in your quiver must be all of a type, the same weight and dimensions with good straight shafts. A decent longbow-man, with good arrows, can put ten into the same gatepost at one hundred yards, inside a minute.'

The boy whistled and asked if he would be allowed to try a shot. Stretch laughed, and passed the boy his bow to try out. Thomas laid down the equipment he was carrying and set himself up in the correct position, sideways on to an imaginary target, and attempted to draw the heavy bow. Even with all his strength, he could only draw the bow to halfway. He looked embarrassed, but Stretch told him not to worry and showed him some exercises to build his upper body strength. Meanwhile, Pretty Boy had run on ahead and placed a circular marker made of woven straw, dyed red and about the size of a dinner charger, on the upper slope of one of the sand dunes. He pegged the marker in place with some hazel sticks, and then paced out one hundred and fifty yards back towards the troop. He threw down his jerkin at the firing point and joined the others, who were stretching and limbering up.

'Maggot, get up here and give us a wind marker.' shouted the captain. Maggot stepped up to the firing point, fitted an arrow to his bow and aimed directly at the target. As he drew the bow to its fullest extent the muscles in his upper torso tensed and hardened and there was a moment when he and the taut, straining bow were inseparable, part of the same colossal war engine. Then he let loose and with a great *whoosh* the arrow was away, rising at first into the blue sky, then levelling off and downward toward the target. A strong breeze was blowing steadily off the ocean and it carried the arrow several feet to the right of the target where it thumped into the sand, and imbedded itself halfway up the shaft. The distance was perfect. Now each archer stepped up to shoot, aiming to the left to compensate for the wind and within three or four attempts they were all peppering the target disc.

They spent much of the afternoon firing arrow after

arrow, up-wind, down-wind, cross-wind, from above, from below. They began at long-range with stationary targets and ended up taking pot-shots at seagulls in flight, with Pretty Boy actually winging one. Thomas ran to and fro, collecting arrows which he was able to pull with ease from the sand dunes. The arrows were still in perfect condition and Stretch explained an important lesson.

'If you use a tree, or a side of beef, for target practice, it'll feel more satisfying, but your arrows will be finished. Snap the shafts off to save the feathers, that'll be about your only option. That's why we use the sand dunes or the soft mud of river banks when we're inland. Look after your arrows, don't waste them!'

They gathered their kit and walked back towards camp as the sun prepared to set down on the far distant ocean horizon. As they reached the road by the southern city gate, a group of men appeared in front of them and blocked their path. The troop was out-numbered by three or four to one and the gang were drunk and belligerent. Stretch recognised one who had abused them earlier in the day; these were the local men who had been drinking in the tavern against the city wall. He noticed Koenig reach for his quiver, but stayed his hand; they were under orders to avoid danger to their guest, lest he be injured, killed or kidnapped for ransom.

'Do exactly as I do.' he instructed his men, and the boy. They pushed through the crowd and several of the gang drew knives. Maggot had a dagger in his hand and walked backwards, waving the blade in a wide arc, covering their retreat. They were spat upon and Stretch felt his rage boiling up, but he steadied the men as best he could.

'With me boys, with me!' he shouted, as they continued to put distance between themselves and the drunken mob, walking though, not running. A tall, dark-skinned man, with the pock-marked face of one who had survived small-pox as a child, called out.

'Les chiens!'

Two handlers came forward from the dark recess of the building, holding a pair of great hunting dogs on heavy leather leashes. The dogs slavered and howled for the chase. They were of a wolf-like breed, and stood as tall as a man's thigh. Each one scrabbled at the dirt with its fore-paws, seeking the purchase that would hurl it forward and at the throat of its prey. Stretch signalled to Maggot, three fingers, to the right. It meant they should split up; him, The Pope and Jones, away to the right around the city wall to create a diversion, while Koenig and Stretch got the boy away safe and straight back to the camp. He judged the moment was upon them.

'Run!' shouted Stretch, and they were away like the wind, the boy keeping good pace with the older men. He looked back once and saw that the Frenchmen had given them a start, for the better sport. As they reached about one hundred yards distance, the handlers let slip the leather leashes and the hounds were away, one veering right to chase Maggot's group, the other after Stretch, Koenig and the boy and gaining fast. He glanced at Thomas, expecting panic, fear, but saw the boy's blood was up. Thomas gave a wild grin and in that moment Stretch knew the measure of the man he would become. Suddenly, Koenig jinked away to the left, behind a small outcrop of rocks, but Thomas and Stretch kept running, laden down with the gear they were carrying and beginning to tire.

They were both aware that the hound was almost upon them, and Stretch pulled his knife and prepared to turn. He saw that Thomas had done likewise, and wondered momentarily where the boy's blade had appeared from. Without a word, they stopped and turned to face the dog. The beast was coming fast, fangs bared and eyes blazing, strings of slobber running back along its snout. The great wolf was ready to jump when there was a *thunk* as Koenig's arrow skewered the animal through the gut, the iron tip exiting through the hound's chest. The dog went down in the dirt, whimpering and pulling at the arrow shaft with its teeth, hot blood frothing and pulsing at both entrance and exit wounds, until Stretch opened its throat with his blade, and all was quiet and still again, except for their hearts which were pounding in their breasts.

Now the men were also coming fast, some with swords drawn. They ran again and were soon within the safe circle of the sentry archer's range around the camp. Their pursuers fell back and, gathering up the carcass of their hound, returned toward the city walls. The three of them found water to drink and squatted down on their haunches against a wall, breathing hard.

'Good Arrow!' said Stretch to Koenig, miming the action so he understood. He had hit dead centre, a fast moving target with the angle changing constantly as the distance increased. It was a superb shot, one of the best Stretch had seen. Koenig gave a big grin and suddenly the hysteria that often follows battle was upon them, and the three of them started laughing uncontrollably.

An hour passed and the full darkness of a moonless night descended. They paced the strip of land in front of their tents, resolving every few minutes to go in search of their friends, and then always deciding to give it ten minutes more. Finally, they saw three figures move into the flickering light of the oil lanterns and there were Maggot and The Pope supporting a figure which must be Jones. He stumbled between them and Stretch could see that his shirt had been torn into strips, and his face bandaged heavily with the cloth. They brought him into Stretch's tent and laid him down on the pallet. The Pope unwrapped the bandage gently, and Stretch could quickly see that the flesh of the left-hand side of his face had been torn away and was hanging in a gristly flap from his lower jaw. The bone of his skull and upper jaw was visible, and the muscles and tendons that controlled the movements and expressions of his face were revealed.

The story unfolded; they had run, just like the others, as fast as they could around the perimeter of the city walls, but found their path channelled by wooden buildings and fences into ever narrower lanes and alleyways. Trapped eventually in a dead end, the hound had caught them and there had been nowhere to set a bow and aim, as Koenig had been able to do. Maggot had drawn his dagger and cut a deep slice into the dog's front shoulder, but it just veered away and leapt at Jones, sinking its fangs into his face then twisting and shaking its head to try to separate flesh from bone. The Pope had struck it repeatedly with a chunk of stone, fallen from the wall, but the dog did not release its grip until its skull was smashed to pulp. They had carried Jones out between them, fighting their way out of the narrow lanes, and Maggot's dagger had drawn blood among the drunken gang several times before they were clear away.

Koenig dug amongst his gear and found a flagon of distilled barley spirit. He forced Jones to swallow several gulps and then poured the fiery liquor directly onto the wound, causing the boy to emit a piercing scream. The big man then demonstrated an unexpected skill and tenderness. He opened a small leather pouch and took out a needle and some fine gut thread. He motioned The Pope to hold the skin flap in place and began to stitch the wound carefully, continuing until the flesh was firmly reattached. As Jones cried out and groaned in agony, the huge warrior made gentle, soothing noises, quiet words in a tongue none of the others understood, as if his patient was no more than a child. When he was done, he forced Jones to swallow the remaining spirit in the flagon, and eventually the young man lost consciousness.

They ate their supper in silence as Jones moaned fitfully in his sleep. Stretch could not stop thinking about their nick-name for him, how it had been funny before and how it had now become horribly ironic, a sick joke. He resolved that none of them would ever mention the words 'Pretty Boy' again. He was not even sure that the boy would survive. What if the wound festered and poisoned the blood? What if the dog had been rabid? All of them were silently thirsting for vengeance, and when Maggot declared suddenly that he was going back to draw blood to avenge the terrible injury they had inflicted on his friend, they found themselves all talking at once, roaring and cursing and bear-hugging each other, pumping themselves up just as they did before a battle. They were about to grab their gear, blades this time rather than bows, when a young but firm voice spoke up above the din.

'Hold! Hold fast, and think!' Thomas was the calmest among them. 'If you go like this they will know you are coming, and they will beat you by weight of numbers alone.'

The four men stood silent as the youth looked each one of them squarely in the eye. He seemed to have grown taller and his voice carried a calm reassurance that even Koenig sensed.

'They were drunk this afternoon, and will be drunker still this evening. One by one, they will go to their beds or collapse where they stand. Above them today at the tavern, I noticed a stairway built into the wall. I think it will lead up to the top. If I can get up there, and you four split up and hide in the shadows, I can signal you their strength. When the odds are favourable you can take the last of them as they leave.' Thomas was suddenly self-aware and blushed deeply. Stretch was dumb-struck, by the common sense of his proposal, and by the fact that this boy had so effortlessly taken charge of the tense and volatile situation. He argued briefly that they could not allow him to be exposed to danger, but Maggot voiced the thoughts of all of them.

'He is part of this thing now. He sees it through with the rest of us, whatever the outcome. And his plan is good.'

Within the hour they were stealthily approaching the city wall again. They heard the sounds of drunken laughter and singing coming from the inn. Stretch and his men concentrated on maintaining complete silence, and they flitted from shadow to shadow to avoid detection. The four men held still, while the boy Thomas made a quick dash across open ground and into the stairwell in the city wall. Seconds later they saw him appear up on the top of the wall, peering down from between battlements. He was able to see down into the common area of the inn where the men were drinking. Thomas raised his hand, which Stretch could see in silhouette against the night sky, and opened and closed his fist four times, fingers splayed. There were twenty of them still, and poor odds for Stretch and his men. They each found dark recesses in which to hide and wait, covering the four directions that anyone leaving the inn would have to take. Hours passed and the gang members began to disappear into the night, moving in groups of three or four and they let the men pass without giving themselves away. As each group departed so Thomas signalled the strength of their remaining numbers, until he was holding up just three fingers.

The dark-skinned captain with the pock-marked face, the one who had ordered the dog attack, was last to leave along with two of his gang. One of them staggered to the side and vomited before collapsing face down in the dirt. The other two made a half-hearted attempt to raise him, but he remained comatose and they moved on. From Stretch's hidden vantage point he could see that they would pass Maggot's concealed position. As they came to within a few yards of where he was waiting, the leader stopped to relieve himself against a fence while his companion walked on and turned a corner, passing close by Stretch's hiding place. He let the man pass unmolested; the one who had set the dogs upon them would be their prize. The leader rested his head against his forearm, leaning against the fence until his bladder was empty. He belched and staggered on, then paused in front of a dark shadow to the side of a heap of dumped rubbish. He seemed to be staring hard, trying to focus on something. Stretch could see him reach inside his cloak to draw a sword or dagger.

'Take him Maggot, take him!' he spoke under his breath, reluctant to call out and force Maggot into action before he was ready. Suddenly, there was a loud whistle from above and their target turned and looked up, bewildered to find a youth up on the city wall, waving to him. Maggot emerged behind him and clamped his hand over the man's mouth, then drew his blade across the exposed throat. Stretch saw the wound open like a hideous smile, dark blood spurting and pumping from the severed arteries. Maggot held him until the life had drained away into the dirt, and then dragged the corpse back into the darkness.

Dawn was not far away when they returned to camp. They were tired but none of them were able to sleep. The Pope scrounged up some breakfast and they lounged around waiting for something to happen. None of them spoke of the murder they had committed, and none of them felt that they had done wrong. By discrete questioning, Stretch learnt that their nocturnal activities had gone unnoticed. The morning was quiet and still. Jones was awake and in agony, as the shock of his injury set in. The wound to his face was swollen and he had a fever, but there was little his companions could do. He would live or he would die, as God willed.

Maggot and The Pope had been discussing something quietly, and spoke to Stretch to seek approval. Maggot took a cake of black tar from his pack and began to heat it in a small copper dish in the embers around the fire. The Pope knelt before the fire and heated the blade of his knife until it glowed hot, then summoned Thomas to sit beside him. Thomas smiled his acceptance, and sat cross-legged on the ground. He took off his shirt and flexed his right shoulder muscle as the first searing hot cut was made in his flesh, forming the shaft of an ascending arrow. The boy winced, but did not cry out, as each knife cut formed the shape. He looked at Stretch who could see his pride in this honour bestowed by men who had followed his command, his contentment with his complicity in the deeds they had done, and with this symbol of his belonging, to carry with him for the rest of his days. Stretch saw the man that Thomas had become, no longer the boy he was when he had joined them.

The day passed without further incident, but early the following morning the camp was astir and it became known that they were to begin the return journey to Calais. Stretch did not know, or particularly care, if the negotiation had been successful; if any resolution of the issue of sovereignty had been agreed. They found a soft berth for Jones on a pile of furs in the back of the baker's wagon. As they were breaking down their section of the camp and packing their gear onto carts and mules, a group of noblemen appeared and in their midst Stretch could see Prince Edward carried on his litter; his infirmity of recent years still undiagnosed by his physicians, together with the knight Erpingham, come to collect his son. Stretch had served the Prince for many years, and the nobleman spoke with familiarity.

'Good morning Stretch. Has your stay been a pleasant one?'

Stretch bowed, to show proper form in front of the assembled nobles, though the Prince would not have expected the courtesy, had they been alone. 'My Lord, it has been pleasant indeed, but dull and uneventful. Not a single arrow fired in anger.'

He looked at Stretch suspiciously. 'I don't suppose you would have any idea why the city elders are giving me grief about the death of the captain of their militia? Found on a rubbish heap with his throat cut.' There was a mischievous look in his eye.

Stretch played it straight. 'Me Sir? No Sir! All quiet in our sector. The most excitement we had was in dealing with a stray dog.'

'Good man Stretch, I would hate to think that we might leave this place with our peaceful reputation sullied!'

The Prince and his retinue moved on while Thomas greeted his father, who wanted to know what he had learned. Thomas promised to recount all he had learned of archery on the long trek to Calais. The boy would travel with his father's people and so they said their farewells. Each of the men embraced Thomas as if they had known him all their lives. They swore on the Virgin that they would meet again, and Stretch even saw tears welling in Maggot's eyes. Thomas's father looked on with a bemused expression, unable to understand how such bonds had been formed in such a short time, and also aware that his son was no longer the timid boy he had left with these soldiers two days ago.

Last to say farewell was Koenig. He gave the boy a bear-hug which nearly squeezed the breath from his lungs. The big man placed his left hand on his own right shoulder and then on Thomas's, which was bandaged under his tunic, and then tapped his index finger on the boy's forehead, looked him straight in the eye and said 'Yenk!'

Just that one word. 'Yenk!'

***

Jacob's leprosy was slowly destroying his body. He had been living at Magdalen House for six months, working in the kitchens, and had become a firm favourite of the woman they called Mother. She was rumoured to be of high birth, daughter of nobility, but nobody was sure and she would not speak of it. She nursed Jacob tenderly, as if he were her own son. As careful as Jacob had become in trying to avoid minor injury, he had not been able to dodge the odd scrape or bruise and they had all failed to heal properly. The tip of his left index finger was a gnarled stump and the old, reopened wound on his thigh had become a mess of warty, lumpen tissue. His face was worst affected, his nose gradually disintegrating, the cartilage and soft tissue becoming fused and unidentifiable as the sensory organ it once was. The roof of his mouth, upper lip, and the teeth and gums in his upper jaw, all became one inflamed mess and it became difficult to eat and drink, and sometimes even to breathe properly. Jacob had completely lost all sense of taste and smell. He lay for several days, close to death, while Mother continued to spoon small drops of vegetable soup into his mouth and mop away discharge from his wounds.

Then one morning Jacob awoke from a long strange dream about birds that had been born without feet and could not land, had to stay in flight the whole of their lives, and himself tracing their flight through a series of unremembered words and gestures. He thought they might have been the House Martins he had seen nesting in the eaves of the roof of his father's smithy; never resting, always in flight. In the dream he was not a leper, he was something else which he could not quite recall. He lay reliving the dream for some time, attempting to find meaning or purpose within it. It was a dream that stayed real and alive even in the waking world. For some reason, the dream left Jacob with the sense that all was not lost, that his life may yet have meaning, that he may still find redemption.

***

CHAPTER 3

(In which an injustice is avenged, the Erpingham family feel the wrath of the Church and plague is visited upon their people)

I could never understand why William Long was so short, slight and almost childlike in appearance; while his son Rufus was tall and muscular with a tendency to fat, red-haired and cheerfully freckled. Yet their characters were identical, as if his soft, thoughtful, resolute demeanour was the only trait passed down from father to son. William is long dead; he was older than Sir Thomas by many years and died in his bed, an old man. Though I remember him well, I am reliant on his son to tell me stories of the time when Sir Thomas was finding his path in life, before Rufus became his lifelong servant and companion.

Rufus and I are walking along the lane from Erpingham village to my home; our cloaks buttoned tight against the bitter January wind. He is carrying a sack of last year's vegetable crop from the market for me; my body is old and weak and I cannot manage such burdens any more. To pass the time he tells me further recollections of his father's stories, which I will transcribe tonight as I huddle around my fireplace.

***

The punishment had been excessive, so any impartial observer would have agreed, for what had been a failed robbery years in the past, in which the monk's involvement had never been fully proven. Sir John and the young master Thomas had kidnapped him from the grounds of the Abbey at St. Benet Holme, dragged him into the nearby woods, stripped him and beaten him relentlessly with wooden staves for almost an hour. William Long knew this to be true as he had been there, holding the horses and had seen it all. Sir John had been drunk and this had proved both a blessing and a curse to their victim, Brother Anselmo, as the viciousness of his temper had been offset by rapidly waning strength in his muscles, and a lack of accuracy in his aim. Several times Sir John had stopped the beating, panting hard and struggling to regain his breath, before a muffled cry from the prostrate man had caused his rage to boil over and the blows to begin again. William would like to have said that the young, sober and usually sensible Thomas had been a restraining influence, but he had laid into the priest with every bit as much gusto as his father.

That was not the story William had decided he would tell in court later that day, as the three of them sat outside the magistrate's chamber, awaiting their summons. The Abbot had raised hell, calling upon the Bishop of Norwich to bring the whole might of the Church crashing down upon the Erpingham family. Sir John had been fighting a rear-guard action ever since and his health had suffered, exacerbated by his heavy drinking. Increasingly, it had been Thomas who had taken on the routine responsibilities of the manor, and William had guided and supported him as best he was able.

Church lawyers had been all over them for months, like a plague of locusts, demanding title to Erpingham lands in recompense for what had been depicted as an attack on the Church itself. At first, Sir John had blustered, bidding them do their worst and declaring there would be corpses to dispose of at the Abbey, not just bruised priests, by the time he was finished. In the end he pulled strings at the highest level, and a deal was done. Prince Edward himself arranged for title to the Erpingham manor and hundred to be transferred to his brother, John of Gaunt, on a temporary basis which all parties knew would be anything but temporary. The income from other remote holdings would be paid to Sir John so that the family would retain their position in society, and they would continue to live in the manor, though as tenants only. By such means are dynasties broken.

As a secondary part of the deal, Thomas, who was by then old enough to begin to find his own way in the world, would join the service of the Earl of Suffolk, William Ufford, at the garrison of Calais. The Church had proved less willing to lay claim to what had now become the property of the King's son, and so there had been a quick about-face and the matter was quietly settled with an agreed nominal fine for a breach of the peace, levied via the magistrate's court. Hence, they sat under the eaves of the courthouse watching rain pour from the sky and run in torrents down the street towards the banks of the Wensum, awaiting their turn. They were preceded by a case contesting the ownership of a breeding sow and piglets, and by that of a local baker who claimed that his wife had been impregnated by his landlord while he was downstairs kneading the dough. The fact that they were kept waiting was simply a reflection that the magistrate, who was on good terms with the Bishop, needed them to know their place.

After several hours their case was called and they filed into the hall which was packed with lawyers, clerks, claimants, plaintiffs and defendants, and assorted onlookers. It had been a hot day and the torrential downpour outside had served to make the timbers of the building itself steam, while many dampened woollen cloaks and tunics were also adding to the fug. A number of local men, here to argue the ownership of various livestock, had working dogs with them which lay quietly at their master's feet, but added to the general damp, earthy, unwashed body stench of the place. William noticed that an old sheepdog near his feet was running alive with fleas, one of which jumped from the dog's nose onto the woollen fabric of its owner's breeches, and then quickly burrowed into the cloth. He scratched his own ankle which was covered in itchy red welts. The recent warm, wet weather had caused a plague of fleas on their livestock and domestic animals and they seemed resilient to all remedies to kill them off. He thought that, as usual, a cold winter would do the trick.

The magistrate called them to the bench and William prepared himself to give evidence if required, recounting events in such a way that the severity of the attack would be softened, to make it appear a drunken prank gone wrong, no more than that. He hoped that Sir John would not be questioned because he had spent the morning drinking wine and was becoming bellicose and loud. William could sense trouble brewing. So could Thomas, who was speaking quietly to his father as the charges were read out, imploring him to remain calm. Anselmo, the plaintiff, was absent from the proceedings; a representative of the Abbot explaining to the magistrate that his injuries precluded travel. As the magistrate was about to call Sir John forward to give evidence in his defence, a senior clergyman from the Cathedral approached the bench and whispered in his ear. With that, the proceedings were bought quickly to a close.

'In the case of St. Benet Holme Abbey against Sir John Erpingham and others, this court finds in favour of the plaintiff. Sir John will pay a fine equivalent to one ounce weight of gold, or lose his liberty for a month.'

The magistrate thumped the bench with a gavel and peered at Sir John to see if he intended to challenge this, and William saw the two guards flanking his desk stiffen up and hold their halberd axes in a slightly more threatening pose. Sir

John just stood up, threw a bag of coins onto the desk of the court treasurer and walked out into the rain, with Thomas and William following fast behind.

Their journey north was uncomfortable and low-spirited, their sodden clothing not quite drying out in the late afternoon sun. Sir John continued to drink wine from a jug he had purchased at the city gate, mumbling to himself about the unfairness of his position, his loss of face, the underhanded way in which both the Church and the two royal brothers had conspired to defraud him of his land and titles, and disinherit his family. He rode ahead while Thomas and William rode side by side, discussing the plan to send the young man to Calais. Thomas was also downhearted about the turn of fortune his family had suffered since the ill-advised attack on the monk, but was evidently excited by the prospect of foreign travel, and William knew that he felt it was high time he escaped the domination of his father, and the over-protectiveness of his mother. He would need to be armed, equipped, mounted on a decent horse, and attended to by at least one good servant. These things would cost money, and William mentally tallied the family accounts to see where that could best be found. He thought that a local tax on villagers and smallholders might be necessary, but quickly decided to avoid such measures if possible, as the ill feeling that accompanied such donations often outweighed the value of the coin itself.

They rode through the warm July evening and into the night; the land around them lit by an almost full moon and it was already growing light as they passed the outskirts of Aylsham. They did not fear the night; three strong armed men on fast horses would not attract the attentions of the robber gangs, who looked for easier prey. As they approached Erpingham village William began to sense that something was wrong. It was early morning still, but there ought to have been a bustle of activity, the smell of bread baking, farm workers heading out into the fields. All was quiet and still. As they approached the first house in the lane a man cried out from an upper window.

'Come no closer, my Lords, if you value your lives. We've locked ourselves in until it passes and, before you ask, none of us in here shows signs. We've all precautions in place, and food and drink for one week. It may just pass us by, and take other sinners'.

'Is that you Jack Cooper? Who has shown the signs?' asked Thomas.

'One of the whores above the tavern showed the buboes in her armpits two days ago. They cut her deep but no pus came, just blood. Jonas was called in and he stripped her down and there were lumps on her thighs as well. She was coughing blood by then so Jonas and the miller dragged her down to the edge of the wood and finished her and burned the body. Jonas said all who were out of their homes at that time must stay out and find shelter away from the village and away from other people, and those that were at home must stay there and lock themselves in. I ran straight back here and got everyone inside and all the animals as well, and here I stay until it passes.'

'Do you know if it has spread further?' asked William, but already Jack had bolted the shutter and gone back inside.

They rode through the deserted village toward the gates of the manor house. Thomas's mother Anne greeted them and they gathered at the table in the great hall to discuss how they could best deal with the crisis. The family was joined by Father John, their parish priest of twenty years, who was wearing a linen cloth which had been infused with lavender water as a mask over his nose and mouth. He had evidently changed his viewpoint that the power of ardent prayer alone was sufficient deterrent to the plague. He brought them worse news.

'There are three families infected. The two elder children of the butcher have died. Robert the chandler is dead, so is his brother. I have ordered them buried in the field behind the churchyard.' The priest was agitated, aware that his morning round to gather news had taken him into close proximity to the dead and infected.

'The fraud Jonas is telling everyone to stay inside. That is wrong. We should gather the village together at mass and pray forgiveness for our sins. The Lord has sent this visitation upon us because we sin, and we must all answer to Him.'

Thomas replied, 'If we are all together in one place, then we may also all die together in that place, even if it is the house of Our Lord.'

William remained silent and waited for either his master or mistress to speak. Sir John was sullen, hung-over and

William was not sure that he fully understood what was going on. Anne asked a question, of no one in particular.

'Should we flee? To Norwich? The coast? Where would be safe?'

Thomas stood up and walked to the window, looking out over the quiet and frightened town. He spoke without turning to face the others.

'We cannot leave. Who would welcome us, fresh from a plague village? I know not if God has sent this pestilence upon us, or if some other force is at work. But everything we know about the plague says we can't outrun it. If we flee, it may follow us and take us still, with many others besides. Jonas is a decent man,' he looked sharply at the priest, 'but he may be wrong too. Learned men say the plague is carried by a noxious mist, blown through the air by the winds, and I favour their view. In any event, we must stay, we must pray, we must bury our dead.' He sat down again and all were quiet.

So began two days of waiting for something to happen. None of them in the big house became ill, but none of them ventured outside the fenced perimeter of the manor house either. On the third morning, William looked out of one of the upper storey windows and saw the strangest sight. He thought momentarily that a giant stork was walking along the road pushing a cart before it. He looked again and it was Jonas the Healer, over six feet tall, very thin, and wearing some kind of conical mask over his nose and mouth, affixed by a strap around the back of his head, which was reminiscent of a bird's beak. William went outside and called out to him. Jonas stayed twenty yards away but stopped to speak.

'So William Long, you still draw breath?' his voice was muffled by the contraption on his face.

'Jonas, my old friend, why do you imitate a bird?'

'It is an invention of my own, though I have not yet perfected the design.' said Jonas with evident pride. 'It filters the miasma; counters its evil intent with healthy and natural vapours. The cone is filled with garlic bulbs. By God it stinks, but I'm alive yet.' He raised the cone to his forehead and breathed clean air. Now he resembled a unicorn or narwhale.

'What is the latest count? Who still lives?' William was aware that Jonas had been out in close contact with the infected; the bloodstains on his cart told him that he had carried corpses to be buried. Yet Jonas seemed fearless.

'I know of seven houses with dead or dying. Problem is there could be twenty more who are not saying, like old Jack Cooper for example. He appeared at his window this morning just long enough to tell me to fuck off; then bolted everything shut again. He had the eyes though, the sunken cheeks. There's pox in that house, I'm certain.'

Thomas joined William at the fence and greeted Jonas. He appeared to have made a decision.

'I'll not sit inside waiting for it any longer. It gets me or it doesn't, God decides. Are you with me, William?'

They walked out of the gates and joined Jonas. Thomas set about him immediately, ribbing him about his bird's beak.

Jonas, all seriousness, demonstrated its design and function. William could not tell what then passed between them on the subject, because he dashed back inside and returned several minutes later with lengths of linen, with which he and Thomas covered their mouths and noses, and bunches of dried lavender on strings, one each to hang around their necks. They decided to call on Jack Cooper again, to see if they could judge the true status of his household. As they approached the end of the main village street, Jonas and William held back while Thomas walked up and knocked firmly on the door. As he did so it opened a few inches, the hinges creaking, evidently no longer locked from the inside. Thomas pushed the door fully open and peered inside into the gloom of the interior. The other two moved forward to join him, Jonas leaving his cart by the doorway.

The stench was awful, a mixture of animal excrement, human sweat and the sweet cloying odour of death. At first they could make out little in the darkness. Then they saw that a young girl sat facing them at the bottom of the ladder that led to the upper storey room. She was in shock and unable to speak, and she looked at the men without comprehension of who they were, or why they had come. Nevertheless, the three men could see no immediate evidence that she was unwell. Their assumption was that it was she who had unlocked the door. Milling around in the small, cramped space were all of the Cooper family livestock possessions, a pig, two goats, a number of chickens and a cock rooster. Jonas quickly shooed the creatures outside. At the back of the room they were now able to discern the naked corpse of a woman, reclining on a low wooden bench. She was not long dead and the first thing William noticed was that the great sores or buboes around her joints which he had expected to see were not in evidence. Thick gobs of blood and mucus had dribbled from her mouth and nose and on the walls and floor around her there were spattered droplets of blood which he guessed she must have sprayed around her in coughing fits before she died. Blood had pooled up, mixed with thin watery excrement, under her buttocks. Her eyes were bloodshot, the whites a deep red spider-web of broken vessels, and blood had trickled from them like tears. The spasms of her death agony had caused her to freeze in an unnatural position, arms outstretched, hands imploring, while her lips were pulled back in a snarl, exposing worn, rotted teeth in receding gums. There was a bowl of cold water and a towel next to her and her nakedness was explained, perhaps the girl had attempted to wash her before she died, or sought to do so after death, and had quailed at the prospect.

The little girl tugged at William's sleeve and pointed to a door leading out to a barn attached to the back of the building. They moved through the door and saw the shape of two smaller children under some rough woollen sacking. He lifted the covering and saw that the two boys had died quickly, before the lungs and bowel had started to disintegrate and fill with blood. William thought it a small mercy, amongst such horror. Thomas and Jonas lifted each body by the hands and feet and carried them through the house and out to the waiting hand-cart, then came back for the mistress of the house. William began to climb the ladder leading up to the upper floor and as his head poked through the aperture he saw Jack Cooper laying on a bed of old straw, sweating profusely and scratching and pulling at his throat. The man saw him and beckoned for William to approach, asking for water.

'I'm sorry Jack.' said William, unable to make eye contact with the sick man. 'God bless you. I hope it is swift.'

With that he climbed down and removed the ladder, laying it on the ground at the back of the room. William thought that now, at least, Jack could not bring his pestilence downstairs with him, and the girl might yet live. They spoke reassuringly to the daughter for a few moments and as the men made to leave she obviously thought she was going with them. Jonas had to restrain her and she was crying and wailing as they closed the door upon her. He took a hammer from his cart and drove a long iron nail through the door and into the jamb, preventing it from being opened from outside, or in. Next he took a pot of thick black tar paint and a brush and marked a large black cross on the door. They began to walk back through the village towards the churchyard, taking turns with the heavy cart, and William noticed several other black crosses on doorways.

He found it difficult to reconcile the horror of their situation and their task with the fact that it was a beautiful summer day, a few light clouds scudding across the horizon, the sun blazing down on an idyllic landscape. Skylarks chased each other up into the heavens, chirping their summer song, and he even saw the quick blue flash of a Kingfisher crossing the pond at the edge of the village green. A black cat lay sunning itself luxuriously on the wall surrounding the village well. William wondered why these creatures were not affected? He thought that if the birds and animals were happy and healthy, then it must give further credence to Father John's assessment that the plague was God's punishment upon mankind alone for the sins they had committed. He could not help but think such horrors as they faced ought to be accompanied by dark foreboding skies and the crash of heavenly thunder.

As they passed the tavern, they heard drunken laughter from within and there were several farm labourers sitting in the dirt of the road, leaning their backs against the tavern wall and drinking from large clay pots. As the men passed, one of the peasants stood and raised his drink to salute the three bodies on the cart, but he fell down again, to the merriment of his friends. They shouted greetings and made ribald gestures, and Jonas's beak caused uproar. 'We drink today, for tomorrow we may die' said one of the seated men with great formality, and then puked spectacularly over his neighbour's boots.

They reached the churchyard and found two of Father John's gravediggers resting in the shade. There were several fresh mounds of earth in the field at the edge of the churchyard boundary. The gravediggers were sullen and unwilling to set to again with their spades. Thomas paid them several coins each, four or five times the going rate, and explained that he would pay them the same each day until the pestilence was gone, and would also pay any other helpers they could muster. He instructed that they should begin one long pit into which they could lay corpses side by side, backfilling as they went.

Thomas and Jonas tipped the three bodies, the woman and her sons, in a pile against the hedge, and covered them with the sacking from the Cooper barn. Father John walked down from the church to join them and said prayers over the corpses, though from a discrete distance. He was about to say mass and asked the three men to join him, but Jonas declined saying they had better things to do. The tension between the two men was palpable. Nevertheless, the three of them knelt to accept his blessing over the work they had undertaken.

So began two weeks of toil for the three of them, visiting each house in the vicinity, dragging out the dead, forcibly restraining those who were trapped indoors with sick family members and were desperate to escape; painting black crosses on locked doors. They returned to the manor house on the first day, but stayed outside and slept in one of the outbuildings, lest they bring pestilence to those inside the house. Thomas received the scolding of his life from his mother, shouted from a distance of twenty yards, angry at her son's foolhardiness. They learned from a servant that Sir John was drinking his way through all the wine in the cellar and had not been sober since they had returned from Norwich.

They became hardened to their task, each corpse no worse to behold than the one before it. They heard last confessions and even absolved half-delirious victims of their sins, as though they were priests. Without ever discussing it, they began to help the worst cases on their way, one of the men pinning down arms while the other clamped the nose and mouth shut to suffocate the victim. They did not speak of their own health, each one amazed that he had escaped infection this long, terrified of feeling the first symptoms, and yet with each passing day a little more confident that he was destined to survive.

When the news reached them that both Sir John and his wife were ill, William expected Thomas to take it badly but, in truth, he just took the tidings in his stride. He commissioned two strong oak caskets to be built by the village carpenter and made discrete arrangements with Father John that they be interred in a vault under the church floor. Mercifully they both passed quickly and within a day of each other. Thomas and William attended a requiem mass at which there were no other mourners, and the young man prayed quietly over each coffin for a few moments. Then they were back to their work, and he did not speak of his loss again. Late that first night, William heard him sobbing in the darkness, but that was the only indication that he saw the death of his own parents any differently to the death of the villagers that he witnessed each day.

A week passed and they suddenly realised that they had

seen no new cases of infection. Another week passed; only one new case. The following fortnight none at all and it seemed that the pestilence had finally left them. By William's best reckoning there were one hundred and twenty seven souls in the village before the plague struck, and thirty one had died, a quarter of their small population. There had been some minor miracles; the Cooper girl had survived, and would join the retinue of servants in the manor house. One woman, Elizabeth Grafton, had contracted the disease, or something very much like it, and then made a full recovery. Much good it had done her, as there had been talk of witchcraft and she was being shunned by those who were once her friends. Jonas the Healer said that the secret of beating the plague could be found somewhere in her survival and, though he did not yet understand how, he invited her to live with him as a servant, to keep her safe from those who feared witches, and to study her closely for clues.

William sent for his son Rufus, who had been working as a farm labourer on the Felbrigg estate. It had been decided that he would accompany Thomas to Calais as his servant. They worked hard to put the affairs of the manor and the family in good order and Thomas commissioned William to look after things while he was away. Finally, as summer turned to autumn, they were ready to leave, Thomas mounted on the best of his father's horses; Rufus on a strong mare with two pack-horses in tow, laden with provisions and equipment. William bid them farewell as they rode out of the manor gates and on toward the adventures that awaited them in the great wide world of men.

***

It had been many years since Mother died and Jacob missed her very much. He was sixteen, or thereabouts, and had already outlived almost everyone who had been at Magdalen House when he had arrived. She had died quickly of an infection one winter, and he had dug her grave and laid her to rest himself. Now Jacob ran the kitchen with several younger leper children to help him.

The leprosy had left his body suddenly, without warning or explanation. He first became aware of this when the wound from a thorn splinter in his thumb had healed normally, once the thorn was extracted. All of his existing scars and deformities remained, but his body was once again able to heal itself of fresh wounds. He had gone to the city gates once, to bring the news to his parents, but he was chased away by the guards and returned to the leper hospital, downhearted.

Magdalen House no longer felt like a sanctuary to Jacob. One of the more recent arrivals, John Blamey, had been a captain of the city militia until the disease struck him. He came intent on crowning himself king of this little empire, and soon gathered the stronger leper men around him. They bullied everyone else into giving up the best food, the most comfortable beds, the warmest positions in winter and the coolest in summer. They took their pick of the leper women, and sometimes the younger boys, particularly the new arrivals, amongst whom the disease had not yet done its disfiguring work. Jacob was young and, though deformed by the ravages of leprosy, found that he was not beneath their interest. He began to carry a knife at all times, secreted within the folds of his cloak, with which to defend himself.

The ex-militiaman, Blamey; began to demand that his food was brought to him in the private quarters he had commandeered in one of the outbuildings. One evening, Jacob brought him a bowl of stew. Blamey asked him to stay and when he declined; two strong men stood and blocked his exit from the room. Jacob drew his knife and, knowing the potentially lethal damage the small blade could inflict on their diseased bodies, the men stepped aside. Jacob walked out backwards, holding the knife out at arm's length. He knew they would come for him later, when he slept.

***

CHAPTER 4

(In which Thomas Erpingham's new servant Rufus Long gets to know his master, and witnesses the making of a man of war)

It annoys me greatly when a row of carrots does not come up straight, even though I had sown each seed carefully along a taut length of twine. Among the many great trials of my life this may seem a petty concern, yet such things seem to trouble me more as I become old and frail, while the importance of major events; the wars fought by kings and suchlike, recede into a cloudy obscurity.

Rufus helps me in my small kitchen garden whenever he is able. He is here today, telling me of the early days, when he and Sir Thomas were still finding their way. I sit down to rest my back and watch him as he continues to hoe the weeds that are constantly threatening to invade my scant parsnip crop. An old man himself now, he still retains the rusty hue of his once bright red countenance. He talks as if it had all happened yesterday.

***

'Who has used a crossbow?' asked their instructor, Captain Hooper, on the morning of their third day in training at the garrison in Calais. He held the machine up for the young gentlemen to observe, gripping the wooden stock in his right hand, one finger resting on the trigger lever. Six young noblemen sat in a semicircle, cross-legged on the ground, while their servants stood in attendance, a few paces back. Rufus could see that the string was loose, the arms slack and that no projectile had been inserted into the weapon.

None were foolish enough to claim that they had; they would not fall for that trick again. Hooper had asked a similar question on their first morning in training about the broadsword, and his master, Thomas Erpingham, had stepped forward. He had been given a wooden practice sword and shield, and joined Hooper on the sanded practice arena. The instructor had told him to attack with the sword using his full strength, and all his skill. Erpingham had charged forward swinging the blade, which Hooper had parried easily with his shield, stepping to the side and delivering a blow with the flat of his blade to the shoulder, with sufficient force to knock the young man to the ground. Thomas had stood up quickly, rubbing his deadened shoulder, but ready to attack again. This time he received another blow with the flat of the blade to the right shin, which left him writhing on the ground in agony, clasping his leg with both hands. Instructor Hooper had helped him to his feet and dusted him down. Rufus was certain that none of the assembled young gentlemen would be making the same mistake again in a hurry.

Thomas glanced at Rufus, rubbed his shin and winked with an expression that said 'No thank you, not this time!' The servant shook his head and was only just able to hide a grin. They had built a good relationship in the weeks on the road, travelling down first to London, then to Dover before a five hour crossing, with them both sick as dogs the whole way. Thomas had been quiet at first, and little wonder thought Rufus, with the horrors he had experienced in the preceding weeks. They were both wary of signs that the pestilence had followed them, but it seemed that God had other plans for them this time. He worried though for his father William, back in Erpingham village, dealing with the aftermath.

Rufus's new master called him 'Red' on account of his hair and complexion, which was why the youth's parents had called him Rufus in the first place. Of course, it would be wrong to claim that they had become friends, what with Thomas born to nobility, and Rufus the son of a commoner. He had thought at first that his master was of that type of nobleman who liked to appear familiar with his people, and had risked calling him by his given name once, but Thomas had reprimanded him sternly and insisted that he be addressed as Sir or Master. Rufus had become accustomed to his master's habits; what time he woke, when he liked to eat, the pattern of his ablutions and defecation, how he liked his clothing presented and other such trivial matters. In truth, Rufus had found him a very easy master to serve. Thomas liked to put problems and conundrums to his servant, and expected an intelligent reply. As they had sat by Dover Castle awaiting their ship, Thomas had presented Rufus with various scenarios relating to besieging, storming or defending the castle and together, via discussion and argument, they had begun a rudimentary understanding of such matters.

They had arrived at the garrison, several days earlier than expected, and Thomas had been introduced to the Earl of Suffolk, William Ufford. The earl was a gloomy character in his middling years with great bushy eyebrows, a prominent hooked nose and a withering stare. He reminded Rufus of a buzzard, and he had looked Thomas over with a keen eye. It transpired that several young men, of decent birth and of sound reputation, had been selected by the King's son, John of Gaunt, to train in the arts of war, the best of them to potentially join his retinue as esquires. Young Erpingham's recommendation had come about as a result of the faithful service his father had given to Gaunt's brother Prince Edward at Limoges, as had his grandfather, many years earlier at Crecy.

Several weeks had passed as they waited for the other young noblemen to assemble, before training would commence. They had settled into their quarters and begun the process of discarding equipment that they had brought with them, expecting it to be required and finding it superfluous or useless, and acquiring new equipment which they had not expected to need. Thomas had deposited a sizeable sum of money with a local banking house and another large sum, on account, with an armourer of sound reputation.

Thomas had spent several days having suits of chain-mail made and fitted, and the various component pieces of armour manufactured. His chosen armourer, a Flemish master craftsman named Jan Vermeulen, had made everything bigger than it needed to be, and packed out the pieces with leather pads and strapping. He had rightly assessed that the young nobleman would not grow taller than his current five feet ten inches, but would bulk out with muscle during the years of training that were ahead. Rufus was aware that in doing so he had saved his master a tidy sum in not having to replace the pieces continuously as he outgrew them, but also thought that it added considerably to the image Erpingham gave when fully encased in armour, of a man bigger than he actually was.

Thomas had given much thought and deliberation to the question of the arms he would carry on his shield, and across his surcoat. His father Sir John had never cared much for such things, considering the fashion for displaying familial emblems overly ostentatious, and just a little effete. With no family tradition to follow, he had opted in the end for a pattern of eight Martlet birds, symbolizing freedom, adventure and constant movement; he told Rufus that they reminded him of the House Martins which had nested in the eaves of the manor house where he had grown up. These stylised birds, drawn in flight without legs or feet, would encircle a plain white shield over a green background, symbolising purity of heart and a new beginning for the Erpingham family.

Hooper pressed the crossbow down into the dirt, as if he was about to fire into the ground at point-blank range. He fitted his right shoe into a stirrup built into the intersection of the stock and bow-arms of the machine, then trod down hard while he pulled the bowstring back into the fully cocked position with both hands, each of which were encased in chain-mail gloves, using all the strength of his arms, shoulders and back. With the taut, straining weapon ready, he slotted a short arrow, no more than eight inches long, into a groove running along the top of the stock. The arrow, or quarrel as they learnt it was named, had a heavy iron tip and four equally spaced tail feathers which would ensure it stayed true in flight. One of the tail feathers also slid into the groove. Hooper aimed at some wooden planking which was stacked up vertically against the far wall of the training compound and gently depressed the trigger lever. As the taut string was released the quarrel fizzed through the air and smashed into the target planking, sending shattered wood splinters in every direction, imbedding itself in the outer wall of the compound.

Each of the young gentlemen stepped up to take a turn and they all found the machine harder to load than it had looked, but easy to fire and very accurate.

They moved on to a demonstration of the longbow. Those first few days had consisted of an introduction to the various weapons of war that each of the trainee esquires would be expected to master. Hooper had already shown them the broadsword, dagger, axe, mace, war-hammer and then finally the bow weapons. Later, they were to see the longer pole-axe, spear and halberd, and the mounted weapons, primarily the lance, both in its solid war version and its hollow jousting form. The details were incredibly complex and Hooper had asked constant questions, testing each man's ability to absorb and remember the information at every turn. The young noblemens' servants did not escape the necessity of this rapid assimilation of new knowledge. They were expected to be able to disassemble, repair and reassemble various weapons, and to maintain all of their master's equipment in perfect condition at all times. In the evenings, Thomas had Rufus test him constantly on what they had been taught that day, and he tested his servant in turn. They both made copious notes, Thomas had a fine hand of course, but Rufus could also write well, some French and Latin as well as English; his father had seen to that, from when he was a young boy.

It was the end of their first week, and Hooper had instructed his trainees to assemble on the beach the following morning, dressed in chain-mail and battle armour. At their supper that evening, the young gentlemen were in a state of high excitement, relishing the chance to begin testing themselves in battle practice. Robert Cranwell, the son of a prosperous gentleman merchant from Gloucester, goaded Thomas about who would demonstrate the greater skill with the sword in the morning. They had become friends during the first week, though it was a friendship tinged with a raw competitiveness which Rufus thought could easily turn sour. They awoke to a clear, cold morning with faint wisps of fog coming in off the sea. As they assembled at the appointed place on the beach, Rufus noticed that none of the practice weaponry had been brought down from the garrison, and he assumed that he and the other servants would be sent back for it once Hooper arrived.

Hooper appeared in due course, accompanied by William Ufford, who was wiping the remains of his breakfast from his beard. Several other noblemen were also in attendance, and the trainees felt themselves tensing up, worrying about how they would be seen to perform in the coming practice fights. Each was aware that reputations, for good or bad, were forged early in such a place, and did not want to let themselves, or their family name, down.

'Good morning my fine young warriors,' shouted Hooper from a mound of shingle above the sand of the beach, 'do you see the spit of rock pointing out to sea, a short way along the beach?' He pointed to an outcrop of rocks about one mile distant. The trainees acknowledged that they did, the truth about this morning's planned activity slowly dawning.

'Run then gentlemen, there and back please. Now run!' he roared, and the young men were away, clanking and squeaking in their armour and chain-mail. The group of servants looked on agape.

'What the fuck are you lot doing, just standing there? Get

after your masters before I have your hides!' screamed Hooper, and they were away too, carrying assorted heavy gear in the packs on their backs. Each of the servants picked out his own master to follow. Several of the trainees had dashed on ahead, running as fast as their cumbersome costume would allow. The tide was not long out and the sand was still full of sea water, which sucked at their metal encased feet as they ran. Each man settled into his own pace, some faster than others. Rufus followed Thomas as he veered away to the right and moved up the incline of the beach to where the sand was less waterlogged. Several of the others followed, but soon found that there the sand was softer and their feet sank into it further still.

Soon, those who had been fastest away were beginning to slow, each step becoming a greater effort as the wet sand sucked downwards on their over-weighted bodies. The steel plates of their armour began to find soft skin to chafe, and bone to dig into. Each movement became increasingly painful and, as the first of them approached the halfway point at the rocky outcrop, some began to ditch their equipment. One man dropped his helmet, so that he could at least breathe and see properly, and stripped off his breastplate, and his servant was quick to collect up that which had been discarded. Rufus could see that Thomas had deliberately slowed to walking pace and had adopted a strange looking waddling gait which was evidently designed to get each foot in turn out of the grasping sand, and forward. He was behind the pace, but still fully armoured and moving in the right direction.

Now the first of those who had been quickest away fell to his knees and had to be helped up by his servant. More and more gear was strewn over the beach, some of it ditched by servants who had not realised that their own physical fitness would also be put to the test. As Thomas approached the rocks and turned towards home, he began to pass others who were struggling to even lift each foot out of the sand. One man was inching forward on hands and knees; another was being supported by the shoulder of his manservant. Rufus was tiring fast with the heavy gear he was carrying on his back. At each step he dragged his feet out of the sand, making a loud slurping sound and leaving a hole as deep as his ankle, which rapidly filled with water. The armoured men were sinking in twice as deep, and he could see that one had given up trying and just sat down on the beach, with both feet firmly stuck.

Thomas and Robert Cranwell were still making slow progress and were the only two who had not stripped off their armour. Behind them, men were inching forward by different means and many of the servants were visibly struggling, being laden down with their masters' heavy armour pieces, as well as their own burdens. Thomas lost his balance and fell and it was Cranwell who helped him to his feet. They continued side by side and reached Hooper and the noblemen together. Behind them, the beach was strewn with men and equipment and it looked as though a small war had been fought and lost that morning. Rufus arrived shortly after his master, barely able to breathe, and close to fainting. Thomas and Cranwell had both collapsed in heaps on the sand, panting for breath and sweating in torrents.

Rufus had noticed that several of the noblemen were exchanging coins, Ufford collecting in the most, and realised that they had been wagering on the outcome, as if it had been a greyhound race. They moved away as a group and only Hooper remained. He spoke quietly to the two trainees who had stayed the course, telling them to remove their helmets and breastplates, and take some water. Gradually, the stragglers came in and soon they were once again a group of twelve, sitting on the wet sand, recovering their composure. They were assembled in a rough half-circle, surrounding the instructor. He stood and spoke to them all;

'Gentlemen, the armour you wear will protect you from the thrust of a sword, or the blow of an axe or the strike of an arrow, if you are lucky. It is designed for you to be able to fight on horseback, and on foot. You will rarely be able to choose your battleground, and you will be lucky indeed if you find yourself engaging an enemy on firm, level, springy turf, where your armour will least encumber you. In any leisure time you have this coming week, I want you to study the accounts of battles in the past that were won, or lost, because of the state of the terrain, because of bogs and marshes and quicksand and wet beaches. You will need to learn to adapt, to think on your feet and to develop the strength in your legs and thighs which will keep you moving through such ground, fully armoured, while men are doing their utmost to kill you.

I have watched you preening yourselves this week in your new armour, looking the part of the warrior, checking yourselves in the mirror glass. Now, there is no need for me to tell you where your equipment is flawed, what needs adjusting, which plates need to be reshaped; the bruises and welts on your body will guide you. So spend time with your armourer, make sure everything fits properly, and worry less about how you look in front of the ladies. The next time we visit this beach, which, by the way, we will do many times before I'm through with you, I want to see you in equipment that works with you, and not against you. I will make men-at-arms of you, if it kills me!'

With that, he strode away toward the garrison, leaving his pupils to gather their gear and make their weary way home. The trainees assumed that, once they had rectified the flaws in their armour, training for warfare would then begin in earnest, but they were wrong. In the coming weeks they attended lectures and demonstrations on horse welfare, herb lore, chivalric obligations, dealing with wounds and injury; including stitching flesh and resetting broken bones, the religious responsibilities of the nobleman, how to kill and butcher cattle and sheep, the basic principles of alchemy and astrology. Their reading, and writing skills and their ability to converse in different languages were tested thoroughly. In almost all respects, the servants were expected to keep up with their masters' newfound knowledge, so that they would be best able to serve and support them in the field. Two of the servants were dismissed for stupidity, and one for having exaggerated his ability to read and write, and they were replaced by locally picked men, who had fulfilled the role in the past. Rufus thought that they seemed to spend as much time in church as anywhere else.

The trainee esquires and, to a lesser extent the servants, were subjected to rigorous physical training, including repetitive lifting of various weights and 'turning the wheel'. This was an old disused water mill, the wheel of which was entered by two men at a time both of whom trod down on the wooden slats until the wheel began to move and then maintained the momentum with the weight and pressure of their downward steps. It was exhausting work; Rufus had attempted it once and collapsed after five minutes' effort.

Gradually, warfare training was introduced into the daily routine. The trainees fought with wooden practice swords and shields, and light wooden versions of the mace and other club type weapons. It became apparent that speed and dexterity were every bit as important as strength; the armour plates, by now bent and flexed to become almost part of their bodies, providing protection from blows but also enabling the men to twist and turn out of trouble, almost as if they were not wearing such protection at all.

Hooper stepped in occasionally to show how to thrust a blade into an exposed chink under a shield, how to seek the open parts of the face shield with a dagger. He was particularly keen that they learn how to use their opponents' strength against them; how to allow a full-on charge to bring the opponent onto the point of a sword or spear. How, once beaten to the ground, to defend against the death-blow and find the weak point at the opponent's feet, to slice through an exposed Achilles tendon or smash a war-hammer down on the bridge of a foot.

Horsemanship was thoroughly tested and each man learned to use the lance to good effect. They attended several jousts and the trainees smashed lightweight, hollow, lances into matchwood on each others' breastplates. They learned how best to unhorse an adversary and how to mount a loose horse, fully armoured, at the run. Rufus and the other servants were expected to maintain their masters' horses, as well as their own mounts, in perfect health and condition, at all times.

The trainee group revisited the beach several times, but now they knew what to expect and prepared themselves both physically and psychologically for the ordeal. Thomas even experimented with different footwear to try to avoid sinking too deep into the sand. The most successful attempt came with a pair of circular iron plates that clipped onto his foot armour under the soles of his feet. They successfully prevented him from sinking too deep, but also stopped him from walking properly and after tripping himself up a couple of times he gave up on the idea and slogged through the ground like everyone else. Each man was increasingly able to keep moving forward, building levels of strength and stamina in the legs and thighs to help them on.

The years passed quickly, and increasingly the trainee esquires were assimilated into the day to day running of the garrison; taking sentry duty, going out on local punitive, or tax collecting missions, acting as bodyguards for noblemen and visiting dignitaries. Their training programme continued, but was by then largely self-organised; Hooper was away looking after another intake of younger, raw recruits.

Rufus was proud to be able to say that his master, along with Cranwell, was consistently top of the class and was often selected by Ufford to accompany him on journeys away from the garrison. When this was on horseback all was well, but when Ufford launched a naval expedition along the coast to Harfleur, it quickly became apparent that sea-sickness would forever prevent Thomas, and his trusty servant Rufus, from becoming accomplished sailors.

They became fully grown men and Thomas did his share, and more, of whoring, drinking and gambling in the town. During those happy, carefree days at Calais, the bond as master and servant between Thomas and Rufus was strengthened, and Rufus knew that he would follow this man, wherever his path took him. They were lucky enough to have several opportunities to return home to Norfolk during those years, and Rufus was able to see his mother and father again, who had kept a good house for Thomas since they had been away. His father looked at his own son with evident amazement; Rufus had left home a boy, in the wake of a terrible visitation of plague, and had returned a man in times of relative peace and plenty, taller by several inches than his old man. His mother had wept as they left Erpingham once more for Calais.

By the time Thomas and Rufus had returned to the garrison, Ufford had returned to England to look after matters on his East Anglian estates and he had been replaced as master of the Calais garrison by the Earl of Salisbury. They learned from him of the recent death of King Edward, following only months after his own eldest son Prince Edward had passed away, victim of a long and undiagnosed debilitating illness. A new King was on the throne, the boy Richard, who had not yet reached maturity and ruled through a council of advisors, chief among whom was Prince Edward's brother, John of Gaunt. Of course, Thomas could have had no idea at the time of the extent to which his fortune, and that of the new King, would be interwoven and dependent.

One day, Thomas was introduced to a tall, dark-haired and fearsome looking knight who was visiting the garrison on his journey back from business in Aquitaine. It was the renowned, much feared and widely disliked John of Gaunt. It was quickly established that Thomas Erpingham, along with Robert Cranwell, would join Gaunt's retinue as esquires. Their future could not look any brighter.

***

Jacob left Magdalen House under cover of darkness. His possessions were few enough; a good cloak with a hood which could be used to obscure his deformities when necessary, a small bundle of spare clothing and food and, hidden away out of sight, the knife with which he had prepared vegetables for the previous ten years. He headed north, away from the city walls and soon veered east into the woods surrounding Mousehold Heath. He was familiar with the terrain from when he was a boy, and followed well-trodden pathways by moonlight. He slept for a few hours just before dawn on a bed of dried leaves and, when the morning sunlight woke him, drank water from a stream and ate some of the bread from his bundle.

Several times during the course of the following days he saw strangers approaching, and he always ducked away behind trees and waited for them to pass. He had only known the company of lepers for many years, and did not know how the people of the outside world would react to his deformities. After many days of walking without any clear direction or purpose, Jacob found himself in a wetland of rivers and marshy lakes. His supply of food was exhausted and he had started to steal eggs and vegetables from households along the way. He had no means of making fire, and ate the eggs raw and gnawed the hard parsnips and turnips as he walked along.

Late one afternoon he came upon some monks working in a kitchen garden which was attached to a great Abbey. Jacob did not approach directly but stayed at the edge of the cultivated land, within a quick dash of the cover of the woodland behind him. He was noticed, and one of the brothers waved him to come closer. He stayed his ground. As darkness fell he saw one of the men bring out a bowl of soup and bread and leave it close to the Abbey wall. When he was sure they had all gone, Jacob grabbed the food and took it out into the woods to eat. He decided to stay close to the Abbey for the time being, and see what opportunities might arise.

***

CHAPTER 5

(In which the esquire Thomas Erpingham witnesses the wrath of the mob, and kills another man for the first time)

A good, long, straight iron nail is a thing of great value, and a lucky find. I recovered this one from the rotting wooden doorframe of a long-abandoned house at the edge of Erpingham village. It had obviously once been driven through the door and the frame to secure the building. I have put the thing to a new double purpose, driving it through the loose plank in the wall of my half-derelict shack; the plank that quivers and rattles when the wind gets up, and into the heavy timber frame of the building itself. I don't drive the nail fully home, leaving about a half inch of the nail-head exposed and I use this as a hook upon which to hang my cloak. I stand and look at the result for several minutes, finding it to be quite satisfactory, before I sit down once more at the rough wooden table, dip my quill in the ink and continue to transcribe the story Sir Thomas had once told me about his first visit to the great city of London.

***

The doorframe had collapsed in a shower of sparks, and Thomas stepped back quickly from the suddenly exposed source of residual heat. It had been three days since Tyler's mob ransacked and then burned the Savoy Palace, there in The Strand; the London home of his liege the Duke of Lancaster, John of Gaunt. The building's timber frame had burned for days, setting fire to several smaller buildings nearby, and now there were just stumps of smouldering ash and charcoal, marking where the great support pillars had once stood. That which was made of stone was cracked and blackened and, already, many of the larger stones had been stolen, to shore up other damaged buildings. The ground beneath his feet was littered with the charred fragments of what had once been some of the finest tapestries, paintings and decorative panels in Christendom. There, close by where Thomas stood, was the spot where the mad priest John Ball had preached a perverted sermon to the throng as the building took light; about the equality of all men, and the need for redistribution of the wealth of the land, and how there was no difference between the high-born nobleman and the common labourer in the eyes of God, and other such foolish and misguided notions. For weeks, the rabble had repeated his piece of inflammatory doggerel; 'When Adam delved and Eve span, who then was the gentleman?'

A little further away, along the shore of the Thames, lay

dozens of bloated corpses, beginning to stink already in the heat of the sun. Among them were any deemed to have been in authority; bankers, lawyers, tax-collectors, and those of rank in the church. Thomas had seen many bodies cruelly abused; castrations, ears and noses lopped off, eyes thumbed out and hanging on glistening strings.

The mob had been recently dispersed; they were saying that the young King had deported himself well, and the leaders would now be hunted down and made example of. Promises had been made in the heat of the moment; had to be made lest the mob would have triumphed, but the reality of the outcome of treason was soon to be made clear. Already, the heads of several captured leaders were on spikes at the Tower, and on London Bridge.

Thomas was there among a group of thirty men, knights and esquires, mounted and armed and sent south by Gaunt to protect his property in the maelstrom of revolt. They were too late. Each of the men wandered about the devastated site, picking up scraps, turning over smouldering planks with the steel toe of their boots; none knew what to do for the best. They were approached by a timid little man who looked about him constantly, fearful of the return of the mob. He was Samuel Reed, one of their master's accountants. In a faltering voice, he gave his testimony:

'When they first arrived, I hid in the grain storage bins across the road, me and several dozen rats. I burrowed down deep and they didn't find me, even when they pissed into the bin to foul the grain, knowing they could not carry it away. I heard them all that night, the priest crying out his poison, and other leaders urging them on. They made a big thing of it, that there should be no loot taken from here, that this should be a clear message of hatred for Gaunt. But that all went out the window once they got started. Parts of the building were already aflame, and I peeked out and saw several men prancing around the street in fine women's dresses and wigs. They dressed up their prisoners in similar attire, then strung them up by the wrists and pelted them with rocks until they were smashed in.'

'Could you identify the leaders?' asked Thomas, 'pick them out if we brought suspects before you?'

The accountant sighed, his soft white hands fluttering with nervous tension, 'I don't know, it was dark. They all looked alike to me; a fierce drunken rabble. Once the place was well ablaze, there were some who began to regret the lost opportunity and dashed inside to grab what they could. I saw one man with a stack of good silver plate, another dragging a great bear fur through the street, another with a bejewelled sword.'

Samuel asked if he could accompany the men for protection, but they sent him on his way promising they would report well of him when they met Gaunt; they were a war party now, looking for blood and he would doubtless hinder them. Eventually, one of the senior men, Edmond de Bamford, called out that they should ride north, that there was nothing left for them to do in that devastated place. Two were sent on immediately at the gallop; they would ride to meet Gaunt and his train coming south from Scotland where, sensibly, the Duke of Lancaster had decamped to, when the trouble had first started. The rest of the men would return to Kenilworth Castle, and await his pleasure there.

There was a cold anger in their ranks as the men rode out towards the city gates. Thomas looked around him and was appalled at the filth and squalor of the streets of this great town. He lifted the hem of his tunic up until the fabric covered his mouth and nose, to keep out the stink and give him some scant protection against the fearful vapours of the city streets. He was country born and, though Thomas well knew the reek of mankind's presence in his own village, he also knew the cool, clean breezes that came down from the coast, the sweet scent of summer hedgerows in bloom, the aroma of fresh bread in the lanes each morning. Here, in the great city, the filth and stench were constant and indescribable. Mounds of human and animal excrement were piled up outside every dwelling place. Flies and maggots proliferated, and rats scurried amongst the filth. Children played in the street, their legs caked up to the knees in dried ordure, and many of them had open wounds and lesions on their emaciated bodies. Thomas had always considered Norwich to be a dung-heap; London was ten times worse.

There were more people abroad than Thomas had ever seen in one place before. Everywhere he looked was a teeming mass of the poorest kind of folk; beggars, thieves, whores, drunkards, layabouts; none appeared to be employed in any useful capacity. There seemed to be hundreds of them crowding every dark, narrow street, countless thousands on the main thoroughfares, each man careful to avert his gaze as the mounted troop passed. There was an unspoken message; we were not involved; it was not us. To be fair, the culprits had been mostly Kentish gangs and a few down from Bedford and other places. How many of these Londoners had watched the proceedings though? Grabbed some small trinket as a keepsake, in the general melee?

Thomas found himself breathing in short shallow gasps; he did not wish to inhale deeply knowing that if plague was really carried in foul air, then this surely was the one place where he was bound to succumb. He was still astounded that he had survived the pestilence that swept through his own village many years ago. He had certainly been close enough to it, carting bodies away to be buried and hearing the gasped pleading and confessions of the dying. Thomas still awoke at night crying out in fear, convinced that he could feel the buboes in his throat, the sickness in his lungs.

The men were all pleased enough to leave that hell on earth behind them as they left the city gates and headed due north up the St Albans road. The wealth that had been destroyed played heavily on their minds; it was not just their master's property, it was the very source of their own income, the thing that sustained them in their positions. Each of them secretly thought of what he could have done with just a fraction of the loot that had been taken or destroyed. Some had expected to profit personally from the chaos of the revolt, and were sorely disappointed with the lack of booty they were carrying away from the scene. As they rode, the roads were full of peasants returning to their home villages. Gallows adorned every crossroads; the swinging corpses of supposed ringleaders were by then replacing those of the representatives of the state who had been strung up by the mob in the previous days.

They stopped at an inn for refreshment before entering the gloom of Hadley Forest. Several men were seated at tables in the roughly fashioned interior, the place seemingly in near darkness after the glare of the sun outside. The innkeeper; an old grey-bearded bear with the inflamed red nose and heavily veined cheeks of an inveterate drinker, was standing behind a counter flicking ineffectually at flies with a dirty cloth. The shutters over the window frames had all been lifted to allow some light in, and some heat out. He served the newcomers with jugs of ale, and his woman was sent to fetch bread and cheese. All conversation had ceased from the moment Gaunt's men entered the room, and one or two customers had sidled out the door and were away before they were noticed. Bamford looked over those who remained carefully and began to question the innkeeper; Who was everyone? Were they locals? Where had they been? The atmosphere grew tense and two of the troop stood and blocked the exit doorway.

One of the customers had a bundle at his feet which he had

been trying to discretely kick back into the shadows under the table. Bamford spotted it and strode across the room, grabbed the man by the throat and threw him to the ground, then lifted the bundle onto the bench and tipped it up. Out fell a crushed and bent chalice, a crucifix in gold and silver, and some large circular silver plate which had been bent into quarters for easier carriage. The landlord cried out,

'He is a passing stranger; we do not know him here!'

Bamford ordered two of his men out to the horses to fetch rope, and the innkeeper and his customers were quickly rounded up and incapacitated. The innkeeper's wife had, quite sensibly, not returned. There was a sudden clamour of innocence, which was ignored, and the captives were led outside. Passers-by averted their gaze, and moved on quickly. With little ceremony, a noose was tied and the rope thrown over a low branch on a nearby oak. The looter's hands were bound and he was dragged under the bough and the noose tightened around his neck. He was babbling incoherently; pleading, begging and praying. Two of Gaunt's troop pulled downward on the rope and the victim was raised, his feet kicking a few inches above the ground. The rope was tied off on another, lower branch and Thomas could see that it was his old friend from Calais, Robert Cranwell, who had tied the knot. They all stood transfixed as the looter began to jerk on the short rope. The noose bit in deeper and the victim's face began to turn red, then purple. His tongue protruded and his eyes bulged and became bloodshot. Urine ran down his legs and splashed on the ground as his feet kicked wildly. There was a sudden powerful odour as the condemned man defecated involuntarily, a dark stain soiling his woollen breeches.

If the others thought they would escape, they were mistaken. Bamford ordered gallows strung on several trees, and from the roof of the inn. An example was to be made. Some of the men struggled and cursed, a few dropped to their knees and begged for their lives, while a group of women, wives and mothers, had gathered and begun a wailing cry of lamentation. Suddenly, the young man whose arm Thomas had been holding jerked away from him and made a run for it. Thomas dashed to his horse and grabbed his sword before chasing the escaper up a pathway towards the woods. Some of Thomas's colleagues made to follow, but he waved them back, saying that he alone would deal with it.

The man had managed to free his hands from the rope that bound him. He was fast on his feet, but so was Thomas; unencumbered by armour, he was making ground on his quarry as the pathway entered the woods. They crashed through undergrowth and jumped over fallen trees and then about two hundred yards into the wood Thomas lost sight of him momentarily. He ran into a small glade and stopped suddenly, panting for breath and looking around him to locate the man's hiding place. With a roar the escaper stepped from behind a tree and swung a stout branch which caught Thomas full in the stomach. He was winded and went down on his knees clutching his midriff, and dropping his sword in the process.

The escaper was upon him in an instant and they grappled and rolled in the dirt. Thomas managed to get on top and smash his forehead down hard onto the bridge of his opponent's nose, causing the young man to scream and clutch his injured face with both hands, all the fight suddenly gone out of him. Thomas stood quickly, picked up his sword and pressed the tip down onto his adversary's chest, above his heart. He leant forward with both hands on the pommel, but hesitated before pressing the blade home. The escaper looked Thomas straight in the eye and pleaded for his life, but Thomas cut him short.

'Look away, or close your eyes, one of the two. Prepare yourself!' he shouted it as an order, a fierce command, but his voice sounded frightened and unsure in the silent woodland glade.

The escaper continued to stare. 'My name is Benjamin. I am a baker. My wife is called Alice. I have two sons and an infant girl. Please let me live'.

'Shut up!' screamed Thomas, 'don't tell me your damned name!' He made as if to thrust the blade in but hesitated once more. For all the practice, all the mock fights to the death, for all Hooper's urging and Cranwell's goading, Thomas knew that he desperately did not want to kill this man.

'I just got caught up in it with everyone else. I don't want the stuff. It's no good to me. Please don't do this. Please let me go.'

There were tears in Thomas's eyes, half blinding him and snot bubbling out of his nose. His hands were shaking and he was terribly afraid. Afraid to take this life from a man he did not know who had done him no wrong. Afraid of his face; his eyes which Thomas knew he would see in his dreams forever. Afraid of damnation for cold-blooded murder. Afraid of not killing him too; of the shame, the disgrace. Afraid that he was a coward.

'Don't look at me. Please.' Thomas was the one who was pleading now. 'Look away.' He said it quietly, gently. Benjamin continued to stare straight back at him, knowing somehow that this was the key to prolonging his life. He said firmly 'Don't do this thing.' Thomas heard them coming through the undergrowth, to check that he had prevailed and did not need assistance.

'Forgive me?' he asked as he leant forward on the hilt of the sword. At first it did not penetrate and Thomas thought that the man may be wearing chain-mail. Then Benjamin's rib cracked and the long blade slid in through flesh and internal organs until it reached his spine. He looked straight into Thomas's eyes, into his very soul, as the blood bubbled from his lips. He was still trying to speak when Thomas saw his eyes glaze over and knew that he was absent, that his words and his stare were finished; that he was gone. Thomas was sobbing quietly, full of hatred suddenly for the corpse lying before him, this baker, father, husband, one-time rioter, looter whose death had shaken him to the core, to whom he had committed this terrible deed that he could never undo. He pulled the blade out; it made a crunching squelchy sound, and stabbed down again several times into the flesh of the corpse's chest and stomach. It was Bamford who pulled him away, led him back to the inn.

'It's alright.' he said to Thomas quietly. He remembered the first one. He knew.

They left behind them seven swinging corpses on makeshift gallows and one bloody cadaver in the woods. They could hear the wailing of the women for a long time after they left. None of the men spoke for some time; all were quiet and thoughtful. Thomas realised that no one was entirely unaffected by death, by the killing of another man.

The remainder of their journey north was uneventful. It was several days before Gaunt's party returned from Scotland, and the troop kicked their heels around the castle with little to do, apprehensive of their master's return and his reaction to their failed mission. Thomas went to mass every day and to confession, but found himself unable to confide in the priest. He told him about peripheral sins, skirting around the fact that he had killed another man, and found himself making up lusts and fornications, a fictitious doubting of Christ's word, the breaking of commandments which never occurred in reality. The priest sensed that Thomas was withholding something and questioned him deeply; perhaps he had heard other men's confession and already knew of the killings? Thomas said his penance without thought or genuine penitence. His mind seemed mired in fog. He could not think straight. 'My name is Benjamin.'

In the end he got blind drunk on strong ale, topped off

with a jar of barley spirit. He recounted the whole episode to his servant, Rufus, describing truthfully his part in the killing and his physical and emotional reaction to it. Rufus did his job well, just listening and saying little. In the morning he mixed Thomas a concoction of his own design; three raw hen's eggs, barley spirit, a pinch (no more!) of their valuable pepper and some other mystery ingredient known only to him, and had his groaning and nauseous master knock it back in one draught. It kicked like a mule, but a bad hangover was averted.

John of Gaunt's party had returned and it was rumoured he was in a foul temper. He called for the senior men, Bamford and one or two others, and questioned them separately on the destruction of his Savoy Palace. He wanted to know when they had set off, by which route; seemed convinced that tardiness may have resulted in the loss of his possessions. Eventually, all thirty of the men who had travelled to London were called together into his chambers. He paced up and down, screaming and ranting, berating everybody as cowards and traitors and sluggards. Each of the men looked down at the floor, terrified of meeting his master's eye. Gaunt was a big man, tall and lean with dark black hair and beard, just turning to grey. Thomas supposed that he could be described as handsome, though he always saw meanness, slyness in the man's countenance which detracted from any positive attributes in his appearance. It was only an assumption, but Thomas felt that his character had been formed by years on end of constant, negative comparison to his elder brother Prince Edward.

Eventually, Gaunt's rage was assuaged and he called for all to sit, and sent for food and ale. Thomas's stomach heaved at the thought, but he raised a jug to his lips along with everyone else. He was to learn in the coming years that this was typical of his liege; fearsome rages which burnt out quickly and were replaced by affable camaraderie in an instant. Gaunt called several men into close discussion with him, singly and in small groups, at the far end of the long table around which they were gathered. Many were sent on errands and missions and left immediately to set about the tasks they had been assigned. Soon there were just a few left and he called Thomas, and Bamford, to join him. Everyone else was dismissed except for Gaunt's bookkeeper, who was always on hand to record his instructions, orders, financial dealings, and to draft letters in a great leather-bound book. Gaunt beckoned Thomas to sit next to him, their backs to the table, feet extended toward the roaring fire. Gaunt was pulling strips of pork off a bone with his fingers and feeding his pair of greyhounds, which were milling around his legs, snapping at the meat.

'Erpingham, eh? I hear good things about you. Ufford spoke well of your time at Calais.'

'Thank you, my Lord'

'I am told that you have drawn blood, since joining my service; killed a man who dared to rob me of my rightful possessions. Did you enjoy the act of killing him?' He looked at Thomas keenly and the young man sensed that his reply would be crucial to his future in Gaunt's service. Thomas opted for the truth.

'No, my Lord. I wish there had been an alternative. I fear the killing was dishonourable; he carried no sword'

'Good,' he replied, and it seemed that Thomas had passed a test, 'I am surrounded by braggarts and boasters and need men who can speak to me honestly; men who know the value of keeping the peace, as well as killing and spreading terror across the land. I have a task for you, which I ask that you undertake willingly Sir Thomas, even though it may seem dull and may take many years to accomplish.'

'My Lord, I am merely....'

'You will be my representative in Norfolk. You will keep the peace. You will ensure that my will is carried out and you will gather the revenues that are due to me without question. Is that understood Sir Thomas?'

'I am your humble esquire, Sir.'

'Oh very well then, if you want ceremony....', Gaunt picked up a toasting fork from the fireplace and tapped it on Thomas's shoulder, 'Arise Sir Thomas, blah, blah, blah! I will not expect you to kneel in the dirt and you will not expect me to fetch my sword from my bedchamber. You are knighted, Sir Edmond is our witness, and the record is made.' He waved to his bookkeeper who was scribbling frantically. Gaunt looked at Thomas then in all seriousness.

'Serve me well Sir Thomas Erpingham. Remember who raised you, and who can set you down again.'

Thomas just nodded; he was in shock and could summon no words. Bamford slapped him on the back and they drank a toast. They were dismissed and joined the remainder of the group in the great hall. Thomas was roundly congratulated by all. His hand was shaken by men of all stations, knights and esquires and servants too. Rufus grinned at him; his own position had been considerably enhanced by his master's promotion. Across the hallway, Robert Cranwell raised his goblet towards Thomas and nodded, but did not come forward to speak and Rufus observed him leaving the gathering shortly after.

Over the course of several days, Thomas's tasks in Norfolk were explained in detail and confirmed in writing, and an income was granted to him in annuity. It was Gaunt's bookkeeper, Michael Swain, who coached him and gave him his letters of authority, and Thomas did not see Gaunt again; he had commenced a tour of his Leicestershire properties, a show of strength with Bamford leading a small army to protect him and demonstrate his power. Rufus prepared for their journey, excited at the prospect of seeing his home and parents once again. So they set out on the road towards home, the birthplace of both young men, both older and wiser than when they had left it. Thomas carried with him two things which he would keep for the rest of his days; a new title, which he had to repeat over and over again under his breath to get the feel of, Sir Thomas Erpingham!, and the image of the two staring eyes of a man called Benjamin, whom he had murdered in the woods.

***

Over time, Jacob made a home for himself in the woods and outbuildings surrounding St. Benet Holme Abbey. The monks fed him on scraps and he foraged in the woods and stole from local villagers. One monk in particular, Brother Anselmo, looked out for Jacob's welfare and in return had him steal items of value to order, trinkets that the monk had observed in houses he had visited. Several other outcasts and misfits congregated around the Abbey and, though they shunned Jacob at first, he soon became a leader amongst them. They became horse thieves, erasing or disguising markings of ownership before selling on the best animals, and slaughtering the old nags for food. Jacob kept a beautiful piebald cob for himself and now the gang were mounted robbers, able to escape pursuit. Soon Anselmo had them holding up and robbing travellers, splitting the proceeds with Jacob and his gang. Jacob found that he only needed to reveal his deformities for most to quake in terror, and hand over their valuables without dissent.

One day, Anselmo left to join the service of a local knight as tutor to his infant son. Jacob kept in close contact though and was often on hand to take and hide, or sell the small items of value that Anselmo stole from his master's house. In the autumn of Jacob's twentieth year, he was tipped off by Anselmo that the lady of the manor and her son would be travelling to Norwich with the harvest, carrying with them much gold, silver and jewels, secreted in the wagon they travelled in. The ambush was set and Jacob led the attack, revealing his face to the terrified woman to frighten her into handing over her treasure. Remarkably, the infant child with her acted with great courage and stabbed Jacob with a concealed blade, injuring him in the leg; a wound which would heal, but leave him with a permanent limp.

The gang fled to the safety of the Abbey, Anselmo following fast behind; his cover blown. He spoke with the Abbot and was hidden away inside the Abbey for several months, to avoid the retribution his actions had surely deserved. The Abbot met all enquiries on the subject with blank incredulity. Jacob and his gang survived on their own resources, without the monk's assistance.

Rather than anger or shame at being bested by a child, Jacob felt a great respect and a strange affinity with the boy; he could not adequately explain why. Anselmo seethed with rage and swore he would have his revenge.

***

CHAPTER 6

(In which we observe a power struggle in the great city of Norwich, and witness the burning of a heretic)

My eyesight is beginning to fail me. That does not surprise me in the least; I have known men of half my years go blind, particularly those who habitually scratch vellum with a quill by candlelight. I own a glass which has the magical quality of raising each word to twice its original size. It is one of several wondrous items I acquired when Jonas the Healer passed away; none of the villagers were interested and, anyway, I am one of the few who can read and write. I peer through it as I scribble in the bright daylight hours, but I have ceased to strain by candlelight.

Sometimes Rufus takes up the pen on my behalf in the evenings, while I dictate from the big old chair by the fireplace. If you read this manuscript you will occasionally observe two different hands, the bulk of the work in my own heavy angular flow, his in a lighter, sharp and scratchy style. The words though, are mine and mine alone, even when it is he who has told me the tale in the first place. We continue...

***

'I had him hung, drawn and quartered, right there in front of his own people, said Bishop Despenser, his hands clasped together and resting on top of his vast paunch. He and Sir Thomas were in private conversation together; walking around the battlements of Norwich Castle, pausing occasionally to look out over the city and beyond. Of course, nothing was ever really private between such men and several of the Bishop's priests trailed behind him at a discrete distance, just within earshot, as did Rufus Long. They were enjoying a welcome break in the proceedings that had been going on all morning in the keep below. The nobility of the county had gathered to discuss appropriate methods for suppressing discontent among the peasantry. Pockets of dissatisfaction kept breaking out into minor insurrections, ever since Tyler and his mob had torched London a few years previously. The Bishop was referring to his execution of the local rabble-rouser Geoffrey Litster, whom he had personally defeated in a minor skirmish at North Walsham, an encounter which was being laughingly referred to in the local taverns as a battle.

'To harness the true nature of power, my dear boy, you must learn to act with fierce vengeance upon those who challenge your authority. Even when your conscience is telling you to be merciful, you must still strike down your foe. Any other course would be seen as weak, and simply invite further impudence. That is why I executed him, and why I persecute his followers still.' The Bishop had slipped his arm affably into Sir Thomas's crooked elbow and now they were walking conjoined, like a corpulent father with his youthful and athletic son, on a stroll after Sunday dinner. Sir Thomas stopped and turned to face the older man.

'Your methods are well known, Your Grace, and your power here in Norwich is accepted and unchallenged by all. But you know who I represent, and he is also a powerful man with many interests here in Norfolk. My task is to represent him faithfully, and my heart's desire is to do so without troubling you; but there are rents owed, annuities unpaid. My master seeks redress.'

'Does Gaunt think I am weak, because I am summoned to parliament over the fiasco at Ypres?' All bonhomie had disappeared from the cleric's voice and demeanour. The Bishop was not long back from his crusade to France in support of the true Pope Urban, and against the usurper Clement who had installed himself at Avignon. He had sponsored and led the expedition which, so it was said, had failed because of his ineptitude in the field. Now it was Thomas who spoke with calm reassurance.

'Your Grace, you have seen off far greater challenges than this. Parliament? They are weak men, all of them, who wouldn't know the sharp end of a lance from the blunt!'

The Bishop had let the mask slip and was all friendliness and smiles again.

'Dear boy, dear boy, you have the look of a soldier about

you, but I suspect you have seen little of the chaos of the battlefield? What was I to do? The Church could not continue with two Popes on the throne, and if I did nothing about it then nobody else seemed likely to try. But my commanders betrayed me, took bribes and looked the other way. They left me to take the blame.'

Despenser was momentarily downcast and, sharing the mood, Sir Thomas confided in the Bishop, who had correctly discerned his youthful frustrations.

'I am a knight, Your Grace, but feel like a charlatan! I have seen no battles, witnessed no great victories, or defeats come to that. Do you know the most exciting thing I have dealt with this year?' He paused for effect, 'a magistrate's case for sheep theft! Five hundred of the bloody things! I ask you, how can anybody steal five hundred sheep without their rightful owner noticing? And I'm supposed to be organising the coastal defenses against the French! Don't make me laugh; a bunch of bloody Norfolk fishermen who wouldn't recognise a Frenchman if they netted one!' The Bishop laughed and put his arm around Sir Thomas's shoulder.

'So, neither of us is entirely content with our current circumstances. But your time will come, dear boy; you will see plenty of warfare if you choose to go looking for it.'

They continued to stroll, pausing to look out over the battlements at the teeming city below. Sir Thomas and the Bishop began to whisper and Rufus guessed that a deal was being struck over the monies owed to John of Gaunt; Bishop

Despenser was a practical man and, though he would wish to appear strong in front of his retinue, he would not relish the prospect of the Duke of Lancaster as an enemy. Rufus looked out over the battlements and nearly swooned with giddiness; he had a great aversion to heights which was as strong as his urge to vomit every time he set foot on a boat. Solid ground was the only medium upon which Rufus Long was truly happy.

They were at the south-western corner of the castle looking out upon the busy, bustling, poorer half of Norwich. The market square, with its great cross at the centre was teeming with life; hawkers, barrows, carts, animals everywhere. The shining new jewel of the city; the great church of St. Peter stood proudly at its southern end. To the right the Madder Market, to the left the Horse Market, both busy, and away to the south the Timber and Swine markets also about their business; the four together forming the hubs of a great seething machine of commerce, fed from the various gateways and roads through the city walls, and by the merchant fleets plying the Wensum from the coast. The city wall itself, pride of the burghers of Norwich; built to withstand the assault of an army, against which it had yet to be properly tested, and against the arrival of the plague, against which it had proved entirely useless.

Rufus Long's father once told him that since the time of the great pestilence which had occurred in his boyhood, killing more than half the population of the city, Norwich had expanded again like a squeezed sponge, sucking in great numbers of people from the surrounding countryside, and from further afield, so that it quickly became impossible to guess that so many had perished.

Sir Thomas and the Bishop continued their walk, now speaking audibly again, the retinue following at a discrete distance. Rufus and the group of priests were equally eager to find out which of the men appeared best pleased with whatever bargain they had struck.

'Of course, my dear boy, your master has the cares of England upon his shoulders and I do not envy him that. I too work tirelessly for my own master,' he looked skywards, 'and in troubled and confusing times, I am obliged to guide my flock with firmness and clarity. You are not, I trust, an advocate of the devil Wycliffe?'

'No, Your Grace, I am certainly not!' replied Sir Thomas, though Rufus wondered if in other circumstances his master might have wished to open up a broader discussion on the subject. He knew that Sir Thomas was no avid supporter of the Lollard cause, but neither was he bitterly opposed to the kind of reforms they espoused. However, Sir Thomas had clear objectives which had nothing to do with discussing the biblical validity of the sacrament of the Eucharist, and there would be little point in entering into discussion with the immensely rich cleric on the need for the church to reject the acquisition of temporal wealth. The Bishop's views were widely known, and he could tell that his master wished to keep the discussion on the safe ground of monies owed, and the balance of power between the Church and secular interests.

'Many have questioned my role in the mother church. 'The Fighting Bishop' they call me, and rightly so. I wish that more of the priesthood would take up the sword to defend the truth against those who have the audacity to claim a more enlightened path. Who does this Wycliffe think he is, eh? A jumped up curate, waving his evil tracts under people's noses and unsettling the peasantry.' The Bishop was becoming enraged, ranting on his pet topic.

'Such matters require a firm hand,' said Sir Thomas, with a placating touch of the Bishop's shoulder, 'but for today we must deal with more earthly matters, like how we ensure that no more Geoffrey Litsters, or Wat Tylers are permitted to come to the fore.'

They had reached the opposite side of the battlements and the two men paused again to look out across the city. Rufus steadied himself against the battlement wall and looked first toward the north; across the Wensum to Norwich-over-the-Water and the great Priory of the White Friars. The main north-south thoroughfare ran straight through Tombland below them and up Magdalen Street towards the north city gate, and then the road quickly disappeared in the woodland beyond. Twenty miles in the distance he could see a faint purple haze where the land rose before meeting the sea. Hanging plumes of wood-smoke betrayed the location of towns and villages along the way and he searched in vain for sight of his own village, Erpingham. Rufus moved to stand at the east facing wall and saw the great Cathedral standing before him, a vast and beautiful monument to the greatness of God, its newly finished spire seeming to pierce the very heavens. Beyond the extensive grounds of the Cathedral he could see the great hospital of St. Giles and then the fortified river crossing beyond. To the south of the Cathedral stood two more great Priories; of the Grey Friars and Austin Friars. This side of the city was quieter, less frenetic and the houses of the richer kind were located here.

The two men were summoned from below and moved down into the castle keep to continue their deliberations around a long oaken table. The afternoon was hot and drowsy, flies buzzing around the remains of their midday meal. Of the twenty or so noblemen and churchmen present, there were an approximate balance of hawks and doves. The hawks were all for making an example; stringing ringleaders up at the gibbet, flaying skin in the marketplace. The doves countered with proposals for poor relief; charitable donations, the release of debtors from the Guildhall as a token of good faith. Mostly, the men were talking to hear the sound of their own voices; nobody listened to what was being said by others, all were mentally rehearsing what they intended to say next. Not one of them moved from his original position on the subject by the slightest degree. All were pleased when the afternoon came to an end and they retired to their lodgings in the city, no further forward in their deliberations, and none the wiser for their efforts. As Sir Thomas prepared to leave, Bishop Despenser invited him to join him in the morning before the meeting resumed.

'We can continue our discussion on the nature of power, my dear boy'

Sir Thomas and Rufus spent the night at the Erpingham family town house, which had been hastily dusted and swept upon the late news of their coming. Food and ale were brought in from a tavern and they both spent an uncomfortable night in fitful sleep; like his master, Rufus was happier by far in the manor house at Erpingham than he ever was in the great city. They were awoken before dawn by one of Bishop Despenser's men, and were taken to meet with him at an undisclosed location. They travelled through the deserted streets, Sir Thomas in the Bishop's litter and Rufus walking behind, along the road out past St. Giles Hospital and across the Wensum via the fortified bridge. Rufus voiced his alarm to his master; suspecting some kind of trap, but Sir Thomas seemed at ease and went along willingly. They arrived at their destination and were met by Bishop Despenser, and a small retinue of priests and servants. They gathered on a grassy knoll looking down on a rough clearing by the bank of the river. A great wooden post had been inserted into a hole in the ground and stood upright, surrounded by a pile of logs and smaller kindling sticks. Another, greater pile of wood lay to the side, in reserve. Rufus was no fool; he knew what this place was, and what they were to witness that morning.

Sir Thomas and the Bishop were in conversation, but they were several yards away and Rufus did not hear much of what passed between them. He caught a snippet; '...recanted, his name is....', 'it's not necessary that I know.....', then their voices were lost again amid a rising whisper as they observed a small procession coming into sight, walking down the hill toward them from the east. At the front walked a priest reciting prayers in Latin, behind him four guards surrounded and supported a slight figure dressed in a white robe, his hands bound behind his back. His head had been roughly shaven, blood seeping from wounds in his scalp and he looked about him without seemingly comprehending what was about to happen. The marks of torture were upon him, livid wounds on his arms and face where the hot iron had been applied; pallid cheeks sunken where his teeth had been ripped from his jaw. As he passed the group of onlookers, Rufus could see that the tips of his fingers were a bloody mess where the nails had once been. He mouthed gibberish and it was obvious that his mind was gone and that he was oblivious to the crime for which he had suffered, and would momentarily suffer more.

Rufus looked across and saw that his master and the Bishop were no longer speaking. There was a hushed expectancy among those who were watching. Several early risers had approached from the city to observe proceedings; word of such things spread quickly, but a strong guard posted on the bridge kept them back. The prisoner was raised bodily onto the pile of logs and fastened to the post by a chain around his neck. The chain was firmly attached to the post with an iron staple so that the body would be maintained in a standing position. The condemned man looked about him without comprehension, opening and closing his jaw like a fish out of water.

The priest who had led the procession asked the captive man if he had anything to say, but the prisoner seemed unaware that he was being addressed. At a signal from the Bishop a bundle of brushwood was lit and quickly blazed in the semi-dark of the early dawn. The bundle was thrown onto the pyre and the rest of the dry wood caught quickly. Rufus had not witnessed a burning before and admitted to himself a morbid fascination; leastways he was transfixed, watching the face of the condemned man for the first agony to register. The old man continued to gape at his audience until the flames began to lick at his feet. He looked downward and then up again at his tormentors, gabling incoherently as his naked feet began a macabre jig, trying desperately to avoid the searing touch of the flame. As the heat and smoke increased in ferocity around him, the man opened his mouth and screamed once, a long shrieking sound which gradually diminished into a deep gurgle until all the breath had been forced from his lungs. As he inhaled, so the fierce flame entered his mouth and nose, and he made no further sound. His shoulders and chest jerked spasmodically, and soon the fire raged so intensely that only his head remained visible. His mouth was fixed open; a circular maw, and as some internal bodily fluid boiled within him there was a loud popping noise, and a great cloud of steam and vapour were emitted from his mouth. This caused a stir among the onlookers and one priest shouted out that the evil had been forced out of the Lollard's body. Now the flame was all-consuming and the body was no longer visible in the conflagration. A smell like burning bacon fat filled the air. Men threw more wood onto the blaze and there was a general sense that the spectacle was over.

Rufus looked at his master to see how he had reacted to the execution, but Sir Thomas was not watching the inferno, he was staring hard at Bishop Despenser, a look of cold hard anger in his eyes which his servant had not seen before. This had been a show of strength, nothing more, and an old man, driven to insanity by abuse and mistreatment, had paid with his life so that Sir Thomas would know who held ultimate power in the city. The Bishop, unaware that he was being observed, stared mesmerised into the flame and drummed the fingers of both hands repetitively on his belly.

As the crowd began to disperse, two men moved in with long iron rakes and began to work the fire, moving half burned logs from the periphery of the heat to the centre. An unidentifiable dark mass was faintly visible in the middle of the inferno and as the upright pole finally burned through and crashed down in a shower of sparks, so the execution site became just another bonfire. Sir Thomas and Rufus began to walk towards the bridge but found their way blocked by Bishop Despenser. The kindly, avuncular character from yesterday was gone; now a vicious animal stood before them; dangerous like a cornered bear.

‘Never question my power, boy, or my willingness to wield it. Attend your master’s business, but steer clear of mine. I will not tell you again.’

Rufus expected his master to respond with an angry outburst, but Sir Thomas spoke softly, gently.

‘My name is Sir Thomas Erpingham,’ he emphasised the three words individually, ‘and I will give you cause to remember that, before we are through’.

They pushed past the Bishop and his guards and crossed the bridge back towards the city. If Sir Thomas had no enemy before, he had one now, and a dangerous and ruthless enemy at that.

***

Over time, Jacob became a fixture at the Abbey and nobody questioned his presence anymore; if they considered him at all they assumed that he was Anselmo's servant, nothing more. One by one, his gang were captured and killed, or imprisoned for the outrageous acts of robbery they had carried out. He was occasionally named by his confederates when they were forced to confess their crimes, but although bailiffs were sometimes dispatched to apprehend him, they generally took one look at his appearance, assumed him to have infectious leprosy, and left him well alone.

Jacob still carried out thefts for his master, but with increasing reluctance. He had taken to following the monks at a discrete distance as they went to the great nave of the Abbey at various times of the day to hear mass and other services, to chant psalms and sing hymns. He would hide in one of the recesses at the back, transfixed by the beauty of the Latin words spoken by the Abbot, the chanted responses, the deep resonance in the great open space under the vast roof of the building.

He had a realistic outlook on the path that his life had taken; at heart he was a decent man but understood that once the leprosy had claimed him, damaged him and then miraculously left him, he had had little choice other than to steal for a living. The option of living the rest of his days on charity was not one he relished. He was a sinner, that much was clear, but the example set by Anselmo and the other monks, including the Abbot, did not lead him to think that his behaviour was exceptional. There was a void in Jacob's life that he was unable to define. For some reason, he continued to experience a repetitive dream as he slept at night on a straw pallet on the floor of Anselmo's cell; one that he had first known long ago as he had lain close to death at the leper hospital, being nursed by Mother, something about birds that lived their whole lives in flight without ever resting.

***

CHAPTER 7

(In which Sir Thomas Erpingham experiences the reality of war, and meets Henry Bolingbroke for the first time)

Sir Thomas had come visiting unexpectedly one afternoon several years ago and found me scrubbing at scrap pieces of soaked rag paper, trying to remove the ink so that I could reuse the pieces to continue my manuscript. Several attempts had already failed, leaving me with shredded masses of unusable pulp. My frustration had boiled over, and as he came in through the door he had to duck quickly to avoid a soggy missile which was sailing through the air at head height.

Within days, a merchant had arrived bearing rolled sheets of the finest vellum from a manufacturer in London; the regular supplier of many of the great monasteries of England. It was the finest stuff imaginable and I still get great pleasure from the feel of the nib flowing across its surface. I am using it now, recording a story he once told me about war and the falling out of princes and kings.

***

They had assembled the trebuchet under intermittent fire, men crouching behind a hastily constructed wall of shields, driving pegs and wedges into the timbers with sledge-hammers. In truth, there was little enough danger from the arrows directed at them from the city walls; they were working at the absolute limit of range for even the strongest archers, and the majority fell well short of their position. The occasional iron-tipped arrow pinged harmlessly off their shield wall, or impaled itself weakly in the soft turf before them. The fact that no projectile reached their position with sufficient force to cause injury told them that the city defenders had no greater weapon than the longbow or crossbow to fire at the attacking army.

Sir Thomas was working with the siege engineers who supervised the great catapult; managing its assembly, disassembly, transportation, maintenance and use, with the help of their siege team of twenty strong men. He had not been assigned this task, but was greatly interested in the mechanics of the machine and, anyway, this occupation was much preferable to him than hanging around the tents of King Richard and the Duke of Lancaster, with all the other young knights and esquires, hoping for a word or glance in their direction.

Sir Thomas would have freely admitted that he had yearned for this life, stuck as he had been in tranquil Norfolk, a glorified tax collector for John of Gaunt. Like much else in life though, he had discovered that what the heart desires most seldom turns out exactly as one envisaged. Sir Thomas had travelled north with the King, and just about every other nobleman in England, at the head of a vast army; some said eighty thousand strong, their mission to engage with and destroy the Scots, once and for all.

The noblemen rode in the van; their colours standing out bold against the rich green summer landscape, burnished armour glinting in the hot July sun. There was much jockeying for position, each knight desperate to ride closest to the King, or at the very least a duke. Behind them the bulk of the army stretched back over several miles; mounted men-at-arms and archers, foot-soldiers, servants, priests, surgeons, messenger boys, heralds and pages, the travelling brothels, the cook wagons, baggage carts and heavily laden mule trains. Each evening as they made camp it was several hours until all were gathered, and in the mornings several hours again until all were on the move.

In their wake lay a scene of utter devastation for miles in every direction. Not a cow, or a pig, or a sheep, or a chicken had survived their ravenous passing. Grain stores had been emptied, fields stripped of crops, kitchen gardens ravaged, and many a village would starve that coming winter because the great army of their own King had passed through their lands. In fact it had proved harder with each passing week to find sufficient food for the great host; word of their coming had preceded them and there were many flocks of sheep and herds of cattle hidden away up in the hills until the army passed by.

Their biggest problem became apparent as they marched around the southern hills of Scotland looking for someone to fight. An army like King Richard's required another army to engage with in formal battle, and such a thing did not appear to exist. The Scottish forces seemed to consist of small groups of mobile mounted troops who were able to set ambushes, and then retreat quickly into the hills. Several times, a troop of the younger knights charged off in hot pursuit, desperate for glory, but the enemy seemed able to melt away before their very eyes. Sir Thomas's liege, the Duke of Lancaster, was seething with anger at what he perceived to be the cowardice of the Scots, and each town or settlement they came upon had paid a terrible price.

Now they were ranged against a proper city; this was Edinburgh apparently, though all such places seemed alike to Sir Thomas. This town had solid defences; walls and turrets and moats rather than just the wooden stockades they had encountered so far, and the English army were preparing for siege. Terms had been offered and rejected, and now the work of the siege engines was to begin. The engineers had almost completed their preparations, and there was something of a race in progress as four other engines were also being assembled, and none wished to be last into action. The great, hinged counterweight box had been filled with heavy rocks and was now in the fully raised position; the siege team had used ropes, pulleys and locking mechanisms to pull it up into place by exerting downward force on the vast throwing arm, made from a whole ash tree-trunk. Attached to the tip of the throwing arm was a long hawser with a rope cradle, into which a large boulder had been manhandled. They were ready for a first test firing.

The lead engineer called his team to safe positions, checked over the firing mechanism carefully, then stepped away several paces to the left and tugged hard on the trigger rope. The great counterweight box hurtled downward, flinging the tip of the throwing arm upwards, the effect of the pivot bearing causing the speed at the tip to be multiplied several times. As the throwing arm accelerated upwards the cable and rope cradle, with its stone projectile, were pulled at first backwards along a greased gulley, and then into a great arc up and over the machine and toward the target. Midway through the cradle's transit, there was a loud snapping sound as one of the cradle ropes broke under the incredible force of the projectile trying to separate itself from the machine, and suddenly they were aware that the boulder had been loosed too early, its trajectory straight upwards and slightly to the rear. The counterweight was hinged so that its path was not abruptly halted as it reached its lowest point, placing unbearable stress on the machine, and it swung on its hinge while the throwing arm gradually settled into an upright position, the ropes and cradle coming to rest in a tangle. All eyes were on the boulder which had ascended perhaps two hundred feet into the air, at its highest point a mere dot in the sky, before it began to descend, becoming bigger by the moment. Sir Thomas looked behind their position and saw men scattering in all directions and then the projectile land with a great crash, turning a baggage wagon into matchwood in an instant, and burying itself several feet into the soft turf. There was silence for a moment and then he heard hoots of derision from the battlements of the city walls.

The lead engineer screamed abuse at his team and there was much discussion and blame asserted about who had last checked the cradle ropes. John of Gaunt, who had been watching from the hill above, rode down and set about the siege team with vicious verbal abuse, and blows from the flat of his sword. Sir Thomas decided that he had seen enough of trebuchets for the time being, and made a discrete exit, making his way uphill to join a group of noblemen who had gathered to observe proceedings. He was greeted by an old friend from Calais, Robert Cranwell.

'Good shot Tom! But shouldn't we be firing at the enemy rather than our own wagons?'

Sir Thomas abused him good-naturedly in return, but was secretly disappointed that his name was being associated with the failure of the catapult; he was as keen as any of them to take home a good reputation and glory from this endeavour, and hoped that this incident would be quickly forgotten.

An hour or so later, the machine was ready for another try and they watched as the siege team worked to raise the counterweight, before the chief engineer went through his preparations again. This time when he pulled the trigger rope the engine operated correctly, and the great boulder was flung toward the city walls in a high arc. The range was long and they heard a crashing, splintering noise as the projectile smashed through several buildings on the far side of the defensive wall. This time there were no jeers from the battlements.

The pummelling of the city of Edinburgh commenced, and all five of the mighty siege engines now had their range. The trebuchets were spaced across a field, each machine about one hundred yards apart, the line three hundred yards distant from the city wall; out of effective range of the defender's weapons. The siege teams worked in sequence so that, although each machine took a full five minutes to prepare and load, a missile hurtled at the enemy every minute, allowing him no time to recuperate from the previous blow. Most of the great boulders landed inside the town, demolishing several buildings as they fell to earth. Occasionally, a lighter stone travelled further and smashed into the rock-face below the castle keep, sending sharp splinters of shattered rock down on the people below. Heavier stones travelled a shorter distance and, though several landed harmlessly short of the wall, every now and again a direct hit was scored on the city walls, demolishing part of the defensive structure and raising a mighty cheer from the English forces.

King Richard and John of Gaunt gave the orders to draw their men up into an attacking formation; foot-soldiers to the front armed with pikes, archers to each flank and mounted cavalry to the rear. This, though, did not represent more than one third of their available force, and many men looked on from the high ground above, wondering if and when their chance would come. At a signal from Gaunt the trebuchet teams began to wrap their stone projectiles in several layers of rough woollen sacking which was then soaked in a hot mixture of tar, pine resin and sulphur, plus other secret ingredients known only to the siege engineers, and then ignited seconds before the boulder was hurled. These flaming comets roared through the air above the heads of the Englishmen, trailing smoke and raindrops of fire behind them, before they crashed down upon the besieged city, setting light to timber buildings and adding raging fires to the problems afflicting the city's defenders. Now the trebuchet teams were forced to douse the flames which had caught the rope cradles and timbers of their own oil-soaked machines before each reloading.

With the city now well ablaze, the order was given that the troops move forward, and shields were raised by all men as they entered the range of the enemy archers. Sir Thomas was on foot, fully armoured and carrying sword and shield, plus a mace and dagger in reserve which were secured by leather thongs at his side. He advanced at the head of a group of Norfolk pike-men, there on service with him as was their due, and shouted encouragement to those who appeared afraid, or wished to lag behind. He made for a section of the wall which had been smashed in by the onslaught of the siege engines, expecting at any moment to feel the impact of an arrow. As they approached to within fifty feet Sir Thomas charged forward, his sword raised and the men following behind him at the run, roaring for blood as they advanced. His assumption was that the defenders would have taken up positions inside the wall and would strike as they entered the breach. He tried hard to remember everything Hooper had drummed into him at Calais, all the lessons, mock-fights, theoretical lectures; but the truth was that he had forgotten all he had been taught and all he felt was the lust for battle raging within him. Sir Thomas had worried incessantly beforehand that he might lack courage in battle; that he might be proved a coward, and the memory of his hesitation before killing the man in the woods on the way back from London was constantly with him. Yet in all honesty he was not afraid. He was enjoying the rush and thrill; had the bloodlust raging within his veins.

There was no enemy. Nobody was there to engage with; all had fled. Sir Thomas and his men moved forward through abandoned defensive positions and saw the burning town laid out before them. Beyond the dwelling places and markets of the city, Sir Thomas could see a long procession of people, soldiers and civilians, walking up a steep pathway toward the castle keep. Many were carrying bundles of provisions, or various kinds of weaponry. There was a crowd at the base of the rock where the path ascended and they were surging forward against a ring of armed men, who only allowed certain members of the crowd through. The people were desperate to escape before the English were among them like wolves. As the bulk of the army arrived, so night began to fall and the town burned. The attacking horde descended into the streets; not only those who had led the attack, but also the great number of men who had been kept in reserve. Once it was clear there was no battle to be fought to gain the town, and not wishing to miss out on the plunder, they had dashed down the hill to join the slaughter.

Sir Thomas was able to observe at first hand the work of the great siege catapults; each enormous boulder that found a target had entirely demolished the timber and daub constructed buildings, crashing down through tiled roofs and multiple stories before bouncing through thin walls and destroying several more adjacent buildings in its path. Much of the town was aflame but there were also many intact, deserted buildings and the English soldiers fought each other to be first into the more prosperous looking houses. Sir Thomas found himself running along a main thoroughfare towards the access point of the castle keep, part of a great howling mob without leadership or discipline and he stopped momentarily, aware that he should take command of the rabble and direct them towards some clear objective. From a building to his left, Sir Thomas saw a group of men drag a woman outside by the hair. They tore off her garments and bent her forwards over a horse-trough. Men held her arms down and her legs apart while their leader began to rut with her from behind, like a dog on heat.

The mob was all around him now, uncontrollable, a vast formless beast intent on bloodshed and murder and rape and torture, and Sir Thomas realised there was nothing he could do to control them. A local man suddenly burst out of the door of his house, carrying a bundle which he clasped close to his chest. He made a run for it, but a thrown mace caught him in the small of the back and he was propelled forward onto his knees, his precious bundle rolling out of his grasp. There was a scramble among the Englishmen to reach the bundle first; momentarily the man was ignored. A soldier ripped off the cloth covering and found himself holding a mewling newborn infant by one leg, the umbilical cord and placenta still attached and dangling from the child's belly. He looked at his prize in bewilderment for a moment, and then threw the baby to one side where it was kicked and trampled upon by the mob. One group of men literally tore the child's father limb from limb, hacking at him with swords and axes, men holding up grisly trophies for each other to inspect and admire. A second group entered the house and dragged out the child's mother, still wrapped in the blood-soaked sheet within which she had just given birth. They raped her and slit her throat, right there in the street.

Sir Thomas was roaring orders for men to gather under his command, but none took any notice. The sight of the blood and murder; the rape and abuse had raised a pounding, thumping rage inside him. Suddenly a small group of local men were found who had drawn themselves into a defensive formation, swords raised, around a building which was evidently the home of their family. Sir Thomas descended upon them with a terrible bloodlust and pushed other soldiers out of the way so he could swing his sword at them, cutting them down, slashing and stabbing. Now there was a roaring sound in his ears and he heard himself cursing and screaming incoherently as he took the life of several men, spattering their blood on the walls of their home, the blade of his sword glinting dully in the light of the burning buildings around him. The night was long and, though he would not forget or deny his active participation in further acts of savagery, Sir Thomas resolved to describe them only to his confessor.

When dawn broke, Sir Thomas was witness to a raging argument between King Richard and his own liege the Duke of Lancaster. In truth this had been long in the making; as Richard had grown to manhood he had been increasingly unhappy taking orders and direction from his uncle. There had also been growing tension over Gaunt's vast wealth and landholdings, which were rumoured to match, or even exceed those of the young King. Richard's close advisors had worked hard at stirring the cauldron of mistrust and suspicion; Gaunt had made many enemies among the King's household, and now he began to reap what he had sown.

It transpired that a messenger had brought news overnight; while the English had been laying waste to much of Scotland, a Scottish army with assistance from the French had slipped past them and laid waste in turn to much of Cumberland. King Richard berated Gaunt publicly over this tactical error, the blame for which he placed firmly with his uncle. Things were said by both men that could not be unsaid and Gaunt, ashen-faced with rage, and with fear that the King could have him summarily executed for the things he had said in anger, allowed himself to be pulled away by several of his retainers. Suddenly the knights and esquires of King Richard and the Duke of Lancaster, who had been side-by-side throughout the campaign, formed themselves up into separate ranks. There was palpable tension in the air which could have turned nasty in an instant but, luckily, some of the older men in each party were able to find soothing words for those who had taken offence, and calm the hot-heads who had reached for their swords.

The great army headed south in fruitless pursuit of the Scottish enemy, though what had once been a united force of eighty thousand was now one great army under the King, marching in uneasy alliance with a smaller force loyal to Gaunt. On the long march home, Sir Thomas found himself riding alongside Gaunt's son Henry of Bolingbroke, the Earl of Derby. He was a confident, affable youth, about ten years younger than Sir Thomas, with the gift of a dry, self-deprecating sense of humour that made it easy to like him. They fell into easy conversation and Henry was desperate to hear of the older knight's exploits in the field. Sir Thomas was reminded of himself as a younger man, keen to impress his elders and to be accepted by them as an equal, but there the similarity ended. He had been a blushing, shy young man, afraid that at any moment he would be exposed as a weakling or coward; this one had all the self-confidence of his father, and, like his father, conducted himself with the regal bearing of a king.

Henry spoke to Sir Thomas with familiarity about King Richard, who was his first cousin and childhood companion. It was evident that Henry still held much residual love for the young King and that they had been friends for most of their childhood, but there was resentment at the way in which the King was now treating his father, and also derision for what Henry perceived to be the King's inherent weaknesses; his nervous, emotional nature and his lack of affinity with any of the noble pursuits which Henry avidly followed; hunting, hawking, swordsmanship, the joust. As each day passed they sought each other out for company and by the time they returned to London, Henry and Sir Thomas had become firm friends.

The falling out between King Richard and John of Gaunt, the two most powerful men in the land was the reason that Sir Thomas found himself, several months later, preparing to embark with his liege and some twenty thousand men, to take ship to aid the Portuguese in their war against the Spanish; the ulterior motive being that Gaunt might be able to use the expedition to further his claim for the crown of Castile and Leon. With the welcome news that his uncle would be abroad for several months, possibly years, King Richard had staged a very public display of reconciliation and the expedition had been given royal support and funding, and was even declared a holy crusade by the Pope. Sir Thomas faced the prospect of a long sea voyage with dread, knowing that he would spend much of it vomiting over the side, but as a loyal vassal to Gaunt, he had no choice in the matter.

It was during the months of preparation for departure that Sir Thomas had come across an old friend from his youth. A man was walking toward him and Sir Thomas was struck by his build; evidently he was an archer, and by the fact that one side of his face was badly scarred, the skin dragging his features downward on that side and fixing his expression into a lop-sided grimace. It was Jones, the one they had called 'Pretty Boy' until the hound had ripped the skin from his face. They had embraced like brothers and showed each other the blackened arrow-mark on their right shoulders. Jones gave Sir Thomas news of the rest of his troop.

'Maggot is around here someplace, still a filthy dog and smelling no sweeter. The Pope we buried somewhere in northern France, he took a blow to the head from a mace and never recovered.' Jones stood to the side as he narrated the story, making sure that Sir Thomas was only able to see the unmarked, expressive side of his face, and it was clear that he was acutely self-conscious of his disfigurement. 'We parted company with Koenig in Calais; he decided to keep walking east and see if he could get back to his homeland, wherever the hell that was. He left us saying 'Yenk' to everyone. Never did learn to speak any English, or anything else anyone could understand come to that.'

Sir Thomas asked him for news of John Stretch and Jones explained that their captain had drawn his bow one day in practice and a tendon of some kind had snapped in his shoulder, leaving his right arm hanging uselessly at his side.

'He spends his days begging on the streets of Shrewsbury and we bring him some money, if we are ever at home.' Jones seemed to accept this as the natural order of things, that an archer's livelihood should cease the moment he was no longer able to draw his bow.

Sir Thomas and Jones went their separate ways; Jones had been Prince Edward's man and was loyal to his son, the King, and so he would not be part of Gaunt's expeditionary force. Sir Thomas estimated that they had several weeks to wait before Gaunt's fleet would be ready to sail and so he sent Rufus Long on a mission north and west on horseback, with a spare mount in tow. He was to take a sum of money to Shrewsbury, to search out John Stretch and offer him a permanent home and position at the manor house in Erpingham, and accompany him there. Rufus was away for a month and returned just as they were preparing to embark. He brought news that the old archer was happily ensconced in the servant's quarters at the manor house and was already giving archery lessons to the children of the village.

As he had fully expected, Sir Thomas proved of little use to anyone for much of the voyage due to seasickness and found himself with much time for contemplation. He began to sense that perhaps a life of warfare would not fulfill him in the way that he had expected; that it would always just comprise a series of long tedious waits for something to happen, interspersed with brief flurries of excitement and activity, and punctuated with much illness and bad food and occasional acts of frustrated depravity. He missed his home and the quiet life that had so frustrated him before in Norfolk. Sir Thomas began to understand that we always desire that which we do not currently have.

***

One day, while the monks were at Evensong and Jacob was sweeping the floor of Anselmo's small cell, he came across a partially completed manuscript on a writing table. Jacob was unable to read, but correctly guessed that this was some kind of religious text; it was apparent that Anselmo was making a copy from a much older document in a great leather-bound book. He stood and looked in wonder for several minutes, transfixed by the exquisite patterns formed by each individual letter. Jacob traced the curves of each word with his fingertip, noting how the width of each line thickened and narrowed, and realised instinctively that this was caused by the contours of the tip of the goose feather quill being turned in the fingers. There was a pot containing quill pens and a separate one with ink, and also several scraps of vellum which had been used for blotting.

Jacob checked at the doorway to ensure he would not be

disturbed. He picked up one of the quills and moved it around in his hand, getting the feel of its shape and size. He held the pen naturally in his right hand, the same hand with which he used a blade; it was lucky that the leprosy had only ravaged his left hand; leaving the fingers as deformed stumps. He dipped the tip into the inkpot and began to scratch with it on the scrap vellum, but he had used too much ink and it just blobbed. Jacob tried again, this time wiping a little of the ink away first. He attempted to copy the shape of the first letter of the document, a large, intricately embellished 'S'. After two or three attempts he had made a reasonable copy.

Several hours later, Anselmo returned to find Jacob meticulously copying the first line of the text, each attempt better than the preceding one. At first he was angry, saying that Jacob had no right to touch his work, but he could not avoid a sneaking admiration for the accuracy and natural skill that the young man had demonstrated. Jacob asked Anselmo if he would teach him to read and write, but the monk declined, saying it was not necessary that a thief had such skills. Jacob grasped the collar of Anselmo's cloak and dragged him forward so that their faces were almost touching; the monk recoiling from the visage of the ex-leper's face. Jacob explained that their former relationship would continue, him robbing and thieving to the monk's order, but only if in return the monk taught him the magical skills of the pen.

In that way, over the course of several years, Jacob became proficient at reading and writing in English, and gained a working knowledge of French and Latin words as well. In time his skills overtook those of his master.

***

CHAPTER 8

(In which Sir Thomas Erpingham participates in the great tournament at Montereau, and tragedy strikes late in the day)

A stone clangs off the roof of my shack and I stand and hobble outside, just quick enough to see several of the village children hide in the trees on the other side of the lane. I shout an obscenity and wave my stick in the air, but inside I am smiling. When I was a boy we would torment an old shepherd who lived in a hut at the edge of the woods in a similar way, inventing terrifying stories about him; that he had been known to kill and eat children and that he was in league with the devil. We would sneak up to his door and knock before running away, and doing so became a rite of passage for any new boy who aspired to join our gang. I understand why they would single me out as an outsider, and do not mind the function they have chosen for me in their game.

Still, they have disturbed my train of thought. What was it that Rufus had been telling me last night about Henry Bolingbroke's poor skills with the lance?

***

Rufus thought it impossible that anyone could sleep the night before a tournament; at least he never could anyway. The build-up was too long, too tense, the excitement too great. He was awake before dawn having dozed fitfully, dreaming of glory and heroism and the adulation of the crowd; the dream marred by anxiety about something that he had forgotten or neglected to do. He was quickly up and about his tasks, taking his master's horses out onto the lush grass meadows of Montereau, allowing them to eat their fill. He watched, incredulous as always, as the horses ignored what Rufus would have thought were the choice tufts of grass, going instead for roots and dry thorny looking stuff, taking in soil and small pebbles along with the vegetable matter, obviously to fulfill some function of their digestion. There was a low mist covering the field which stretched away to the south down a slight incline. He heard the drumming of hooves, horses at the gallop, and then saw the mist disturbed down at the lower end of the meadow, rolling and boiling as some force came through it until the disturbance was suddenly resolved into a pair of horses, their riders low in the saddle, on an exercise gallop. These were the horses of the French champion, Charles de Grugy, who was scheduled to meet his master, Sir Thomas Erpingham, at the lists later that afternoon. The riders waved toward Rufus, and he returned their salute; there was no animosity between the grooms.

Rufus, and his master Sir Thomas, had been there preparing for several days, in the company of Henry Bolingbroke who, following the questionable wisdom of his role in the revolt of the 'Appellant' Lords against King Richard the previous year, was lying low until the dust settled. Henry seemed happy to allow his father, John of Gaunt; recently returned from Iberia, to smooth things over at home while he and a few close friends, including Sir Thomas, indulged in their passion for martial honour at the joust.

Nothing was straightforward in the company of Bolingbroke, and their train of baggage, spare horses and equipment had filled three large trading ships as they crossed from Boston to answer the challenge of the knights Charles de Grugy, Jean des Barres and other famous tournament champions of France. Their party could have been mistaken for a small army, off to war, rather than a company of twenty or so knights, esquires and servants, intent on a few weeks of drinking, fighting, roistering and gambling. Henry's own train included all the trappings of royalty on the move; the finest tapestries and wall hangings, bed linen, clothing, cutlery and plate, and in the evenings he entertained in his tent every bit as lavishly as when at home in one of the many family castles. He was spending vast sums of money on this trip, wagering on the outcome of the jousting and also on the less noble sports of cock fighting and greyhound racing, and buying expensive souvenirs for himself and his retinue, tapestries and exquisite fabrics, jewels and silver and gold, ornate cutlery and plate, so much in fact that they would need to charter a fourth trading ship to get it all home.

Sir Thomas was now thirty years old, hardened by several years at war in Scotland, Spain and Portugal in the service of John of Gaunt, and now in close companionship with Gaunt's son, Henry Bolingbroke; part friend and advisor, part bodyguard. Rufus never ceased to be amazed at the change in his master over the past ten or fifteen years. When he had first left Erpingham village with him in the wake of a plague epidemic, Sir Thomas had been unsure of himself, full of self-doubt, shy and bashful, but also personally fearless, reckless even. His character had been a strange mixture of formal language and behaviour, interspersed with jokes, vulgarity, a nudge or wink, the taproom language of the common labourer; almost as if he had been trying on different characteristics and mannerisms like clothes, to see which fitted best. Now all that was gone. Sir Thomas had become supremely self-confident, but not in an overpowering or unpleasant way. He just knew exactly what he wanted, what action to take for the best potential outcome, or what his opinion was on any subject, and spoke his mind openly without subterfuge or deceit. Rufus was certain that it was this characteristic that had endeared him first to Gaunt, and then to his son Bolingbroke; men who were constantly surrounded by those who would curry favour by giving false praise or opinion.

To Rufus he was open, honest and forthright; he would castigate his servant if he felt he had neglected his duties, and praise him roundly if he had surpassed himself. Sir Thomas shared confidences too; intimate things sometimes and Rufus was sure that he only did so because he knew that no judgement would be passed, or opinion expressed too forcibly. They were an indivisible unit; Sir Thomas relying totally upon Rufus for all the mundane things which made his life possible, and Rufus upon his master for his livelihood, his station in the hierarchy, and the excitement that came with a life of danger and adventure.

The dawn had come with a clear blue sky and a light warm breeze from the south which rapidly dispersed the early mist. People were arriving already, some in fine carriages or born on litters, with servants carrying baskets of food and wine to provision the long day ahead; some walking in the dirt of the road with a parcel of bread and a jug of ale. The tournament, which would continue for several days yet, drew avid support from all layers of society; it was perhaps the only time that Rufus had seen the lord and the commoner, the knight and the servant milling around together without visible division of class, at least not until the tournament itself began when the best viewing points were always reserved strictly for those who could afford them.

Men approached to ask how Sir Thomas fared, in what form was he? Rufus basked in the vicarious fame of his master, acknowledged to be one of the finest knights of all Christendom at the joust, but was non-committal; much would be wagered that day on the outcome of the various matches, and he had good reason not to want to alter the odds available on his own master's performance at this early stage of the day.

With his morning duties completed, Rufus headed for the big tent for breakfast. Their quarters here were lavish to say the least; the French noblemen who had invited the English here were keen that their hospitality be remembered as the finest, finer indeed than any English nobleman could offer. Rufus settled at a long bench, the table covered with bowls of hot soup and stew, good bread, cold meats and fish, jams and preserves. He was about to swallow a mouthful of chicken when a great thump on his back caused him to choke and spit his food onto the floor. It was Sir Thomas, already dressed for the day ahead in the chain–mail he would wear beneath his armour. He sat down next to Rufus and began to fill a charger with vast quantities of food.

'So Red, the horses are well? Good. What's the word on this Frenchman?' he took a great bite out of the leg of a roasted fowl, and a swig of ale to moisten the meat.

'He's supposed to be moderately good with the lance,' Rufus shrugged, as if there was little to tell, 'they say he is difficult to unhorse, holds his mount well'.

Charles de Grugy had a decent reputation at the joust but was known more as a swordsman. The smart money today would be on Sir Thomas at the joust, but if they should decide to meet with sword and shield then the Frenchman would be a slight favourite.

'I want you to shorten up the harness on the left side when I ride the mare today, keep her head down; help me keep her straight. She keeps trying to veer right after I've set my lance.'

Sir Thomas was always doing this; tinkering with the set-up, trying to iron out miniscule faults. Rufus said that he would see to it, knowing full well that after the first run he would want it reset to its original length.

'What do you know of his style? Will he hit low? Should I hold my line or anticipate a move?'

Sir Thomas always expected that Rufus would have done his homework on everyone he would meet in combat. In truth, this was the part Rufus enjoyed most; seeking out information from grooms and servants, watching other men at practice, listening in to drunken alehouse conversations. Rufus began to tell his master what he knew, but they were suddenly joined by Bolingbroke and a group of noblemen who sat down to their breakfast. Rufus stood quickly to leave, aware that his station ought not to permit him to stay seated amongst these lords, but Henry waved him back into his seat.

'Stay with us, master Rufus. We may have need of your expertise this morning.'

Bolingbroke's performance with the lance at practice had been mediocre at best, and a long discussion commenced about possible causes. With each run, as he set the lance to impact upon the oncoming rider's shield or breastplate on the nearside, and so have the best chance of unhorsing him, he seemed to allow the tip of his lance to over-swing outwards slightly, striking the off-side of the breast-plate and causing the tip, as often as not, to skim off the burnished metal and away harmlessly to the side. Each of the noblemen gave suggestions; the harness set-up was wrong, his posture needed adjustment, his grip on the lance was incorrect. They each gave an opinion in such a way as to appear helpful, without sounding condescending; after all, none of them was his match at the joust, with the exception of Sir Thomas. Henry asked Rufus directly for an opinion, but the servant was reluctant to speak up in such company, until Sir Thomas encouraged him to speak his mind.

'My Lord, I have noticed, perhaps, a slight tendency to set the lance a little early. May I suggest that you try to count the pace of your horse's stride in your head, and then make yourself set the lance one stride further than your arm wants it to happen.'

Bolingbroke thumped the table, and bowls, goblets and food were sent up in the air.

'There!' he roared, pointing at Rufus. 'There is a man who knows his business! Thomas, how much would it cost me to make you part company with young master Rufus?'

'Alas,' replied Sir Thomas, smiling, 'I fear that I would cease to function at all without him!'

There was general laughter and now the conversation moved on to talk of a possible crusade the following season to join the Teutonic Knights in their war against the heathens in Lithuania. The noblemen seemed up for the idea, to a man, and Rufus left them to plot and scheme while he excused himself and walked out of the big tent into the bright morning sunshine. His morning tasks were done and for an hour or so he had free time to enjoy, as he saw fit.

The great arena, in which the main events of the day would be staged, was surrounded by tiered rows of seating; reserved exclusively for the rich and noble. Bolingbroke and his party, when not engaged in combat, would be seated there, entertained with the very best food and drink served by the most beautiful young servant women. Behind the seating area were the great tents of purple cloth, emblazoned with silver and gold banners, where each party of noblemen or dignitaries was to be housed for the duration of the tournament. A little further, behind the tents and out of sight of the main arena, were the practice grounds, stables, smithies and armourers forges; all roped off and guarded to ensure the general public was kept out. Beyond this was a low hillock which would be used as a viewing area for the mass of the poorer folk; offering a reasonably good view of events, but at a distance that made good eyesight a pre-requisite. There were men who would earn their bread and beer that day by describing the action as it happened to those older folk with poor vision, and those who had gone blind.

Rufus walked up and over the hill and was greeted by a scene of great chaos. Here was the field where the mass of the common folk had gathered for what was in effect, a feast day, carnival, fairground and market all rolled into one. Families and groups of friends had staked out areas for themselves and erected rough tents and cook-fires, with carts and wagons pressed into service as makeshift sleeping quarters. The demarcation lines between each family's chosen space was bickered and quarrelled over, blows often being exchanged before agreed lines were drawn up and staked out with posts and rope. Already, the smoke from many cooking fires was rising, and the smell of bacon and hot bread filled the air. Tradesmen and merchants of every kind were setting up their stalls, and brisk trading was already taking place. Rufus walked through the mass of people, taking in the sights and sounds as he went, one hand firmly on his purse, lest he fall victim to the pick-pockets and cut-purses that would also be about their business that day.

He passed a stall selling religious relics, lucky charms, and ointments and potions against ailments ranging from 'vapours of the head' and 'flaccidness of the member' via all other known ills to include a remedy for the bubonic plague. The proprietor had on display a finger-bone of Saint John the Baptist, which he declared loudly had been verified to be genuine by various scholars of the great religious houses of Christendom. Rufus was certain that if he added together all the finger-bones of John the Baptist he had seen on his travels, there would be enough to fill a hay-cart!

A little further along, a rough circular pit had been dug out and lined with sand. A man stood guard over several wooden cages with wire fronts, in which his fighting bantams strutted to and fro, awaiting their own tournament later in the day. He heard a low animal grumbling roar and looked up to see a bear which had been chained to a tree, an old scabby, sick looking beast which was being encouraged by its handler, who wielded an iron poker, to rear up on its hind legs. Next he happened upon one of the first of many wrestling matches that would be held that day, the champion of each village or district taking on all comers, with much of the financial wealth of his friends and neighbours riding on his performance. There were no discernible rules; certainly it seemed that attempts to gouge out an opponent's eye with the thumb were not penalised. As he watched, the man who was attempting to do so was kicked hard in the groin and sagged to his knees, doubled up with pain. His adversary kicked him again, this time full in the face and the gouger toppled unconscious to the ground, blood and several teeth spattered on the dirt around his prostrate body. The victor went to collect his purse but there was controversy about the legality of his victory; one group of onlookers unhappy about the second blow while their man was on his knees, a second group declaring it to have been an acceptable response to the attempted blinding. As a scuffle broke out between the opposing factions, Rufus returned to the tournament area and his duties for the day ahead.

The action commenced at about noon, but with the poorest fare that would be on offer that day. Inexperienced young esquires attempted to bring themselves to the attention of their masters by tilting ineffectually at each other, and with their swordplay using blunted weapons. For the most part they were ignored as most of their intended audience were either feasting and drinking wine before the afternoon entertainment proper began, or preparing themselves for combat. One of the first of the major matches took place in the early afternoon and this time everybody was in attendance and watching the action; this was the much anticipated clash between Henry Bolingbroke and the French champion, Jean des Barres. If it seemed a little strange to many of the onlookers that such an important match was taking place so early in the day, Rufus at least knew the truth; that Henry wished to acquit himself with honour, then spend the rest of the day drinking and gambling on the outcome of the matches that would follow.

The two protagonists entered the arena, mounted on their chargers and led by two grooms each, with servants carrying spare lances and a variety of other weapons. There was a rumble of approval from the crowd; Henry's horse was decked in the finest white and red skirting, the armour protecting its head glinting in the sun, while Henry himself rode tall in the saddle, his great shield emblazoned with the heraldic symbols of the House of Lancaster, his lance tipped with a red and white pennant. He acknowledged the crowd with a salute, dropped the visor on his helm and cantered to the far end of the lists. Bolingbroke's opponent, Jean des Barres, was also finely attired but with a little less flash and a little more purpose about his overall appearance.

At a signal from the herald, the crowd was hushed and both men spurred their horses forward, galloping toward each other on either side of the low barrier fence. The distance between them, about one hundred yards, was closed rapidly and Rufus saw both men set their lances, aiming to strike a blow on the opponent's shield or breastplate and, with luck, unhorse him. Henry's lance-tip missed by inches; again he had allowed the lance to veer too far to his left, deflecting off the outside of his opponent's armour. Jean des Barres' lance made clean contact with the outer edge of Henry's shield, but the Englishman was able to flex his shoulder backwards at just the right moment to deflect the force away from his body. They gathered their mounts at the far end of the lists and turned to face each other for a second time, Bolingbroke muttering to himself, the French knight signalling one of his grooms to fetch a new lance; the tip of his original weapon having been chipped and blunted by the impact on Henry's shield.

They charged forward again and this time Rufus saw Henry deliberately pause for an additional second before setting his lance. Both men were on target; Henry's lance impacted dead-centre on his opponent's shield; the weapon shattering into a thousand splinters and shards of wood, which flew in all directions. The Frenchman managed to stay in the saddle; meanwhile Henry had shifted his torso to the right at the last moment avoiding what would have been a clear hit for des Barres. Both men took fresh lances and closed again. This time, both knights made a clean strike. Henry was unhorsed, tumbling instantly to the ground to the sound of a great gasp from the crowd, while the French knight was thrown back across the rump of his horse, one foot out of the stirrup. He held on dourly for several strides and then he too fell to the ground. The grooms rushed forward, one from each camp to gather in the horses' harness and lead the beasts away, the other to bring swords and shields for the continuation of the combat.

Henry stood and dusted himself down, took the sword and shield from his groom, then walked purposefully toward his opponent. Jean des Barres also had sword and shield in hand but had discarded his helm. He was staggering about drunkenly, obviously suffering some kind of shock or injury from the impact of the lance. Henry approached him cautiously, circling his opponent with sword raised. The crowd was hushed, expecting the 'coup de grace' at any moment. The Frenchman was not defending himself; he leaned forwards, resting both hands on the sword's pommel, the tip pointing downward into the dirt. He was trying to clear his head, to concentrate through the bells pealing inside his skull. He attempted to raise the weapon but staggered forward, unable to cope with the shift in weight. Everyone could see that he was unable to defend himself properly. The herald looked ready to step in at any moment.

The crowd was quiet, expectant. Suddenly, Henry dropped his own sword and shield to the ground and stepped forward to hold his opponent around the waist, supporting him. Jean des Barres willingly dropped his own weapons and Henry took the arm of his opponent and raised it aloft in a salute of triumph. The crowd went wild, and both men were cheered and applauded as they left the arena. Henry's action had endeared him to what had been a hostile crowd. Rufus thought it typical of the man; that he knew instinctively how to win over men to his side, and he felt certain that this was a skill that would serve Bolingbroke well over time.

Later that afternoon Rufus was back in the saddling area, helping Sir Thomas to prepare his equipment and assemble the various pieces of his armour, discussing tactics for the combat ahead. He explained that he had overheard a conversation between the French grooms, who had wrongly assumed the Englishman would not understand their tongue, that de Grugy had injured his ribs on the left-hand side in practice the previous day, and would be keen to protect himself from blows to that part of his armour. It was the kind of information that might just give Sir Thomas the edge in what was seen by many as a closely matched pairing. As they were speaking, a representative of their opponent arrived to offer terms. Charles de Grugy wished to make four runs with the lance, followed by up to three strikes each with sword and shield; the weapons with which he was most skilled. Thomas was challenged to fight with sharpened blades, the safer option of using blunted weapons was one he would have eschewed anyway, and for a purse that was roughly the equivalent of the entire annuity he received each year from John of Gaunt. He accepted the terms unequivocally.

'Isn't there somewhere you should be?' asked Sir

Thomas, when all was ready. Rufus grinned and ran off to find an acquaintance of his, an old Jewish money-lender who also brokered wagers at tournaments and on sporting events generally. He followed the tournament circus around Europe and was known and trusted by those who wished to wager discretely. It was never his own money at risk; he simply matched bets between parties and took his commission from the winner. His business done, Rufus was back and ready as they were summoned by the heralds.

They arrived in the arena to a fanfare of trumpets and a great roar of expectation from the crowd. The French knight arrived moments later to equal acclaim and both Sir Thomas and his opponent made a point of bowing to the local Duke and Duchess who were hosting this extravaganza. The Duke held aloft a golden pendant, a thing of great beauty which was studded with rubies and emeralds, and announced that this bauble was to be added to the prize purse for the winner. The crowd murmured their appreciation of the gesture and the two mounted knights rode the length of the tiered seating area, acknowledging the crowd with open hands raised in salute. Sir Thomas rode up to Rufus to collect his lance, winked once before lowering his visor and then cantered off to his starting position. At a signal from the herald, both men dug their spurs hard into their mounts, and closed rapidly at full gallop.

Their first pass was uneventful, neither man had his aim quite correct and the lance tips both missed their targets by a fraction. The crowd was silent, hushed, barely even breathing.

The riders turned at the far end of the low fence and spurred their horses into the second tilt. This time Sir Thomas made clean contact on the Frenchman's shield while his opponent's lance caught him high on the rim of his helm; knocking the headpiece half off. Both men remained securely mounted. Sir Thomas rode across to his groom and called for a cloth. He removed his helm and wiped blood from a gash on his forehead. He wrapped the cloth around the wound and then forced the helm back on over the makeshift bandage. Taking a fresh lance, Sir Thomas lined up for a third run. This time his horse reared up when the spurs dug in, and was slower away than de Grugy's mount. With a fractionally delayed start, he had less time to set his lance as his opponent reached full galloping speed several seconds earlier; nevertheless, Sir Thomas's aim was good and he caught the Frenchman a glancing blow on the breastplate, a strike which would have unhorsed a lesser opponent. De Grugy's aim was true and it was only the last-second twist in the saddle and lean to the left by Sir Thomas that avoided a direct hit, the lance tip scraping along the inside of the Englishman's raised shield.

As they held their mounts ready for a fourth and final charge, both protagonists raised their lances in salute to the other, acknowledging the quality of the combat. The crowd was near delirious with excitement, and money was passing from hand to hand all over the assembled audience, as final wagers on this part of the encounter were agreed. This time, although both men aimed well, both were also able to move their torsos dexterously out of harm's way, and no blow was struck by either lance. This small disappointment for the crowd was quickly forgotten as the two warriors dismounted and prepared to meet each other with sword and shield. Rufus was feeling reasonably confident; by his assessment Sir Thomas was slightly ahead after the joust and needed only to perform as he knew his master was able to with the sword, for his wager to be secured.

The men circled each other cautiously, shields held in close and high, swords held pointed forward at half-thrust; feeling for range. De Grugy swung first, a great half-circle swipe with the blade directed towards the midriff, which Sir Thomas parried with his shield, the force of the impact momentarily numbing his shield-arm. He replied with a downward stroke aimed at his opponent's shoulder and the Frenchman had to use his own sword to parry the stroke; the clash sounding out across the arena. According to the terms of the challenge, each man was only allowed three clean strikes before the heralds would call time and decide on a winner, so neither wished to waste his efforts. Several times their swords became locked together and the contest became a trial of strength, both men attempting to push the other away so that he could get in a clean blow. After several minutes and a number of inconclusive attempted blows, and with both men starting to tire, de Grugy raised his sword high for a downward blow. Sir Thomas parried with his shield and, noticing that his opponent was holding his own shield too low, protecting the painful ribs on his left side, dummied to the right, then switched quickly to the left, striking a crushing blow down onto the left side shoulder armour of his opponent. De Grugy went down on one knee, dropping his sword and clutching at the front of his left shoulder; from what Rufus could see, a broken clavicle was the most likely injury.

Sir Thomas stepped in to administer a third, decisive stroke but the Frenchman raised his right hand to signal that he yielded, and the crowd went wild and Rufus was jumping up and down and punching the air and Bolingbroke was bear-hugging the Duke and the peasant horde up on the hill were surging forward to get better sight of their new favourite and Sir Thomas was raising his sword in the air to acknowledge the crowd. Rufus was feeling about as good as he had ever felt in his life before; sometimes the world is a wonderful place to be, and he would not have swapped it for all the glories of heaven at that particular moment.

So they rested for a few days, some nursing injuries, some dining out on their exploits at the lists, some counting their winnings, others regretting poorly executed manoeuvres, still others aggrieved that they had not yet had their chance to shine. It was from among this later group that Bolingbroke selected his team of seven for the melee, the tourney between two teams, each man in full battle armour carrying a variety of weapons, the winning team determined by the last man standing. The number and type of weapons had been specified and agreed in advance; two men on each side would carry the pole-axe, three the broadsword, two the mace. The crowd was gathered in great anticipation of the event. There was some wagering, yes, but this tended to be more of a blood sport, enjoyed for the pure spectacle and was the closest many in the audience would ever get to a real battle.

The combatants met as if on the battlefield itself, laying into each other with full strength and murderous intent. Some chose to fight individually; others paired up and fought back to back, keeping each other safe from a blow from behind. When a man was knocked to the ground, he had the option to yield else his opponent was permitted to strike once more in an attempt to incapacitate him. If he failed to stand after this blow, he was declared 'hors de combat' and must retire.

The melee lasted for almost an hour and at the end it was an English esquire who was still standing. He was helped off the field by his servants, to rapturous applause. He rested for several days while, for others, the feasting and fighting continued. They heard rumour that he was passing blood with his urine. He deteriorated quickly, some internal trauma draining his life away fast, and died the following Sunday. Bolingbroke and the other noblemen had Holy Mass said over his body, and paid the local Abbey a large sum to ensure he was buried well, with a fine stone monument. The Abbot reluctantly agreed; the church was against the sinfulness of the tournament, particularly as it tended to raise revenue which did not find its way into church coffers. So they mourned for several days before beginning the long journey home to

England; Sir Thomas weeping openly for the loss of a friend, as they left the body of the esquire Robert Cranwell behind in the care of the French monks.

***

Jacob tended his master's wounds as best he could, but it was obvious that some of the damage was permanent and a full recovery unlikely. Many of Anselmo's ribs had been broken in the assault and he was only able to breathe with great difficulty. For the first few days his body stiffened up and swelled as the soft tissue tightened around the damaged bones and muscle. Then the bruising began to come out in livid browns, blacks and yellows and the extent of his internal injuries became clearer. For several days he passed blood with his stool, and his loose and broken teeth prevented him from eating anything other than weak gruel.

The Abbot called in to visit several times, questioning Anselmo about the reason behind such an attack, but Anselmo declared it to have been a random thing, brought about by strong drink. As the weeks passed, he began to regain some of his strength. One morning he asked Jacob to accompany him and they went to one of the storage barns behind the Abbey. Anselmo moved several pieces of old screening and planks aside and revealed a low hidden doorway. They both passed through it and went down a flight of stone stairs. Jacob found himself in a dank cellar, dimly lit by light filtering down from cracks in the ceiling and the flooring above. Among several old crates and boxes was a trunk. Anselmo took a key from his pocket and unlocked the clasp. The chest was stuffed with gold and silver coins and fine jewels; much of the loot that Jacob himself had stolen to the monk's order was here.

Anselmo made his proposal quietly but clearly, and without any preamble. The contents were all for Jacob, on condition that he killed the Erpinghams, father and son.

***

CHAPTER 9

(In which Sir Thomas Erpingham finds himself on an unexpected pilgrimage to the Holy Land)

Not that long ago Sir Thomas was sitting there, at the low bench near the doorway, red faced from drinking a surfeit of my latest batch, his white locks hanging in tangles down over his wrinkled old brow and his legs splayed out, feet resting on two low stools. He had his breeches rolled up above the knee and was showing me some scars on his kneecaps, obtained he said in the course of following Christ's last journey up the hill to Golgotha, on hands and knees. I filled his cup again from the stone jug of mead, just to lubricate the story.

***

If the first of Henry Bolingbroke's crusades to Lithuania had been fairly inconsequential, the second descended rapidly into farce.

King Richard had been perfectly happy to see the back of his handsome, popular and charismatic, rebellious cousin the first time, and when Henry had finally returned from the east to great fanfare, and wildly exaggerated tales of his courage and heroism; announcing almost immediately that he would return to Lithuania the following season to continue to crush the heathen, Richard had done everything in his power to aid the second expedition on its way.

According to popular legend in England, the Teutonic Knights were a fine group of ex-patriot Englishmen who had, upon returning from crusades to the Holy Land, set themselves up in north eastern lands close to the Baltic Sea with the sole intent of bringing Christianity to the heathen peoples of Prussia and Lithuania. This they had successfully achieved in Prussia, carving out vast new rich and fertile territory for themselves, and were in the process of doing the same in Lithuania, where they were beginning to discover that the heavily wooded and river-strewn terrain did not lend itself to conquest so easily. It was while forcing a long and difficult path up the forest-enclosed bed of an ancient river, that it was believed led to a Lithuanian stronghold, that the main force of the Teutonic Knights had found itself joined by a group of flamboyant and over-excited Englishmen trailing miles of extravagant and superfluous baggage behind them. Marshall Rabe, the leader of the Teutonics, had been gracious enough in accepting Henry's additional force and had asked the Englishmen to join him on a long circuitous surprise attack though the forest, while the bulk of his men continued the difficult river approach.

By all accounts, upon reaching the Lithuanians' fortress

base, Henry and his small group of knights and esquires had acquitted themselves well, fighting bravely until the attack became bogged down in a long and desperate siege. Sir Thomas Erpingham, together with one of Henry's marksman archers, had been first to the top of the outer defensive wall, raising the banner of the House of Lancaster and in the process reinvigorating an attack which had been about to be repulsed. Bolingbroke himself was in the thick of the action, sustaining bloody but superficial wounds to his chest and shoulder. The fortress was eventually won, following a five-week blockade and bombardment, and the defenders were slaughtered to a man, only women and children spared who were marched away to be forcibly baptised before entering a life of servitude in the castles of the Teutonic Knights. That the captured stronghold proved of little tactical or strategic value, being just one of several such outposts in the vicinity, did not detract from a general euphoria amongst the Englishmen, who felt that they had been the deciding factor in a battle of major significance.

With the winter rapidly approaching, Henry had sent messengers home to England with spectacularly embellished accounts of his activities, ensuring that he would be feted as a great hero on his return, before settling down with Sir Thomas and a few other chosen companions to a warm and comfortable winter as guests of the finest houses in Prussia. Meanwhile news of his adventures had spread at home and when, early the following spring, his ships returned to England to a hero's welcome, it was much to the chagrin of an envious King Richard. Looking back on it, Sir Thomas felt that this had been the key moment which would set in train the calamitous events of the following years.

The preparations for Henry's second crusade had been even more extravagant than the first and Sir Thomas, who had observed carefully the limitations imposed by the surrounding terrain in Lithuania on the previous jaunt, and who was responsible for sourcing the ships, equipment and livestock required, could not help but think that they would be better off travelling light; no more than each man could carry himself and with horses sourced locally in Prussia. Henry would have none of it though, and continued to demand that he went to war embellished with all the trappings of a great prince. So Thomas ensured that the Prince's huge bed was dismantled and packed, along with all his bedchamber furnishings, his best dining plate, silver and golden goblets, wall tapestries, his greyhound's wooden sleeping hut, and several barrels of Henry's favourite wine and foodstuffs, among many other bulky, heavy and entirely inappropriate items.

Stories of Henry's spectacular successes the previous season had encouraged a number of copy-cat crusades by young English noblemen, keen to make a name for themselves, and without exception they had proved more trouble than they were worth, demanding that heavy and useless equipment be dragged around the countryside by the Teutonic Knights' servants and then prancing about on the periphery of battlegrounds in beautifully burnished armour, and generally getting in the way. By the time Henry's force had disembarked in Prussia for the second time, Marshall Rabe had had enough and Henry found a message waiting for him to say that his services would not be required in the forthcoming campaign, together with a large sum of cash to offset Henry's expenses, and to soothe any rancour.

Henry had sent the majority of his retinue home with the story that he had changed his mind and would now set forth on a journey of penitence to the Holy Land to thank God for his many blessings, and to seek forgiveness for his sins. Sir Thomas was one of the few who were selected to accompany him. With immediate plans now clarified, Henry had spent several days writing to his wife and children in England, to his father John of Gaunt with a request for additional funding, and to various other persons and institutions regarding the upkeep of his properties and the collection of his income for the coming months and possibly years.

With Henry busily filling the satchels of several messengers, Sir Thomas begged a spare scrap of vellum and took the opportunity to write home to his new wife, slipping his letter in among the official papers, along with silver coins to ensure its safe delivery. He had married Joan, daughter of a prosperous Suffolk family of minor nobility, the previous year. To her many other suitors she had given the impression of being a quiet-natured and serious young lady, a little distant and cold; only Sir Thomas would see the playful, mischievous side of her nature and it was this difference in behaviour, rather than any spoken preference, which assured her parents that she had chosen a husband. In many ways, it had been a typical marriage of country nobility, joining two East Anglian families of status and modest wealth to ensure ongoing affluence for the generations to come, but that did not mean the couple did not love each other very much. Sir Thomas's courtship had been light-hearted and frivolous and at times Joan, and her parents, had wondered at the seriousness of the proposition this young knight offered; there had been plenty of other viable options, men of property and substance who did not disappear for months at a time to take up challenges at the joust. Joan though, had decided upon Sir Thomas against her father's instinct for what was best, and had quickly settled into her role as mistress of Erpingham manor and was equally at home in the large city house under the lee of the castle keep in Norwich.

They did not see much of each other in those early years and in fact their relationship would always be curtailed by long periods of separation. This would eventually lead to their relationship becoming cordial, rather than warm; a mutual shyness to be overcome each time Sir Thomas returned from a period of absence, though all that was far in the future as Sir Thomas prepared for departure for what would be the greatest journey of his life.

If Joan had worried for her husband's faithfulness while abroad, she need not have. In most other ways, Henry

Bolingbroke and his party behaved as a young group of noblemen were expected to behave; feasting and drinking and gambling and fighting at every opportunity, but though several of his men spent as much time as they could in the brothels and with the serving wenches, Henry did not and neither, following his liege's example, did Sir Thomas. Henry was exclusively faithful to his wife and family and took his religious obligations seriously, so while he could with justification be described as narcissistic, truculent, avaricious and ambitious; he was also faithful, devout, charitable and self-effacing. Thomas found these strange mixed characteristics appealing, and so to some extent modelled his own behaviour to mirror them.

The journey ahead of Sir Thomas was one of unimaginably vast distances, of strange cultures and languages, of great mountain ranges and warm blue seas, of Biblical peoples and places, and he was excited about the prospect more than he had been about any previous adventure. To date, he had travelled east to Prussia and Lithuania and several times to northern France, regions with climate and landscape no different than could be found in his own county of Norfolk. He had a vague recollection of his time as a boy in Aquitaine, but could recall little about the landscape. This would be the first time he had travelled south and he had been told by those who had done so of the climate he would experience in the Holy Land; heat so fierce in the summer months that you could crack a hen's egg upon a rock and watch it cook before your very eyes. He only half believed that such a thing was possible.

Finally, with letters home sent, equipment sorted, route maps studied, guides hired, accommodation reserved at the finest houses and castles along the way, and Gaunt's money and blessing for the venture received, the great caravan had set off down one of the well-trodden pilgrim roads south. For several days, Sir Thomas did not see much change in the landscape around him; vast areas of woodland interspersed with fields of grazing cattle and sheep, small farmsteads with wheat and barley growing tall and golden in the bright early autumn conditions, small villages surrounding castle keeps and older wooden fortified buildings, like the motte and baileys at home.

They erected tents each evening and lived a luxurious life in comparison to the pilgrims they passed on the road. Every few days they came upon a house or castle of substance and Henry was welcomed as a famous prince of England, staying for several days and often taking advantage of the hunting available in the locality, before moving on south and east. They spent several weeks in the great city of Prague being lavishly entertained by Emperor Wenceslaus of Bohemia, a never-ending party so raucous, so drunken and so dissolute that Sir Thomas feared they would never leave; would die of over-consumption and alcohol poisoning. Eventually they moved on, livers swollen and bellies distended, as gradually the land around them became hilly and then mountainous; Sir Thomas stood agape one morning, in awe when he saw the mighty Alps before him for the first time.

They stopped again for several days in Vienna, where the Duke of Austria used his influence to ensure a galley would be awaiting Henry and his party in Venice to take them down to the Holy Land, and back. Sir Thomas found their journey up and over the mountains fascinating, the heightened senses of hearing and vision, the cold crisp clarity of the mind brought about by the rarefied air near the summit. The long decent down narrow passes with the great Italian plain stretched out below them. Then the long hot tramp across the flat northern plains until finally they reached Venice; a city that Sir Thomas had read about, but found beyond his power to comprehend, the magnificence of the buildings rising from the salty lagoon, everywhere around him visible wealth beyond imagination, an empire of the sea that made small English pretensions seem pathetic by comparison.

Henry had set himself up in some style close to the Doges' Palace and St. Mark's Cathedral and, because this was a religious pilgrimage rather than a pleasure trip, interspersed his sumptuous partying with many devout visits to the churches of the great city. Sir Thomas found himself, during the interludes when Henry did not require him to be in attendance, exploring the major canals and lesser waterways of Venice in one of the proliferation of small boats for hire, piloted by a local man who was able to recount the history of each of the palaces, churches and bridges they passed, along with much gossip about the latest scandals among the Venetian nobility.

When Henry had tired of the local hospitality, he took just a few of his closest friends, including Sir Thomas, on the final leg by sea down to Jaffa, in the galley that the city elders had provided. For the first time in his life Sir Thomas was able to enjoy a sea voyage; dead calm conditions prevailed and he felt none of the sickness that usually afflicted him upon water. The galley was rowed the entire journey by Venetian prisoners, captured pirates who had been the scourge of the Adriatic sea-lanes, and were now to be worked to death in the bowels of the galleys.

It was on their arrival at the teeming port that Henry had begun to behave as though this trip really were a religious pilgrimage, rather than a pleasure jaunt, by declaring that they would walk the thirty odd miles to Jerusalem, rather than ride or be carried in litters. As they progressed across the hot and barren landscape, Sir Thomas observed that the local population of peasants seemed little different to those of more familiar northern lands, except for their darker, Arabic features and complexion; certainly their level of poverty seemed no different and the swarms of beggars which descended upon the party were as avaricious and persistent as any in England or France. Their guides were Saracen soldiers, fierce, quiet men who carried long curved scimitars and vicious daggers. Henry had done his best to ensure their loyalty by paying them several times the going rate, half up front and half upon the party's safe return to the waiting galley. His expenditure was eminently sensible; abduction and ransom for huge sums of money at pain of death was commonplace for rich travellers in the Holy Land, but this was a time of comparative peace, when the rulers of the eastern lands were keen not to provoke yet another western crusade, and so the eminent English prince and his party were probably safe enough.

In the fabled city of Jerusalem, which Sir Thomas had imagined would be like some heavenly oasis, all shimmering gold and cool fountains, he found instead a raucous, crowded bedlam, made more unbearable by the heat and the flies and the stench of humanity. Henry's party were taken to various dubious looking places of biblical fame; the place where Jesus was flogged before being forced to carry the cross was now a dank cellar below a bazaar where fragments of the true cross were on sale; the Garden of Gethsemane was an olive grove where jars of the miraculous olive oil produced by its crop were without doubt the most expensive to be had in all Christendom.

At the foot of the hill leading up to what their guides had assured them was the mound of Golgotha, the place of Christ's execution, Henry and his party joined a number of poor pilgrims who had gathered there to follow Christ's pathway on hands and knees. They had not travelled more than a few feet like this when Sir Thomas discovered that the hard stony ground would cause this journey to be a torture like none he had experienced before. Several of their companions gave up after a while and continued on foot, but Henry seemed determined to see it through; seemed to have the religious zeal that Sir Thomas had once heard William Long describe of the Flagellants, men who had toured England at the time of the great pestilence, whipping their own flesh into a bloody pulp to seek God's forgiveness. So Henry and Sir Thomas climbed ever upwards, blood pouring from lacerations on their palms and their knees, each seeking their own personal redemption. At the brow of the hill, laying prostrate on a great flat stone which had been laid to mark the place where Christ's cross had once been planted, awash in a sea of hawkers, beggars, priests and penitents of every kind, Henry and Sir Thomas prayed fervently for several minutes and then quietly agreed that they had had quite enough of religious pilgrimages, and should return to England forthwith.

Of their journey home it is probably true to say that these would be the last carefree days, without duty to family or liege that either man would experience for many years to come. The familiar pattern continued; two or three days at most camping quite luxuriously at the roadside, followed by several days as guests of some local nobility, hunting and feasting until the host's resources had been thoroughly depleted, before moving on. Henry seemed determined to spend every last penny of the allowance his father had sent him, and purchased the most extravagant souvenirs and gifts for himself and his friends that he could find.

Their journey through southern Europe and the Middle East had bought Henry's party into contact with merchants and travellers from Africa and the Far East and he had acquired various exotic animals to join his menagerie at home. An early favourite; a large constrictor snake which for several days had travelled looped around Henry's neck and torso, decided to bite him painfully on the thigh and Henry had grabbed for his sword and chopped the thing into pieces before it could do any more harm. An African trader had sold him an Ostrich which travelled in great style on the back of an open cart, accepting with regal dignity the bread and cakes which fascinated peasants offered it at every village on route. This and several other exotic creatures would spend short uncomfortable lives in England, being fed unaccustomed foodstuffs and dying off rapidly in the cold English winter. Henry had not thought to try to acquire a breeding pair and so by the following summer the first Ostrich in England was no more.

He lavished expensive clothes on his retinue, dressing his knights and esquires in matching outfits of the finest material and cut. While the party was travelling north up the Italian peninsula, Henry found a bolt of the finest silk for sale at the premises of a merchant of fine quality fabrics. He bought the material, paying the exorbitant asking price without attempting to haggle and then, a few days later, gave the thing to Sir Thomas as if it was some trifling item of little value. Though Sir Thomas could not initially think of what he might do with such a thing, he did know of a fine embroiderer in London who would doubtless be able to make an exquisitely patterned garment of some kind from it.

Sir Thomas and his servant Rufus had been reunited in Venice, where Rufus had spent rare days of leisure while his master had been in Jerusalem, and they shared stories of their experiences as they rode north on the busy pilgrim return routes. At last, as their ship docked at the port of London and Henry dashed off to visit first his wife and children, then his father John of Gaunt and finally King Richard, Sir Thomas and his servant spent several days overseeing the disembarkation of Henry's newly acquired livestock as well as the countless rare and wondrous items he had purchased on route; Rufus doing his utmost to ensure the local wharf-men did not pilfer too much.

Their journey back to Norfolk several days later had been uneventful and Sir Thomas settled quickly back into quiet married life at home and the duties as Gaunt's representative in Norfolk which he had otherwise neglected in recent years. His journey to the Holy Land had burned away some of the wanderlust that had kept Sir Thomas on the move for several years; in truth he was now a man of early middling years and began to seek satisfaction in quieter pursuits than tournaments and wars and the endless round of partying that accompanied Henry Bolingbroke. He and Joan found great pleasure in the time they were now able to spend together, and it was only their inability to make a child, despite their best efforts, that was to cause Sir Thomas any anxiety over the coming few years. It was in such domestic contentment that he was to receive the urgent message from Henry Bolingbroke which would change his life forever.

***

Anselmo's rage knew no bounds when he heard that Sir John Erpingham had perished in an outbreak of plague; felt that he had been cheated of the right to inflict personal revenge for the beating he had received and his loss of face, and he seemed doubly determined that the young man Thomas should pay the price in full. Jacob was dispatched on reconnaissance missions to Erpingham village and to the Erpingham family town house in Norwich itself, travelling by night and keeping himself hidden from scrutiny under the hood of his cloak. At first it seemed likely that his mission would be thwarted; discrete enquiries revealed that the young man was abroad and that it was not known when he would return. Anselmo reluctantly accepted that patience would be required and settled to the normality of life at the Abbey as his wounds slowly healed. Jacob continued to act as his personal servant, and occasional thief, while gradually making himself a familiar presence on the periphery of the Erpingham estate; becoming known as 'that poor beggar' who would carry out the odd chore for a penny or a bowl of stew. It became evident over a period of several years that Thomas would only return to his home county occasionally and when he finally did come home on a semi-permanent basis it was as a knight of the realm and a man of substance in the local hierarchy of nobility.

Jacob was careful not to get too close; the old man William Long still lived and would doubtless recall Jacob's unique facial disfigurement from the attempted robbery all those years ago, though the old mistress had perished of the same pestilence which had taken Sir John, and Jacob was sure that Thomas would not have a clear recollection of the event from his childhood. He steeled himself to carry out the brutal task that his master had ordered, his mind captured by the lure of Anselmo's chest of gold hidden in the cellar, but sometimes in the long reaches of the night he tried to envisage what his life might come to after such an event, in what way the treasure might alter the hard terms of his existence. It was on such nights that he settled finally to a restless sleep, dreaming again of the birds that were born without feet and lived their lives in constant flight.

***

CHAPTER 10

(In which King Richard exiles his troublesome cousin, and Sir Thomas Erpingham is faced with a life-changing decision)

In the early years, I had lived at the manor house with the servants but there had been certain difficulties which obliged me to find a new home. It was Sir Thomas himself who had offered me the tenancy of this shack, for nothing more than a peppercorn rent. It had been the home of the village beekeeper, a popular local man by the name of Michael Sheringham who had died in the wave of pestilence that had taken Sir Thomas's parents. Its location, a good two hundred yards along the lane from the village itself, was the result of the unpopularity of the swarms of bees surrounding the original apiary's home in the village square.

Sir Thomas had explained his grand plans to me, that the hives should be stocked and tended once more; my lack of experience with the husbandry of bees was passed off with a shrug, the building itself was to be refurbished and established as a public house and inn, specialising in the sale of mead. Like many a grand plan, the refurbishment never happened, but I do preside over an inn of sorts, leastways people come here to drink and slap a penny down on the table when they remember to do so. It is a refuge for storytellers, every bit as much as a home for drunkards. Sir Thomas once told me a good one, about how he came to be exiled from the land of his birth.

***

Other accounts will state that it began with a chance meeting on the road, with accusation and counter-accusation of treason, fraud and murder. It did not. It started with an argument over a game of chess and would end with the exile of Henry Bolingbroke, and the death of a king.

While Henry had been away, carousing his way around Europe and the Levant, his cousin King Richard had become a hardened, callous man, driven to adopt a nature that ill-fitted his gentle demeanour by personal tragedy and by a series of challenges, uprisings and outright rebellions. Within months of each other, both Henry Bolingbroke and the King had been widowed by the plague, Richard going into prolonged and public grief over the loss of his childless Anne, Henry behaving rather more stoically over the passing of his Mary, mother to his five children. As Richard suffered his personal grief, so the affairs of state had gathered around him like a besieging army. Chief among his concerns had been the anger and disappointment of many of his noble subjects over what they saw as the gifting of Aquitaine from the Crown to the

House of Lancaster in a deal that he and John of Gaunt had concocted to try to bring permanent peace between England and France. Added to this was the constant irritant, like a flea on the skin, of his Irish lords going native and rebelling against English rule. And, as if that was not enough to contend with, Richard had taken it upon himself to mete out vengeance, served cold after several years, to each and every one of the noblemen who had opposed him in the Appellant's Rebellion. The crown of England rested upon a troubled brow.

One afternoon, in the great hall of Eltham Palace, Richard and his retinue had been relaxing after a long, acrimonious conference regarding the Aquitaine question, drinking wine and playing with wooden bowls and skittles for wagers that had commenced with pennies but soon escalated to purses full of gold coin. There were no women present and the atmosphere of increasingly reckless gambling, drunkenness and aggressive masculinity had brought proceedings to a point where boisterous fraternity could trip over into antagonism and violence in an instant. There was a constant malicious interplay going on between the men, aimed at gaining kudos with King Richard, which was based on finding fault or weakness with aspects of each other's character or the things that were said, then gathering in groups to pick on a man and make him seem small and inconsequential. Because of this, no man among them dared to say anything interesting or controversial or which might be seized upon by the others as a sign of weakness. The conversation was therefore of necessity trivial, curt and aggressive in its nature.

Henry Bolingbroke, who had lost heavily at bowls and was now playing chess with Thomas Mowbray, the Duke of Norfolk, called Sir Thomas Erpingham across to their table to adjudicate.

'Thomas, Thomas, Thomas.....' slurred Henry, who was drunker than most in the room at that early hour of the afternoon, 'This here Thomas.....' he waved dismissively at his opponent across the board, '...has not learned the rules of the game properly and wishes to move his King several squares as if it were a horse!' He was slumped back against duck-feather cushions, legs splayed beneath the table and with a glassy-eyed expression. Sir Thomas Erpingham, who had seen Henry drunk many times and knew the warning signs, was confident that belligerence would shortly follow.

Thomas Mowbray, who was also drunker than was good for him, defended his move with passion. 'It is known, Sir, as the King's Leap, and has been recognised by the great masters of the game as integral to the rules. You Sir....' pointing his finger with wine fuelled malice at Henry, '...can claim no greater knowledge of the game than I, schooled as I have been by the great Mendoza of Seville!'

Henry looked to Sir Thomas Erpingham with a contemptuous expression, then back to Mowbray. 'Mendoza? Who the fuck is this Mendoza, that I should give a toss for his opinion?'

'Ha!' said Mowbray as if Henry's question had betrayed

his lack of contemporary knowledge on the subject. He glanced around the room to see who was listening and who might come to his aid, but the others were deep in their game of bowls and seemingly unaware of the developing row. Sir Thomas Erpingham, who was a modest chess player at best, and had in fact been taught to play the game by Henry himself during long nights encamped on their various adventures, had never heard of the great Mendoza either and attempted to dissipate the situation by moving pieces around on the board, looking for alternative continuations for both players.

Neither Henry nor Thomas Mowbray spoke for a few moments, both unwilling to attempt to diffuse the confrontation, both aware that the next word spoken might force an escalation to violence which their wine befuddled brains half-welcomed. Henry took a long, deep swig of his wine, much of the rich purple juice spilling down the front of his tunic. With a loud belch, he rose to his feet and swept the pieces off the board where they clattered and skittered noisily on the tiled floor. Mowbray also got to his feet and, not to be outdone in dramatic gesture, smashed the wooden chessboard in two across his knee and threw the pieces to the floor. Suddenly the room was silent, expectant as the two noblemen squared up to each other, noses an inch apart. Sir Thomas Erpingham backed away; he knew which way this was headed, and that none of the possible outcomes were good ones.

Henry commenced poking Mowbray in the chest as his rage boiled over, and he began to say things which in the present company were better left unsaid.

'You Sir,' he spat the words with venom and hatred, 'are a vile cunt of the worse kind. You embezzle money from your own king. Don't deny it! Eight hundred thousand for the defence of Calais? Siphoned off into your own coffers! You urge treason in whispers; court dissent and spread malicious gossip. And worse than that, you had my uncle Gloucester killed. By God, I will have satisfaction for that!'

Thomas Mowbray was stunned by the onslaught, particularly by the accusation that he had been involved in the murder of Henry's uncle the Duke of Gloucester, an act which had almost certainly been carried out at the direct order of King Richard in cold-blooded revenge for disloyalty during the Appellants' Rebellion. Henry was treading on dangerous ground indeed. At a loss for any adequate verbal response, Thomas Mowbray punched Henry Bolingbroke full in the face, breaking a tooth and splitting Henry's lip which commenced bleeding copiously down his chin and onto his clothing, blood mingling with the wine stains. Henry wiped away some of the blood with the palm of his hand and looked at it with a puzzled expression then threw a punch in turn, but his aim was out and he missed Mowbray's jaw by several inches. Now Thomas Mowbray went on the verbal offensive.

'I am sick to death of you prancing about the country as if you were king. Everyone knows your ambition. I'm surprised your head is still attached to your shoulders you mangy fucking dog!' This insult caused Henry to go into paroxysms of fury and he had to be restrained from throttling Mowbray by several onlookers including Sir Thomas Erpingham. By now, Thomas Mowbray was also being restrained and both men were doing that 'Let me at him!' thing that men tend to do once they are safely held by their friends and the danger of immediate combat has passed.

You will hear it said that Mowbray was the one who issued the challenge to trial by combat, but it was not. Henry spoke the challenge and Thomas Mowbray accepted it, both statements within clear earshot of the other men in the room. With that, both were dragged away from the great hall by their retainers before either could say anything further to harm their position. King Richard sat at the great table watching proceedings implacably as the last two surviving members of the group of nobles who had opposed him in the Appellants' Rebellion set themselves up for his revenge.

The following morning, Sir Thomas Erpingham met an ashen faced Henry Bolingbroke as they both prepared to depart for their respective homes. Sir Thomas felt that Henry had been stupid, setting himself up for unnecessary trouble, but he tried to be conciliatory.

'Well, that could have gone better.' he said with a wry grin.

Henry seemed crestfallen, he was badly hung-over and well aware of the precarious position he had placed himself in, in front of the King. 'I've tried to get an audience with Richard this morning but he's seeing nobody. I need to talk this down

Tom, before the King decides to rid himself of us both. He's after my hide anyway. What the hell was I thinking, saying all that stuff?'

'It may not be too late,' replied Sir Thomas. 'Go to him now, force an audience. He knows that Mowbray is a snake. You should strike while the iron's hot and get it over with.'

But Henry did not do as Sir Thomas had suggested, instead he headed north to his home, leaving King Richard to scheme, and Thomas Mowbray to seethe. So it was that Sir Thomas was contentedly dealing with domestic matters at the manor house in Erpingham village several days later when the messenger arrived with an urgent communication from Henry Bolingbroke to say that King Richard had convened a chivalric court to settle the matter once and for all. The court, under tacit guidance from the King, had determined that Bolingbroke and Mowbray would meet at the lists and that the winner would be declared just and righteous while the loser would be taken to the gallows and hung by the neck until dead. Henry had requested that Sir Thomas act as his second.

This was hardly a request for help; more a command and Sir Thomas knew that he would not escape involvement in the episode, or its outcome. He wondered vaguely about John of Gaunt's position in the matter; thought that Gaunt would almost certainly step in to resolve a petty dispute that could potentially lead to the death of his own son, but it was to become apparent in the coming weeks that Gaunt was losing his power over the King, and was becoming a peripheral figure at court. Henry was in a state of near panic, seeing clearly the trap that Richard had set for him, and by no means confident that he could win the day in combat, man to man with Mowbray, who was considered at least his match with lance and sword.

Sir Thomas had joined Henry and begun the preparations for combat, choosing weapons and armour carefully, trying out various horses to determine which would be best for the joust, and practicing with sword and shield until Henry was about as ready as he could be. The event was becoming a great talking point among the nobility, many of whom would be in attendance on the big day, and substantial wagers were being discretely struck on the outcome. Sir Thomas had sent Rufus Long to track down the old Jewish money lender who had brokered many wagers for him in the past and found that Mowbray, with his slightly superior record with the lance was a warm favourite.

When the day of reckoning arrived, the chosen field was decked out like a major tournament and a vast crowd was in attendance; lords and commoners too. Both Henry Bolingbroke and Thomas Mowbray had arrived in fine style and were mounted and ready when King Richard ascended the viewing platform and waved to the crowd assembled below. Heralds were dispatched to each protagonist to enquire if they wished to temper their accusations and sue for peace. Of course, neither could do so without losing face and so the herald ensured that each party was fully cognisant of the terms and rules for the forthcoming contest, and then indicated to the crowd that the combat would shortly commence.

As the two knights spurred their horses forward to take up position at each end of the list, so King Richard had stepped forward and raised his hand indicating that he wished to speak. The action was momentarily paused; the crowd hushed and expectant.

'My noble friends, I wish you to know that I take this matter unto my own heart, and my own hand.' a murmur of shock pulsed through the crowd; this was the King indicating that he would pronounce judgement himself, without the need for combat. Several whispered arguments broke out about the potential for refund of wagers in the event that no combat took place. The King spoke for several minutes, praising both Bolingbroke and Mowbray for the chivalrous way they had deported themselves in their preparation, then sat down and indicated that a page should read out his proclamation. There were gasps of disbelief when it became apparent that Richard had decided to banish both men from his kingdom, Henry for ten years, Thomas Mowbray for life. Both Henry and Mowbray attempted to reach the King, to plead with him, but a heavy armed guard kept them at bay while King Richard, deaf to all entreaties, commenced his journey home.

Both men would be allowed ample time to make their preparations, and during the coming weeks Henry did get an audience with Richard, who seemed to be softening in his resolve, indicating that his cousin would not, in reality, be expected to complete more than a couple of years in exile and would be allowed to maintain much of his property and income. The outlook for Mowbray seemed harsher, and no indication of a shortening of his life term was apparent. As Thomas had previously suggested to Henry, perhaps King Richard knew the man to be a snake after all.

Several weeks later, Sir Thomas and his wife Joan were walking arm in arm in the meadow behind the manor house at Erpingham. It was a cool day with a brisk wind coming down from the north and both were well wrapped in furs to keep themselves warm. Sir Thomas had spent the previous days visiting local noblemen to try to make arrangements for the safety and security of his property and income during his coming enforced absence; there had never been any question about him not accompanying Henry abroad. To stay would have been an outright denunciation of his loyalty to Bolingbroke and the House of Lancaster. Sir Thomas was no friend of the King, or of Richard's court, and would not have survived long in the absence of his liege. An old friend and neighbour, Sir Simon Felbrigg and another local knight Sir Robert Berney had agreed to jointly oversee the estate in his absence. Now there was just one last question to settle.

'Come with me. Please'

Joan did not speak at first; she watched a swan fly in from the east and settle at the far end of the carp pond.

'I would not relish the nomadic life,' she replied. 'And we have a home here that needs a mistress. You may be away for many years and there may be war and sickness and privation to endure. I am no adventuress. Let me stay here and I will ensure a warm and comfortable house awaits your return.'

'I will miss you.'

'And I, you. Now go.'

They kissed briefly, and neither knew that the days they would subsequently spend together in this life could be counted on the fingers of one hand.

***

When Jacob brought news to Anselmo that William Long had finally died, and that the young wife of Sir Thomas was the new mistress at the manor house, the monk felt that the time had come to enact his revenge. Having ascertained that Sir Thomas was abroad, he felt emboldened to make a return visit to the Erpingham manor house, knowing that there were none left alive who would remember or recognise him, except perhaps for some old serving wench or field labourer, who could be bribed or threatened into silence.

He arrived at the manor gate on horseback, the hooded Jacob also mounted, but holding back a few paces. Joan of Erpingham welcomed the monk into her home, as she would have welcomed any other travelling man of God, and made arrangements for his servant to be fed, and his horses tended. They sat talking of mundane things, Anselmo saying that he was a friend of Joan's husband from years before and asking after his wellbeing, though he gave a false name in case Sir Thomas had told his new wife the story from his childhood of the deceitful monk who had robbed and betrayed his family.

As evening drew in and their supper was over, Anselmo led Joan in prayer, saying the rosary and the evening benediction. They agreed that Joan should visit the Abbey as Anselmo's guest for mass on the coming Sunday and that in the meantime he would be welcome to stay as an honoured guest in the Erpingham home. Joan had her servants make up a comfortable bed in a warm corner of the great hall, close to the embers of the day's fire. When the hour grew late she bade him goodnight and went up the stairs to her own bedchamber. Anselmo paced the floor for several hours, muttering to himself, trying to muster up the courage to enact his terrible vengeance. When he felt certain that the last of the servants had retired to their beds and the house became quiet and still, he drew a small blade from the folds of his tunic and began to ascend the stairway towards Joan's bedchamber. From the shadows, a dark hooded figure emerged and followed him silently up the stairs.

***

CHAPTER 11

(In which both Richard and Henry raise the stakes, and Sir Thomas Erpingham is forced to gamble with his life)

I supplement the meagre income I receive from the sale of my honey brew by tending the churchyard; scything back the long grass around gravestones, cleaning the stained glass windows, sweeping leaves from the porch. In truth, I do little enough hard graft; it is more that I potter around and make myself appear useful. Father Cedric, our new priest, leaves a few coins for me on the ledge by the vestry door each Friday and these I take to the village market on Saturday mornings to convert into a small sack of oats, some hard bread, whatever vegetables are available and occasionally a piece of rabbit, a pigeon or even a fish.

Rufus joined me in the churchyard one morning last week and we sat in the shade of the great Yew tree and talked. He felt it was time that he told the story of the great gamble that Sir Thomas was part of, and how both luck, and stupidity, had played their part in the outcome.

***

Sir Thomas had been sick as a dog as the small boat tacked northward against a modest breeze and a slight swell, while Rufus, for some unknown reason, had suddenly acquired his sea legs and a sailor's stomach, and was heartily tucking into a bowl of beef stew. The small flotilla of ten boats had safely navigated the English Channel and was now headed north, a mile or so off the coast of Norfolk and headed for the mouth of the River Humber up on the Yorkshire coast. Sir Thomas was in nominal command of the vessel, which sat third in line of the small convoy; a nobleman commanded each boat with its contingent of thirty or so fighting men, while Henry Bolingbroke and the ex-Archbishop Thomas Arundel led the fleet, ensuring that the colours of the House of Lancaster on their masthead were visible to those who watched the convoy's erratic progress from onshore, a message of hope to raise the temperature of latent rebellion throughout the land.

While the waves of queasiness tormented his stomach and the hot vomit bile burned the back of his throat and nose, Sir Thomas thought back on the events of the previous year that had brought him to this hard uncomfortable berth on a small boat in a churning sea, heading towards God only knew what.

Henry Bolingbroke's exile, in and around the great French city of Paris, had become characterised by boredom and a lack of clear direction or purpose. This led to an acceleration of the heavy drinking and feasting to which Henry had always had a predilection. Little of note happened to ease the monotony of wealthy idleness, and Henry's only occupation had been writing a long series of letters to both King Richard and to his father in an attempt to get his sentence of banishment rescinded. While Henry's fortunes had been placed on hold, he fared far better than Thomas Mowbray, who wandered aimlessly around Europe, painfully aware that he lacked the family connections at home that might be able to rebuild his reputation at court, and died eventually of the French Pox in a cheap lodging house in Venice.

Then two events occurred in quick succession which forced Henry out of his torpor. The first was the news of the death of his father John of Gaunt, the man who had been the most powerful and, for many, the least loved nobleman in the kingdom, followed swiftly by King Richard's decision to annex all of Gaunt's possessions, and in the process extend Henry's banishment for life. At the time, Sir Thomas had felt that King Richard must be entirely confident of his support among the nobility to have made such a drastic move; must have been aware that Henry might attempt to prise back his inheritance by force of arms, and felt sure that he could deal with any attempt at retribution by his cousin.

Henry had gathered his faithful retinue around him in a tavern on the outskirts of the French capital, well away from the spies who swarmed around the French court. He made his proposition to which most of the men in the room reacted with shock and disbelief. His clearly stated intention was to sail to

England at the head of an army and reclaim the House of Lancaster's possessions by force. Sir Thomas had been one of the first to speak.

'My Lord, you know me to be a brave and loyal servant, and you know that I would lay down my life in your service, but we are two, three hundred strong at best. Where is our army to be sourced and then provisioned? Where is our invasion fleet? We have few enough friends here in France.' He spoke for most in the room.

'Thomas, my good and loyal friend,' replied Henry Bolingbroke with a smile. 'I have strong intelligence from England that the King's subjects have had quite enough of his avarice and the extravagance of his court. He taxes them until they bleed, and then some more. We need a fleet, yes, and a fleet will be found. But the country is up and ready; we will draw support as we go. By travelling in small number, there will be no suspicion of an invasion and knowing my cousin he will dismiss us as a genuine threat'.

'It would be a great gamble, My Lord,' replied Sir Thomas, with a wild grin 'and the odds would be stacked against us.'

Henry had seen this look before; the feral expression on Sir Thomas Erpingham's face before he went into battle against a larger force, or engaged an opponent of greater reputation at the joust, and with his closest companion onside, Henry felt increasingly confident in the success of his plan.

Next to speak was the ex-Archbishop Thomas Arundel,

who had also suffered banishment from the kingdom and had now allied himself to Henry's cause.

'If I may offer the humble opinion of a simple cleric,' said Arundel, who as Archbishop of Canterbury had been one of the most powerful and wealthy churchmen of England before he had displeased the King several years before. 'There can be no question that this is the correct course of action. Without the wealth of the House of Lancaster restored, you good Sir,' waving a blessing at Henry, 'become no more than a beggar at the French court'.

'Then we are agreed,' said Henry 'but we must be discrete. As far as our good hosts here in France are concerned, we travel south to Spain on a family visit to see my sister. I do not wish to land in England to find myself ranged against a great defensive force and be thrown back into the sea. We will get one chance at this; just one.'

So with the best effort at secrecy, the plan had been put into action, though of course there were spies in King Richard's employ even among Henry's closest circle, who ensured that word of the expedition did get back to the English court.

All of Sir Thomas's experience of warfare in the previous twenty years had led him to the conclusion that the most important factors determining the outcome of war were not force of numbers, strength of arms or tactical skill, but the less predictable qualities of luck and stupidity. Luck, both good and bad, were indeed about to play a serious part in the fulfilment of Henry's plan, but Sir Thomas would spend the rest of his life puzzling over the stupidity of King Richard's decision at that point, knowing full well of the threat from his cousin in France; to ignore that threat as if it did not exist and go on a half-baked punitive expedition to tame his wild subjects in the bogs of Ireland, leaving the timid and inept Duke of York in charge of the defence of his realm. For a monarch so cunning, so devious, it would always seem to Sir Thomas to be the most foolhardy of actions.

As the small fleet finally anchored at the mouth of the Humber, close to the small and inconsequential town of Ravenspur, Henry had his closest confidants transfer onto his vessel for a final council of war before the invasion, if the landing of such a small number of men could be referred to as such, commenced. When the tactics and routes for the following day were shared and understood by all, he drew Sir Thomas aside to task him with an unpleasant duty. Letters had been found in the possession of two of the esquires of Henry's retinue, detailing the size and armament of the invasion force, and what was assumed to be their planned route to London, which had been intended for the eyes of King Richard. The two were now under guard on Sir Thomas's boat and Henry wanted an example made.

Returning to his vessel, Sir Thomas had the two traitors dragged up from the small and fetid hold beneath the waterline and he addressed them in front of the thirty odd men of his command.

‘Know this,’ said Sir Thomas, speaking to the onlookers, rather than the accused, ‘there are only two possible outcomes of our endeavour. The first is that we regain our rightful lands and properties and live out our days in peace and prosperity with our families. The second is that we dance a jig on the scaffold until we are almost dead, then have our bowels ripped from our bodies and our limbs torn asunder. Which do you choose?’ he looked from man to man. Nobody spoke a word. They could see that Sir Thomas was pale and looked ill, but knew also of his seasickness so did not assume that his pallor was because of the act he had steeled himself to carry out, as both warning and example. ‘Until our mission is complete, there will be no mercy, no compassion for the traitor, or even for the man who wavers or is undecided. Each man we meet along the way will be for us, or against us. Harden yourselves. This is what we must do.’

Sir Thomas stepped forward to the first of the prisoners, drawing a knife from his belt. The man began to speak, to beg for his life. Thomas spat in his face and rammed the blade into the man’s gut, low down, just above his member, then ripped the blade upwards through the soft flesh of the belly. As a great mess of intestine burst out of the stomach cavity and dangled down below his groin, so Sir Thomas pushed the man backwards, over the side of the small ship and into the vast ocean where the chains around his wrists and ankles ensured that he sank immediately below the waves. The second prisoner tried desperately to cover himself, throwing himself to the floor and curling up into a foetal position. Sir Thomas took him by the hair and opened the man's throat with his blade, then threw him bodily overboard after his companion.

'Mark this well,' said Sir Thomas, wiping his blade on a rag, 'and be certain of your loyalty.' With that he pushed through the crowd of men and entered his small cabin. Rufus joined him there and poured his master a draught of strong barley spirit, but wisely did not speak.

The following morning, the invasion force, such as it was, disembarked and was met by a small, friendly and loyal group of Lancastrian supporters from Pickering Castle, and it was there that Henry set up his first base on English soil. By the end of the first full day, Henry's force had doubled in size, men coming in from the surrounding towns and villages to join his cause. Sir Thomas, who had steeled himself to act with ruthless efficiency in defence of his master's endeavour, interviewed each of the noblemen who rallied to the Lancastrian banner. Though he could see that many of them were delighted at the return of their champion from banishment abroad and were genuine allies, he also knew that several were simply playing it safe, waiting to see which way the wind blew, and these he marked out for close scrutiny in the coming weeks. During the whole of this period which was to last several weeks, when the outcome was in the balance, Sir Thomas was to behave with a ruthless and vicious efficiency which was far removed from his natural character; interrogating, sometimes torturing and often killing any who opposed Henry. It was as if he had realised that his normal tolerant, liberal attitudes would lead him only to failure and his own demise in the coming struggle. The man who knew him best, his own servant Rufus Long, kept his own council during those days and looked at his master as if to a stranger.

The luck that had held for Henry so far, continued to bless his progress. A great storm commenced, now that his small flotilla was safely ashore, and this prevented news of the invasion going south by sea. His route progressed by linking up the castles that had until recently been in the possession of his family; Knaresborough, Pontefract, Doncaster, Derby, Leicester and Kenilworth. Each stronghold either welcomed him with open arms, or put up a brief show of resistance, just in case Henry's ambition was thwarted and they would be able to claim that they had held out as long as they could for King Richard.

Sir Thomas would aver for the rest of his days that he did not know when Henry's plan to wrest back the possessions of the House of Lancaster had become expanded into a plan to usurp Richard's throne, but he would always claim that the distinction was irrelevant; death would have been the outcome of failure, in either endeavour. By this time, several powerful lords had allied themselves to Henry, including the Earl of Northumberland, Henry Percy, and the once insignificant invasion force of a few hundred was now a powerful army of several thousand. At the same time, many southern noblemen, including Sir Thomas's old enemy Bishop Despenser of

Norwich, had rallied to King Richard's banner, currently in the care of a terrified Duke of York who set out with a small force of less than three thousand reluctant men toward Bristol, in the hope of meeting up with King Richard; by now alerted to the very real danger at home and on his way back from Ireland via Milford Haven.

By the time the Duke of York's small and reticent army had briefly engaged with, and then gone over to join Henry's greater force near Bristol, King Richard was to make another terrible tactical error. With the bulk of his army now landed at Milford Haven he had a chance of meeting Henry in a decisive battle, one way or the other. Instead, he sneaked away into the night with a small retinue and ran north, covering the length of Wales in just a few days to take refuge in the mighty fortress at Conwy.

Sir Thomas had always assumed that Henry's invasion would culminate in a great and decisive battle between the opposing forces, and he had steeled his resolve to fight to the death at the side of Henry Bolingbroke, if that proved of necessity. Now it began to appear as if there would be no such clash of arms. With Richard having fled, his own army at Milford Haven began quickly to disintegrate, many looting what they could of the royal treasures and drifting off into the hills, many more changing allegiance and joining Henry's army, now so vast that it was becoming unwieldy. The Lancastrian force had now begun to track Richard's flight north, moving through areas both loyal to the King, where their progress was greeted with sullen acceptance, and those where Henry was greeted as would have been a messiah; Gloucester, Ross, Hereford, Leominster, Ludlow and finally Chester where Henry set up his headquarters, right in the epicentre of King Richard's support in the north-west.

They say that bad things come in threes, and so it seemed to Sir Thomas, did acts of stupidity. With all chance of military victory gone, King Richard's only hope had been to flee the country, to Ireland or even France, and there build his own invasion army to retake his kingdom. Instead, probably made overly confident by the memory of using the force of his own character to save his throne against the odds during earlier rebellions, he trusted to the power of negotiation. Although Sir Thomas had been at Henry's side for the entire adventure so far, and was undoubtedly Bolingbroke's most trusted lieutenant, it was two other men who conspired with Henry to achieve King Richard's final downfall. Henry Percy, the Earl of Northumberland, and Thomas Arundel, ex-Archbishop of Canterbury agreed to entice Richard out of his fortress with seemingly easy terms which would include him remaining on the throne. The fact that Sir Thomas was excluded from this fiction meant that he was not troubled in later life by feelings of guilt for the underhand way in which Henry tricked his cousin into surrender. Trusting the honey-tongued promises of these two men would be King Richard's fourth and final act of gross stupidity.

Sir Thomas had been given an important role in the plan

which saw him lead a group of one hundred armed men up into the hills above the coastal road where they waited, hidden from sight, on the appointed day. He could not help but be awed by the beauty of his surroundings; the green mountains with their great flint and slate outcrops, the endless expanse of the Irish Sea, blue and still with just the faintest trace of white wave crests out toward the horizon, the distant brown line of the land out along the Wirral peninsular, the empty road stretching away toward the west and the great castle of Conwy, all of it so different from the gentle contours of the coast of his own native Norfolk.

Soon, Sir Thomas observed a small party comprising Northumberland, Arundel and their personnel pass along the road toward the east, their mission to give false assurances to King Richard at Conwy, and to draw him out into the open was evidently complete. Several hours later and another group of perhaps twenty men rode east, amongst them the King of England. Thomas waited until they had passed and then led his men down onto the roadway, in order to block any retreat by King Richard's party. Richard and his men rounded a bend in the road and found themselves confronted with a sizeable force under the banner of the Earl of Northumberland. Knowing at last that he had been deceived, King Richard turned his horse and kicked hard, attempting to gallop back to Conwy, but found his path blocked by a second group of mounted men. While his guardsmen were quickly surrounded and disarmed, the King was approached by a mounted knight.

‘Sire, it is over,’ said Sir Thomas, taking the King’s rein in his hand. ‘Come with me now to Rhuddlan, where your cousin would speak with you, and put all to rights.’

‘You, Erpingham?’ said the King, ‘I had not expected that it would be you.’

‘It is over.’ repeated Sir Thomas, and led the King’s horse away.

***

At first, Jacob tried to drag the corpse by the hands along the floor but found that he could not navigate the stairway in such fashion without making a noise sufficient to wake the sleeping household. He managed to lift the body up and over his shoulder, the cadaver was lighter to carry in this way than he had expected, and was able to creep down the stairs into the darkened great hall without being discovered. He paused once, barely breathing as his foot kicked an unseen object, a cup or bowl, which skittered noisily across the floor. At last he felt confident that none of the household had awoken and he moved on, carefully placing one foot before the other. Soon he was moving by moonlight, out of the manor gates and, keeping always to the shadows, along the lane and into the woods. Jacob walked deeper into the trees and then forced his way through a tangle of weeds and bramble into what he hoped would be a secluded and invisible spot come morning. He dumped the body on the ground and went back quickly, but silently, to the outbuildings at the back of the manor house, where he was able to find some farming equipment, amongst which were a good spade and a mattock. He was thankful for the near full moon which had illuminated his search. It took Jacob several hours to dig out a shallow grave; the roots were thick and the ground stony, but when he felt he could get no deeper he straightened up and tumbled the dead body into the hole. Jacob started to backfill, but paused before covering the head. He knelt down in the mud and closed the two staring eyes of his erstwhile master Anselmo, then searched for something among the folds of the soil spattered cloak. Jacob found what he was looking for and, covering up the face with a fold of cloth, he continued to spade in the soil. When he was done, Jacob trod down the newly disturbed earth as best he could, then spread bracken and fern fronds and dead leaves all around the small clearing. Then he sat back against the bole of an old tree to wait for the dawn so that he could examine his work in the daylight; half-dozing through the night, but jerking awake at the slightest sound, fearful of discovery and pursuit.

Joan of Erpingham awoke the next morning to the vague recollection of a nightmare in which she had seen a man with a knife standing over her bed, and another hooded figure standing behind, reaching out toward her attacker. In the morning she wondered why the monk had left without leaving word.

***

CHAPTER 12

(In which the throne is usurped, and Sir Thomas Erpingham is rewarded for his service, but loses his greatest treasure)

Before he drank himself into an early grave, old Stretch the archer gave me his worn leather quiver. This was on account, as it were, of some of the many gallons of my mead he had consumed, but not paid for, at my table. His seemed a comfortable and happy death, if such a thing is possible, and he had confided to me that he harboured no great regrets to ponder in his final days. Oh, that we might all be blessed with such an ending!

I had been looking for a suitable vessel in which to store my manuscript, ever since I had returned from the village one afternoon to find that the local children had ransacked my few possessions; tearing and trampling upon several sheets of completed prose. There was no great harm done, but now I roll my sheets up and store them in the container that had once housed a captain's arrows. I tuck the piece up under one of the roof beams, along with my eyeglass, quills and ink, whenever I leave the house. I am off to visit with Rufus Long today, who has the gout in his toes and cannot raise himself from his bed. He has promised to tell me of the most difficult years of Sir Thomas Erpingham's life. Sir Thomas himself would never speak of the time immediately following his ambush of the King on the coastal road between Flint and Conwy, and so we are reliant on that which his personal servant Rufus Long saw, heard and could still remember after all these years.

***

In the days following the kidnap of King Richard, Henry Bolingbroke's hold on his prize had seemed to be precarious to say the least. Sir Thomas had found himself in the role of chief guard and gaoler of the King on the journey south, and had already been instrumental in foiling several half-baked rescue attempts by the time they were able to deliver the King safely to the Tower of London. Knowing that the burghers of London were no friends of the King, who had taxed them mercilessly in the past, and with the strongest of guards posted, Henry felt confident that no further rescue would be attempted. He retired to Hertford Castle with a group of trusted advisors in order to consider his options. For a man who had seemingly achieved his objective, Henry was fretful, paranoid about perceived threats and plots against him and most of all baffled about what he should do next. It was as if he had thought through, with great care and deliberation, every aspect of the invasion and of chasing down and arresting his quarry, but had given not a moment's consideration to what would inevitably follow.

The only historical precedent for an enforced abdication that he and his advisors knew of was that of his Great-Grandfather Edward II, who had at least been encouraged to comply by the promise that his own son, the future Edward III would succeed him. The plain fact was that Henry Bolingbroke had a dubious claim to succession at best, the infant son of his eldest uncle the Duke of Clarence, being formally next in line.

'Well?' asked Henry of his inner circle, 'Find me just cause. Something that Parliament and the Church will wear. I will not be cheated of the crown by some legal trickery, or the meddling of the Church.'

None of his assembled companions spoke at first until, reluctantly, Thomas Arundel cleared his throat and made a suggestion.

'If the legitimacy of your cousin's claim to sovereignty could be disproved, My Lord, then all might be made to fit? There are men of learning who could be tasked with finding such evidence.'

He was referring to an old rumour, no more than a piece of court gossip, that the birth years of two of Henry Bolingbroke's ancestors had been switched to make the elder of Henry III's two sons, known ignominiously as Edmond Crouchback, appear the younger and therefore be disinherited. If true, this would have made Bolingbroke's claim to the throne stronger than Richard's anyway.

The meeting broke into a cacophony of argument, some supporting this line as the best approach, others wanting a straightforward impeachment of the King on the grounds that he had served his subjects badly; had mistreated them, and overstepped his office in extorting taxes and fines beyond reason. Amid the shouting, Henry became aware that Sir Thomas Erpingham alone sat quietly, seemingly agreeing with neither position, and called for silence.

'Thomas Erpingham, you have been at my side throughout. What would you counsel?'

Sir Thomas seemed unwilling to speak, and others sought to continue their argument, but when eventually he stood and spoke the room fell silent. It had been there, in the room and all around them; a solution which none dared voice. Sir Thomas now did so.

'My Lord, we have crossed many bridges on this journey together, and burnt them all. We cannot choose now to step away from our path. What would be our bargaining position? If your cousin is returned to power, regardless of by what means, then we are dead men, all of us. While he lives we can have no security. It is clear what must be done, otherwise all that we have risked so far has been to no purpose.' Sir Thomas sat down and did not speak again during the rest of the meeting.

Henry looked distraught, as if the possibility had never occurred to him.

'I swore an oath to my cousin when we were boys that I would never do him harm, would protect him always, come to his aid when asked. You would have me do this?' he looked around the room at each man's face.

With that, the meeting once more disintegrated into a babble of conflicting argument, and Henry seemed willing to allow the others to formulate a plan without any clear directive from him. Sir Thomas had wondered if this was a subtle ploy designed to ensure that blame could be directed elsewhere if the plan proved flawed, or whether Henry had simply found his self-confidence dented, now that the suggestion of the murder of Richard had been voiced. Eventually, some sort of consensus was reached and it was agreed that Arundel would commission the best scholars from the universities and monasteries of the land to find evidence of Henry's birth-right to the throne, while another group led by Henry Percy would have an abdication contract, predicated on Richard's misrule of the kingdom, drawn up for the King to sign.

Several weeks later, Sir Thomas had found himself one of the party of noblemen commissioned to take the charter of abdication to the King for his signature. The official line following this meeting was that after some discussion about, and amendment to, a number of minor clauses in the text, Richard had signed 'with a flourish and a happy face', though when Sir Thomas later described the scene to his servant Rufus Long, he said it had been more grimace than grin.

A meeting of parliament had been hastily convened at which the abdication was ratified with little opposition, and Henry had used the occasion to step forward, as all present had fully expected him to do, to claim the crown. Riding high on a wave of popularity, both among the nobility and the common people, Henry was swept to power. In the meantime, the quest to prove Henry's claim to the throne by reconfigured ancestry had proved a dead-end, and was quietly dropped.

A period of great anarchy had commenced throughout the land, many using the sudden regime change as a pretext for reneging on debts and contracts, and Henry's early weeks as King were much taken up with issuing a series of proclamations to attempt to restore order. During this period he had quietly arranged for the deposed King, now officially referred to as Richard of Bordeaux, to be removed from the Tower and taken to a secure cell in Pontefract Castle, where it was planned that he would languish indefinitely, while Henry pondered a suitable solution to the problem of his cousin's continued existence. His thoughts occupied with many problems; it was more by luck than judgement one night at Windsor Castle that Henry and his family escaped a plot to murder him, overthrow the Lancastrian regime and restore Richard to the throne.

A time of rumour, misinformation and uncertainty ensued, when news came tinged always with the political affiliation of its source. Richard was alive and free and leading a great army toward London. Richard had been killed by a mob in London; his relocation to a cell in Pontefract a mere fiction. Henry had been captured by forces loyal to Richard and would stand trial for treason. A great invasion fleet was on its way from France.

No story heard could be either fully trusted, or safely ignored. Men stood ready to switch their allegiance at a moment's notice, depending on which party appeared to be in the ascendency.

Rufus Long had been unable to confirm or deny much of what he had heard, but about three things he was clear. Sir Thomas Erpingham had led one half of the Lancastrian forces to victory over the rebels at a short, but vicious battle at Cirencester, this Rufus knew for the truth as he had been there, and suffered a wound to his shoulder in the process. But Rufus strongly refuted the claim made by French propagandists that Sir Thomas had then executed several of the rebel leaders; Sir Thomas Blount, Sir Benedict Cely and others, abusing them cruelly as they died; claiming that he and his master had been at Windsor at the time on other business for the new King. Of those who joined the rebellion but were subsequently allowed to live, he saw with his own eyes the pitiful scene at parliament, when Henry Despenser, Bishop of Norwich was forced to embrace his old enemy Sir Thomas Erpingham and beg his forgiveness, his dominant position in Norfolk finally ceded to the younger man.

One of the rumours abroad at that time was that Richard was ill, unable to take sustenance from anything he ate, but whether this was true or just further disinformation from Henry's court was impossible to gauge; nobody except his gaolers saw the ex-King alive to prove or disprove the story. Impossible legends were born; that Richard had been seen at the head of a great host, dressed in white with a golden orb suspended above his head, while from the other side came the story that a great eagle had landed on the highest tower of Henry's home at Kenilworth and nested there, a sign that his ascendency to the throne was blessed.

One morning, Sir Thomas instructed Rufus to pack for a journey and prepare two good horses. He said nothing of their destination, or purpose. They travelled north, staying at common inns under false names. At length they reached Pontefract, and Rufus at least knew that their journey must be upon business relating to the imprisonment of Richard, though his master remained silent. Sir Thomas waited until nightfall before approaching the castle walls and then waited again for several hours, watching for a sign or signal from within. Rufus knew better than to speak, or ask questions. In the early hours of the morning, a light flickered on in one of the upper windows and Sir Thomas dismounted and walked across the drawbridge and into the bowels of the castle. Rufus followed him, noticing that no guards seemed to be on duty, and that nobody challenged the presence of two strangers. At a doorway leading to a stone stairwell down into the lower levels of the great fortress, Sir Thomas bade his servant wait while he proceeded alone. Rufus waited for what he thought to be no longer than fifteen minutes before his master reappeared. Sir Thomas did not speak and again Rufus knew better than to ask any questions. They left as they had come, and travelled south through what remained of the night in silence. Neither man ever spoke to each other about that night, or that journey again.

Two days later and news began to filter south that Richard had at last succumbed to the illness which had caused him to be unable to take sustenance from his food. Henry went into public mourning for his cousin and a great procession was arranged bearing the body south in an open coffin, so that all the subjects of the crown could see that the old King was really dead.

Henry Bolingbroke's subsequent coronation as King Henry IV had been the final act in the great saga of his usurpation of the throne of England, and of Sir Thomas Erpingham's part in it, though the repercussions would echo on into the years and decades that followed for both men, in different ways. Those who had stuck by Henry in the bad times were to find themselves rewarded fabulously, beginning with being given roles of honour in the service of coronation, Sir Thomas himself carrying Henry's ceremonial sword at the head of the procession through the great hall of Westminster Abbey.

Titles, wealth and property were soon to follow. Henry heaped lucrative positions upon Sir Thomas, such as Warden of the Cinque Ports and Constable of Dover Castle, but these roles were sinecures; any tasks required being carried out for him by deputies. He was made a Knight of the Most Noble Order of the Garter, an accolade reserved for only those members of the nobility in highest standing with the King. He would also receive the incomes from many of the East Anglian estates that had been previously in the possession of supporters of King Richard, along with his own fine London residence on the banks of the Thames which, incidentally, he rarely if ever visited. Almost all of this newfound wealth would eventually find its way back into Norfolk, and particularly the city of Norwich, which was to gain many fine churches and civic buildings at Sir Thomas Erpingham's expense in years to come.

In those first few years of Henry's reign though, Sir Thomas found himself almost constantly at court, or dealing with the affairs of the King, and had little time to spare for his home county, or indeed for his ever-patient wife. In the same way that he had taken a young Henry Bolingbroke under his wing when the King had been growing into manhood, he now became mentor for the young Prince Henry, eldest son and now heir to the throne of England. Sir Thomas did his best to coach the young prince in the arts of nobility, kingship and the chivalric code, but both he and King Henry often despaired of the boy, who showed every sign of being even wilder than his father had been at the same age. As young Henry approached manhood he seemed to take great pleasure in riling his father, who was desperate that his eldest son should embrace the great responsibility of his destiny as future King, and cement the usurpation of the throne by his succession. The young Prince behaved with a total disregard for his social status, drinking in low taverns with the mob and gambling in the worst of the London dens. Sir Thomas was discretely commissioned by the King to keep an eye on young Henry and to ensure that he burnt off his youthful energy without coming to harm. Prince Henry liked the older man, who had a fearsome reputation in battle and at the joust, and welcomed Sir Thomas into his company of young noblemen. Sir Thomas often found himself called upon to tell late night stories of his exploits at the lists, or during the battles to secure the crown for the young man's father.

While Prince Henry enjoyed himself to the full, boasting that he could enter the lowest drinking and gambling dens to be found anywhere in the city, keep the company of cutthroats, thieves and villains of every sort and emerge the following daybreak with impunity; he remained unaware that his safety was often only assured by Sir Thomas discretely revealing a hidden blade to discourage a cut-purse or would-be kidnapper, or paying bribes to local gang-masters to ensure the party of young noblemen remained unmolested.

It was around this time that Sir Thomas was dispatched on a mission to France to negotiate the betrothal of young Princess Marie to Prince Henry, a mission that seemed to progress without a hitch until the young lady in question refused point blank to leave the convent which had been her home since birth. He returned in the ignominy of embarrassing failure, but Prince Henry at least was quite happy enough not to be married off at such a tender age, even if his father was less than pleased with the outcome.

Though Sir Thomas continued to receive great wealth, title and property from his King, there eventually developed a coldness between them which was to last for many years. Some thought that King Henry never recovered his inner spirit after the events of the usurpation; that his self-confidence and self-esteem had been broken upon the rocks of falsehood and betrayal. Others believed that Henry felt unable to forgive Sir Thomas for some act he had carried out during those wild and dangerous times, and sought to assuage some of his own sense of guilt for usurping his cousin's throne, by projecting fault onto his accomplice. Henry was to spend vast sums in endowing chantries all over the country to buy peace of mind in this life, and forgiveness in the next. In any event he was to die just thirteen years later, bought low by an affliction of leprosy which some felt was no more than he deserved.

Sir Thomas often felt he had spent every waking hour since he had joined Henry Bolingbroke in banishment, looking after the affairs of his liege, and had only seen his wife Joan on the briefest of occasions since. It was in the midst of these tumultuous years that he sometimes found himself with a great desire to spend a little time in peace, rediscovering the simple delights of domestic life. He never felt able though, to simply escape to the leafy lanes of Erpingham village; feeling obliged to remain a short ride away from rescuing the young Prince from some scrape or other. Eventually, he had decided to send for his wife to join him at last in his new London residence. She travelled south, staying overnight in the great houses of the nobility on route, and died in an epidemic of sweating sickness, which had been decimating the city of St Albans at that time.

***

When dawn finally came, Jacob saw that he had been right to wait until morning before making good his escape. There were clear signs of his nocturnal activity everywhere; deep footprints in the mud, broken branches and crushed fern. He did his best to cover up these tell-tale marks and also applied more dead leaves and bracken to the site of the shallow grave, which appeared to him to be obvious to any passer-by. At least, thought Jacob, he had accidentally chosen the site well in the darkness; it was not near any path that appeared to be in regular use.

When he had finished and was as confident as he could be that the grave would not be discovered, Jacob crept back toward the house to see if he could detect any commotion that might indicate anyone had witnessed his strangulation of Anselmo, or his removal and hiding of the body, but all seemed well; just the normal sounds of a waking house. When he saw Joan looking out over the home farm from an upper storey window, looking sleepy, dishevelled and a little puzzled, but not alarmed in any way, he began to sense that he had avoided detection, for the time being at least. Jacob cleaned and then returned the spade and mattock to the place where he had found them, then retrieved the two horses from where they were tethered at the back of the barn, lucky that none of the servants were yet about in that part of the yard, and walked them away into the trees.

It was night time before he reached the grounds of the Abbey and Jacob tethered the horses out in the woods and made his way stealthily toward the outbuildings behind the great dark mass of the Abbey walls. He forced the door of one of the barns and felt his way in the darkness, moving piled up sacks of goods and stacked timber until he reached the low hidden doorway that his master had shown him several years previously. Moving down into the basement he located Anselmo's trunk and taking the key from his pocket, opened the lid. The contents gleamed dully in the half-light.

Jacob took two empty sacks and filled them with gold and silver plate, ornamental jewellery and figurines, chalices and candelabra. When the sacks were full he tied the two openings together so that they could be slung over the shoulder, or a horse's flanks. He then filled two smaller bags with gold and silver coin. There was still much treasure left in the trunk, but he knew that he could carry no more and left the remainder for the monks to eventually find, and do with as they pleased.

***

CHAPTER 13

(In which a new King is on the throne, while Sir Thomas Erpingham helps build a new city, and sees his work consumed in flames)

The winter just passed has tired me greatly and, though the spring brings warmth to my bones, I cannot help but think that my time on this earth is almost done. I have begun to cough all the time, a deep racking spasm that almost, but not quite, brings up some foul phlegm lodged within me. My prayers are simply that I will live long enough to complete this manuscript, though I cannot imagine who would ever choose to read it, or why. As I weaken, so I find myself writing less and day-dreaming more. I have begun to make small illustrations around the margins of the text; rough sketches of archers shooting their arrows, miniature men-at-arms wielding swords and maces, the heraldic symbols which noblemen use to adorn their coats of arms. In truth, I am no artist; the drawings are childish at best, but they amuse me and help to pass the long hours of each day.

I have first-hand knowledge of the time of which I

currently write. Some of the events I witnessed myself, others Sir Thomas had confided in me. The story tells itself, but there is one fact that Sir Thomas never admitted to anyone, least of all me. I have become convinced that for all of his middle-aged infatuation, he did not love his beautiful second bride, even though he was the envy of the county and her smitten with him and would do anything for him, and gave him all she had except that which he desired most; a child.

***

On a warm Norfolk evening in early summer, it seemed as though the whole city of Norwich had turned out to welcome their great benefactor Sir Thomas Erpingham and his new bride; another named Joan, a young widow of famous beauty. For Sir Thomas, six years had passed in mourning, and none thought it inappropriate that he should be wed again, least of all Sir Thomas himself. Dressed in the finest garb, and with the Lancastrian double 'S' motif on a golden chain hanging heavy around his neck, Sir Thomas wore his beautiful young bride on his arm as if she were part of his costume. The crowd loved every minute of it. The women whispered jealously of her immaculate complexion, of her long golden hair, the exquisite delicacy of her figure, the fine cut and radiant hue of her dress and jewellery. The men leered and spoke side-of-mouth obscenities as they drank their beer. City dignitaries tripped over each other in the race to be first to present him with fine wines and foodstuff to refresh the newlyweds after their long ride from London.

Sir Thomas was tired and wanted nothing more than a simple supper in his own house and a decent night's sleep, but would have to endure first a number of interminable speeches from the Mayor, the Sheriff, local aldermen, merchants and high-ranking churchmen, and then some sort of civic dinner. He whispered something in his wife's ear which made her blush and make as if to scold him. Sir Thomas, though thickening through the torso with middle-aged portliness, and with hair and beard turned almost completely white, still had all the lasciviousness of his youth, and the lack of respect for civic pomposity which he had always displayed.

With the speeches finally done, and after Sir Thomas had addressed the great crowd which had gathered outside the Guildhall; playing skilfully upon their prejudices against, and distrust of everything outside of the county of Norfolk, and by stoking the fires of support for the Lancastrian house over that of the old regime, the party moved out of the public gaze and into the home of one of the leading men of the city, William Appleyard. An old friend of Sir Thomas Erpingham's, he had served as the first Mayor of Norwich several years previously, when Sir Thomas had used his influence with the old King to secure a charter for the city, enabling among other things the election of a Mayor and Sheriff, and ensuring that the status of Norwich as 'second city' of England was formalised, and had recently completed a second two-year term in that office as well.

Taking seats at a table in the great hall, the newlyweds were presented with a spread of the finest food and drink available anywhere in the county, and spent the next couple of hours feeding each other titbits and generally behaving like first-time-smitten youths. The couple seemed oblivious to the other assembled guests, all of them local dignitaries and representatives of the leading families of the county. Appleyard feigned patience with their infatuated behaviour, which many in the room thought rude and unseemly, but was actually keen to separate the newly-weds so that he could speak to Sir Thomas, man to man, on a number of important matters.

Eventually, with the meal finished and most of the other dignitaries having left, Appleyard sensed his opportunity and approached Sir Thomas, only to find at that moment a great gaggle of supplicants, who had been queuing at the door for the chance to speak with the great man, had burst in and surrounded Sir Thomas, each of them waving a written petition. Erpingham's personal servants, under the command of Rufus Long, were quick to restore order and were about to throw them all out, when Sir Thomas indicated that he would speak with them, one at a time. An orderly queue was formed and each man was able to sit with him for five or ten minutes to present their petition. Sir Thomas heard each man out, asking a number of salient questions and gave either a judgement, or promise of funding, or indication of his preference in the matter under discussion. William Appleyard sat back to wait and after half an hour of this, Sir Thomas's new bride indicated that she would return to the Erpingham city residence to rest. As she left, surrounded by her personal servants, she stopped to whisper something in Sir Thomas's ear, and now it was his turn to blush.

Finally, with the hour grown late, the last of them was gone and Appleyard found himself alone with Sir Thomas. They had long been friends and, once all servants had been dismissed from earshot, treated each other with a fraternal irreverence which in other men of their high standing could easily have caused rancour, or offence.

'I see you still pick the ripest apples, Thomas,' said William Appleyard with a smile. 'Are you not worn out, a man of your many years?'

'The sap still flows in an old oak tree!' replied Sir Thomas with a self-deprecating shrug. 'As I am sure you know yourself!'

Both men were at the nicer end of the spectrum of drunkenness; there would be no insult taken here and they both relaxed in each other's company. Appleyard sought to move the conversation on to a subject of mutual interest.

'Do you bring other treasures along with you, apart from this Aphrodite who awaits your company at home tonight?' asked William, pouring them both a cup of wine.

'I bring the blessing and goodwill of our new King,' replied Sir Thomas, 'Who seeks the same assurances that all kings seek; that the city of Norwich and the county of Norfolk are loyal, and will remain so.'

'I trust you conveyed all such assurances?'

Sir Thomas grew serious. 'This new King is not like his father was in recent times; seeking a quiet life above all else. He wants war, soon, with France and he will expect support without question from the county. Accept his largesse now, but do not image that it comes without a heavy price.'

Sir Thomas called out for the master of his household, Rufus Long, to join them and then sent him to retrieve a scrolled vellum document from one of the trunks with which they had travelled up from London. They spread the document on the table and weighed down the four corners with wine goblets. Rufus held a candle to light the text as Sir Thomas began to talk through its content. The document was, in effect, a promissory note setting out funding to be allocated to the city of Norwich for building works; new civic structures, extensions to priories, much needed repairs to Cathedral buildings, new parish churches, the laying of paved or cobbled streets. The sums involved were immense, far more than could ever have been raised by local subscription. Among the signatories were prominent noblemen and churchmen of the new young King's court, including Sir Thomas Erpingham in his formal role as Steward of the Royal Household. At the bottom of the list of signatories was the red wax seal of King Henry V. It was as if a great sack of gold had been placed upon the table.

Sir Thomas gave Appleyard the news that he had been selected to oversee the great works; to decide upon the proportion of funds to be allocated to each project, to ensure the money was spent wisely and to report back, via Sir Thomas, on progress. They talked long into the night about which were the first priorities, whether church should be allowed precedence over secular interests, which pet projects should benefit and which should be forced to wait at the back of the queue. It was agreed that the Dominican Friary in the city would be a priority case; the Black Friars receiving a greater proportion of the funds than any other non-secular establishment, and it became apparent to Appleyard during the course of their conversation that a significant proportion of the promised funds were to come from Sir Thomas Erpingham's own private coffers. It was late in the night when Sir Thomas finally left his friend pouring over the parchment, enraptured by the sudden change in his city's fortunes, and not a little perturbed at the scale of the task before him.

For several days, Sir Thomas busied himself in the city while his wife Joan began to alter almost every aspect of the internal layout and decoration of their city residence. She invited many of the wives of the local nobility to join her in this endeavour, and soon Sir Thomas found that he would come home in the evening, expecting peace and the warm embrace of his beloved, only to find a cackling flock of hens had descended upon his domain, screeching their loud opinions about different samples of wall-hangings, and commissioning expensive furniture and table decorations on his behalf. After several weeks he could bear the intrusion no more and decamped, with Joan, to the manor house at Erpingham. For a while all was well, but soon Joan became bored with country living and asked if just a few of the ladies from Norwich could visit to help her pass the time. It was not long before the manor house was also invaded, the finest ladies of the city having decided that if one was not to be seen in the company of Lady Joan of Erpingham, then one was absolutely nobody in society at all.

Sir Thomas was forced to find peace walking in the fields and on the pathways of the village. He realised that the last time he had done so was when plague had afflicted the village, many years previously, and he saw many of the houses which had been daubed with the black cross of death, now thriving family homes with the smells of baking emanating from within and healthy, well-nourished children playing outside. He spent time speaking with the people of the village, some of whom remembered him from his childhood, and nearly all of whom mentioned the local legend that as a small boy he had fought off an armed band of brigands, when on route to market. They told him of local concerns; trouble with merchants from Norwich who set unfair prices, boundary disputes with farmers from other villages, threshing equipment and grain storage facilities which were in great need of repair. In each case Sir Thomas offered either financial assistance, or to intervene with the relevant authority. There was just one concern that all his people voiced, about which Sir Thomas was able to do nothing, and that was the fierce drought that had afflicted the whole of East Anglia that summer, shrivelling up crops in the field and turning green woodland into tinderbox dry brush.

He visited the parish church at Erpingham on several occasions to pay his respects at the grave of his parents and became friendly with Father Cedric, whom he had not previously known. Together they discussed the long-term possibility of adding a new bell tower to the west end of the nave and Sir Thomas gave assurances that he would help to fund the project. It was during one of these visits that he showed Father Cedric a sketch of a brass effigy he had commissioned in London, of his father in full battle armour, which was to be imbedded in stone above the vault in the aisle of the church, under which his parents lay.

Matters of national concern were never far away and, though Sir Thomas succeeded for most of that summer in dealing with his responsibilities at court by fast messenger, it became apparent that King Henry felt his chief steward had holidayed for long enough, and should soon return to London to help in the preparations for Henry's planned invasion of France. On his final visit that year to Father Cedric, Sir Thomas presented the lowly parish priest with a most beautiful embroidered silk chasuble, which would have graced the garment collection of any Bishop or Pope. It was made from the bolt of silk that Henry Bolingbroke had given Sir Thomas as they journeyed back from the Holy Land together many years previously, and he had paid for the finest craftsmen in London to embroider it with patterns and religious images, to his exact specification. He had planned to present the chasuble to the new Bishop of Norwich, Richard Courtenay, who had succeeded the short lived successor to the old Fighting Bishop himself, Henry Despenser, with whom Sir Thomas had found an unexpected empathy and even a reluctant friendship in the last years of the fat old cleric's life. However, in a flamboyant and eccentric gesture, typical of the new middle-aged and wealthy Sir Thomas Erpingham, he had decided on a whim that the beautiful gift would go to a more deserving home.

It was late summer and with preparations made to return to court, leaving his wife for the time being happily ensconced among the good ladies of Norfolk, Sir Thomas had just one more civic duty to perform; to attend a great council of the Norwich civic officers as guest of the Sheriff, which was to take place in the Guildhall. Among other items on the agenda was to be a formal vote of thanks to Sir Thomas for all the intercessions he had made with the royal court on behalf of the city of Norwich.

While the great and mighty were lionising each other in the Guildhall, another citizen of Norwich, Simon Jermy, had been attempting to burgle the house of his employer, John Spence, who was away visiting with relatives in the village of Taverham. Simon had long suspected that Spence, a prosperous timber merchant, had been hoarding silver coins in his bed-chamber; indeed Spence had intimated as much when they had been drunk together one night in the Maid's Head tavern. Simon worked for Spence, supervising the unloading of timber from the merchant ships which plied the river, and had recently taken to drinking and playing dice with the wharf-men down at the sheds on the banks of the River Wensum. He had gotten in a littlc too deep, and this robbery of his employer would mean his redemption from gambling debts which had turned nasty. There had already been talk of an example being made, of injury and disfigurement as punishment for his non-payment of the debt.

Simon had broken into the house with ease; a latch securing a trapdoor above a delivery chute into the basement had only to be prised with a blade and he was in, and able to make his way around the rooms of the house without leaving any other trace of the burglary. He made his way to the bedchamber and started to look around for potential hiding places. It was difficult to see properly in the early evening gloom, and Simon decided to light a candle to aid his search. As he did so, he was suddenly startled by the sound of loud knocking at the front door. Fearing that he had been discovered, Simon dropped the candle and ran toward the back of the house. He could hear shouts from the street and dashed out of the building via one of the rear doors, which had been locked to entry from outside, but opened easily on a latch from within. Simon ran down an alley which ran parallel to the street, cursing his luck and praying that he had not been observed, and identified. The watchman, who had been employed by John Spence to deter just such an attempt at robbery, used his keys to enter the front door and gave each room a perfunctory check to ensure nobody with still within, then re-secured both the rear door and the delivery chute, before retiring back to his house across the street, where he was soon dozing again in his chair.

In John Spence's now deserted bed-chamber, the discarded candle had almost gone out as it rolled across the floor and under the bed, but the tiniest orb of blue flame managed to survive at the tip of the wick and, as the candle came to rest against the cotton bed-covering, it grew again into a bright yellow flame, kept fed by the rapidly expanding pool of molten wax beneath it on the wooden floor. The area of bed covering just above the flame grew hotter and turned brown, then began to smoulder and smoke, before suddenly bursting into flame. Quickly, the straw bedding caught too and within a matter of minutes the entire bedchamber was well ablaze.

A strong warm breeze had been blowing all day from the south-east, the kind of wind that threatens, but never quite delivers, stormy rain. As the flames from within the bedchamber began to penetrate the roof of the house, catching light to the dry mud and reed packing between the roof beams and the slate tiles, so the breeze fanned the fire, increasing its intensity and ensuring that it quickly spread into the roof of the adjoining building to the north. John Spence's house was on Ber Street, just behind the Timber Market; part of a long row of terraced properties which culminated a few yards from the base of the mound below Norwich Castle. Behind the building to the west lay a maze of poorer dwellings, mostly rickety timber tenements leading towards St. Stephen's quarter and the Horse Market. Swiftly, the fire began to rage north along Ber Street, and west into the housing beyond. The drought that had afflicted the county that whole summer had dried out timber and thatch to the extent that the merest spark was enough to set an inferno raging, and very quickly the fire began to spread throughout the city.

By now the alarm had been raised and men and women raced desperately to get their possessions out of their homes and away to safety, before the flames engulfed them. City wardens ran from street to street giving as much warning as possible, though often the thick, acrid smoke preceded them, giving people ample warning of the conflagration to come. Looting started, and it was difficult to be sure if the man lugging an expensive item of furniture up the street was its rightful owner, or an opportunist thief.

The wind which had ensured the fire's progress north and west also helped to ensure that its effects were minimised to areas south and east of its starting point. The inferno did engulf the dwellings around the base of the castle mound on the east side, rapidly burning along King's Street and the eastern edge of Tombland, but the great buildings of the Austin Friars and Grey Friars Priories, and the Cathedral itself, were only marginally affected. In part this was due to the kindly wind direction, but also because their proximity to the Wensum enabled men to fetch bucket after bucket of water to drench the walls.

To the west of Ber Street the inferno raged unabated. On this side of the city were the poorer dwellings and these tended to be made entirely of wood, rather than brick or stone, and to be terraced together in a dense maze. The fire was now so intense that any attempt to fight it was beaten off by the heat. Men simply ran for their lives, no longer intent on rescuing their meagre possessions, and in any case, there was less on this poorer side of the city worth saving. The only areas that survived relatively unscathed were those that were surrounded by open spaces, such as the new church of St. Peter at Mancroft and the cleared land around the market cross.

The city dignitaries had long since been alerted and many had dashed away from the Guildhall to see to their own properties and possessions. Sir Thomas Erpingham, along with William Appleyard and one or two others took charge of the evacuation of the city, quickly agreeing a makeshift plan of defence. Each man moved swiftly to take command at one of the northern Wensum crossings; Coslany Bridge, the New Bridge at St. George's Plain and Fye Bridge at the northern end of Tombland. As frantic crowds gathered, they hurried people across the bridges, commanding them to ditch the superfluous burdens of their possessions at the side of the road, then set the young and the strong to work, hunting out buckets and receptacles of every kind with which they set up human chains carrying water from the river to douse the buildings on the northern side of the Wensum. Sir Thomas thought it their only chance; if the flames were stopped by the expanse of the river, and any fire that did cross were to find only dampened wood, then the entirety of Norwich north of the river might yet be saved.

By now all of the western districts of Mancroft, Wymer and St. Giles were ablaze and effectively lost, while the great castle mound was an island in the midst of the inferno. Sir Thomas had established his command post just to the west of Fye Bridge in the Colegate area and could only look on as the fire began to engulf the half-rebuilt shell of the Black Friars Priory, which had been one of the main recipients of the funding he had helped to secure for the city. With everything south of the river and west of Tombland now aflame, Sir Thomas began to direct a stream of refugees to head east along Colegate Street and seek sanctuary at the great Priory of the White Friars at the north-eastern edge of the city, and if no room was to be found there to head south again, crossing the Wensum, which was at least fordable due to the prevailing drought conditions, and then to head for the Great Hospital of St. Giles, or the Cathedral itself. He prayed desperately that the wind should not change direction and veer round to come from the west.

As midnight passed and it seemed as though the river itself had been sufficient barrier to the flames, so the wind continued to carry smouldering clumps of ash from roof thatching, high into the air above the river and the citizen's defensive line. Eventually, one or two of these floating faggots caught in the parched thatch of the buildings up along Magdalen Street and soon they were ablaze too. Now all of Coslany and everything west of Magdalen Street was engulfed until the flames licked the great stone walls of the city. The rest of that long night passed in a blur of smoke and steam and fire and the screams of those who were trapped and the wailing of those who had lost all. Sir Thomas found himself, many hours later, as a smoke-laden dawn broke across the devastated city, huddled with a thousand others in the great nave of the Cathedral, wondering why God had brought such calamity upon him, and upon his city.

***

It was the turn of the young leper boy, whom everybody knew as Fetch, to bolt the front door of Magdalen House and sit guard just inside the doorway during the evening hours. He was in the process of doing so when there was a loud knock on the door. Fetch opened it fearfully and saw a man in a dark cloak, with a hood obscuring his features, standing on the pathway. The stranger carried two heavy sacks slung across his shoulder. These he dropped in the doorway, making a clanging sound as the contents hit the stone floor. Without a word, the man turned and walked back down to where his horse was tethered; mounted up and was gone. Fetch called for the senior men of the house and together they opened the sacks and began to sort through the wondrous contents. They were used to receiving anonymous charitable donations from those wealthy citizens of the city who sought to ensure themselves a place at The Lord's Table in the next life, but were unable to believe the scale of this largesse, which would ensure the comfort and sustenance of the leper inmates for many years to come.

During the following weeks a strange phenomenon began to be reported in the poorer towns and villages around St. Benet Holme Abbey. People would awaken to find that coins had been left on a windowsill or gatepost; sometimes copper, occasionally silver or gold. It seemed that the poorer the household, the larger denomination of money was left. Nobody could explain this strange but welcome event and over time the bounty diminished and then ceased entirely, leaving stories and rumours talked about in the public houses and marketplaces. Legends were born from these stories which would still be in circulation many generations later.

With just a few pieces of gold and silver remaining in his purse, Jacob rode through the Magdalen Gate and into Norwich for the first time since he had been a child, flipping a coin to the gate-keeper to ensure he was not challenged. Halfway along the street he looked to the left-hand side of the road to try to identify the building that had housed his father's smithy when he had been a child. It was there still, hardly changed, and he dismounted and cautiously approached the old building. The door was ajar and Jacob peered into the gloom. He saw an old smithy forge which had evidently not been fired for many years. In the corner sat an old woman, peeling vegetables over a wooden bowl. She looked up at the sound of the door creaking and Jacob could see the thick opaque cataracts on both her eyes.

'Can I help you?' asked the old woman. Jacob said nothing and placed a handful of gold coins on the table beside the seated woman. He walked quickly outside, remounted and spurred his horse away, heading north toward Erpingham, trying desperately hard to remember what his mother had looked like on the long-ago night when he had been driven away from his home by men with stout Ash-poles.

***

CHAPTER 14

(In which the new King sets out to regain his ancestral dominions in France, and Sir Thomas Erpingham goes to war for the final time)

Rufus Long has declared himself to be bed-ridden; utter nonsense in my opinion, but I will admit that when I last saw him his feet and legs were swollen and purple looking, the blood no longer moving freely through his veins. In order to complete my manuscript I must drag myself to his bedchamber at the manor house to record his testimony, and I do so simply because there is nobody else left who can recount at first-hand experience the story of Sir Thomas Erpingham's final battles; at Harfleur and then the long march to a muddy field that has become known by the name of a nearby village; Agincourt.

The story Rufus recounts is less about the glory and honour and chivalry they tell of in the taverns, more of blood and filth and disease and wasted life. Still, he survived to tell it, and says that it happened like this.

***

It had seemed to Rufus Long as though every man of fighting age in England had descended upon the city of Southampton that summer. Every inch of usable space upon the heath, and along the front of Southampton Water, was covered by canvas tents and tethered horses, by cooking fires and piles of weapons and the paraphernalia of war. Out on the water the fleet had gathered in a vast chaotic armada, vessels of every size from the King's own flagship to the smallest tender, and there was no space for any ship to manoeuvre in safety without risking collision and incurring the wrath of the captains of the craft around them.

Rufus had walked down to the water's edge to gather his thoughts and find some momentary peace. In recent days he had been assisting his master, Sir Thomas Erpingham, with the arrangements for the execution of the noblemen Scrope, Conisburgh and Grey, whose foolish plot had been revealed to King Henry by Edmund Mortimer, the Earl of March, the very man with whom they had sought to replace him on the throne. All the arrangements seemed to have been delegated to Erpingham; the secure incarceration of the accused, the sham of a trial, the commissioning of local carpenters to build a scaffold down in front of the Bargate, the finding of a willing hangman, the policing of the crowd. It seemed that his master's reputation as an executioner from the days of Bolingbroke's invasion had stuck, yet Rufus knew only too well just how distasteful Sir Thomas found such tasks. The corpses of the conspirators now dangled on short lengths of hemp rope, for all to see their foolish ambition exposed for nothing more than a treasonable dream.

Feeling the pleasant warmth of the August sun on his shoulders, Rufus gave a couple of coins to the cook of a troop of archers from Huntingdon in exchange for bread and ham and a jug of beer. He sat on a low wooden post close to the water's edge to enjoy his luncheon and let the world pass him by for a few minutes.

He would be travelling with Henry's invasion fleet as Sir Thomas's personal servant, in addition to the indentured men under Erpingham's command; twenty men-at-arms and sixty archers, all of them mounted. Theirs was to be one of the smaller troops, with some noblemen contracted to bring almost a thousand men, many of whom though would arrive with less than their agreed quota. Still there would be an army of close to twelve thousand men ready to sail, though nobody yet knew of the objective of the invasion, lest spies forewarn the French court of King Henry's plans.

Having rested and eaten his fill, Rufus stood and brushed the breadcrumbs from his tunic, let out a great, satisfactory belch which carried across the still water, and headed up through the town toward the heath where Sir Thomas's men had been mustered. As he entered the makeshift camp he was greeted by Sir Walter Goldingham and the esquire Hamo Strange, two of the senior men of the Erpingham contingent, who asked Rufus for news of their possible date of departure.

Rufus indicated that, with the Mortimer conspiracy crushed and its plotters dead, Henry seemed impatient to embark and get the expedition under way, and so they should be prepared to move at a moment's notice. He looked around the camp and saw men preparing their equipment, checking weapons and sharpening blades and arrow-points; impatient to get started. They looked well-fed, strong, frightening men; experienced killers all.

Sir Thomas was not with them. Immediately following the executions he had dashed off to find his armourer for a final fitting of his new suit of armour. It had been a close call as to whether the equipment would be ready before embarkation, with Erpingham running the risk of the ignominy of not being able to lead his troop into battle for the want of the necessary protective kit, or worse still, having to borrow ill-fitting pieces from other men-at-arms. The trouble had begun many weeks previously, with Rufus constantly nagging Sir Thomas to try on his equipment early, leaving ample time for adjustment, and his master barely listening, so engrossed was he in the work to repair the burned-out city of Norwich, and re-home its destitute citizens. Finally, with just days to go before the journey south, Rufus had been able to corner his liege and force him into a reluctant fitting. What Rufus had observed, and Sir Thomas would have vehemently denied, was that he had put on several stone in weight, and several inches in girth, in the years since he had last waged war, and the armour was impossibly, embarrassingly tight. Sir Thomas had bluffed and blustered and sucked in his belly, but was finally forced to admit that he was no longer the Adonis he had once been, and sent for his armourer to drop all other commissions, and come to his aid quickly.

It had been Sir Thomas himself who bought the news that they would begin embarkation with the following tide, in the early hours of the next morning. Looking like a knight from an Arthurian legend with his long white hair and beard, his heavy, powerful-looking frame encased in highly burnished armour under a surcoat emblazoned with the Erpingham arms and the Cross of Saint George, Sir Thomas led his men down to their allotted place on the waterfront in the chill grey pre-dawn, to await the allocation of their ship.

To have transported an army of twelve thousand men across the English Channel, and disembarked them safely, in battle order, would have been a relatively simple task. It was the horses that complicated matters; made the enterprise a logistical nightmare for Henry's planners. All the civilians; the physicians, servants, priests, cooks, baggage-handlers, scribes and heralds were simply rowed out to their transports in small skiffs and tenders, ascending the sides of the larger vessels by rope or ladder. Heavy equipment was taken out in similar fashion and winched up onto the deck by rope and pulley. This process had enabled many of the vessels which would comprise the invasion fleet to remain at anchor out in the deep water. These were ships of every shape and size, pressed into military service and away from their normal business, so men found themselves billeted on-board among the remnants of the ship's previous cargo; soon blackened with charcoal dust or forced to find a comfortable berth where pigs had recently lain in their own filth.

Those ships designated for horse transportation were either designed specifically for the purpose, or had been quickly adapted. They were shallow drafted vessels, without much of a keel, which were towed in towards the shore by rowing boats, stern first, at high tide and then allowed to settle onto the sand and silt as the waters receded. Rufus could see hundreds of similar vessels beached along the waterfront, but was soon forced to concentrate only on what was going on with the embarkation of his own troop. A great hinged wooden gate in the stern was swung open, and Rufus could not help but be concerned that the opening would only just be above the water-line when the ship was fully laden at sea. Heavy planks were lowered down, side by side to form a ramp, each plank studded with iron rivets to enable some degree of purchase for the horse's hooves. Another set of planks were laid on the inside, forming a low bridge. Quickly, the first horse was spurred forward by its rider. At first the beast shied at the unfamiliar bulk of the vessel but the mounted soldier whipped his steed forward, and with a rush the horse was up the ramp, clattering hooves ringing off the iron studs, and then was swiftly down the other side and into the interior of the ship. Now the rider dismounted and walked his horse forward by the bridle along an aisle between wooden stalls forming a herring-bone pattern along each side. As he reached the furthest stall forward, he led the animal in, tied off at the rail and then climbed up and out of the stall, which was just wide enough for the horse. A trough of feed kept the horse from worrying about his new surroundings and the soldier then ascended a ladder onto the foredeck which was to be his home for the duration of the voyage. Behind him, the process was repeated until one hundred horses and their riders were onboard.

Now the sailors pulled the planks back on board and stowed them away, then closed and bolted the great horse port. Taking buckets of soaked straw and a tar-like resin, they commenced caulking the gaps around the gate until all appeared watertight. Up on the foredeck, the men milled around, seeking out the best places to set out their kit and rest in some degree of comfort for the voyage to come. Sir Thomas, together with Rufus and one or two of the noblemen in his retinue, was housed in a small cabin which was usually the domain of the vessel's captain, and they also quickly staked out a bench, table-top or corner of the floor for themselves.

Gradually, the tide came, floating the great ship off the mud and allowing it to be towed out again into deep water, and as the long morning dragged on into afternoon the signal finally came from Henry's flagship, the Trinity Royal, that the expedition was officially underway. Sir Thomas settled in for his customary bout of sea-sickness, and by the time the first ships were leaving the Solent and entering the slightly choppier waters of the English Channel, he was vomiting spectacularly over the side, along with a number of his men.

The voyage proved uneventful and, having sighted the French coast on the morning of the next day, they spent a further day and night tacking along toward the west. As Rufus had suspected, the improvised gate through which the horses had been loaded was no match for the sea and all attempts to keep the aperture water-tight were to prove flawed. The job of bailing out the hold, which would otherwise have filled rapidly with water and caused the ship to founder, was allocated to the grooms, who were soon ladling bucket-loads of a foul broth of seawater, horse excrement and urine over the side. Rufus looked out across the ocean and saw ships afloat as far as the eye could see, good visibility and kind winds meaning that each captain felt confident to plot his own course; happy that he would not lose sight or intended direction of the bulk of the fleet. He wondered if a greater armada had ever set sail in all of Christendom.

Two days after leaving Southampton, the fleet came to anchor at the eastern side of the Seine estuary and Henry called his captains together on his flagship for a conference before the invasion began in earnest. Sir Thomas was rowed across between the great ships in a tiny skiff, and clambered up the rope ladder to board the fleet's flagship, feeling every one of his fifty-eight years. Henry set out his plan of campaign, and ensured that each of his commanders understood the part he and his men were expected to play. He then detailed a scouting party to go ashore, check out the lie of the land, estimate the strength and location of any opposing forces and reconnoitre the town of Harfleur to see what defences might be ranged against them. This had been the first time that Harfleur had been openly mentioned, but when the fleet had spied the French coast and turned west rather than east, most had surmised one of the two towns guarding the entrance to the river Seine, Harfleur or Honfleur, would be their objective. Henry commanded his young cousin Sir John Holland to lead the scouting party, which would consist of a dozen of his best men. As he picked them out, Henry's eye landed on Sir Thomas, but seeing that the old warrior was looking pale and unwell with the rolling swell of the ship, he passed him over to choose other, fitter men.

Holland's party were gone for several hours and returned with the astonishing news that there did not seem to be an opposing French force anywhere in the vicinity, and that the good citizens of Harfleur seemed to be going about their business as if the wrath of God was not about to come crashing down upon them.

So the disembarkation process commenced, in a reverse of that which had seen them loaded and underway, made easier by far by the welcome fact that there was no enemy in sight to harry the English when they were at their weakest, during the slow laborious unloading and gathering together of mounted troops into their various companies and formations. It was several days before all was ready, and after gathering intelligence locally through a combination of threat, torture and bribery, seeing the merchant fleet safely away to collect those who had missed the tide or been left behind for lack of space on ship, and the fighting ships prepared to blockade the town from the sea, King Henry gave the signal and the great army set off to attack the walled city of Harfleur.

Sir Thomas had been almost instantaneously reinvigorated on being reunited with dry land, and had set about putting the men under his direct command into good order. His primary role in the coming campaign began to become established; now in his late fifties, even Sir Thomas himself had to admit that his days of being first man in amongst the enemy were over. He found himself bolstering the courage and morale of those young men for whom this would be a first taste of war by talking to them quietly and confidently, and cooling the blood of the hotheads, who were all for charging off ahead in search of honourable combat, just as he himself had done on that long ago trek through the wild lands of Scotland. In general, the younger men had a great affection and respect for the old man, knowing the stories of his adventures with the King's father, and of the great courage and prowess Sir Thomas had once shown in battle, and at the lists. Of course there were one or two who objected to the interference of an old man, whose day had surely passed, but they were in the minority and he was regarded as more an asset than a liability to the campaign by all who came in contact with him.

Rufus had ridden alongside his master at the head of their troop as the great army breasted a hill and looked down at last upon the city below. His eye was immediately drawn to a great flood of water lying across the valley between them and the city walls; it was to become evident in the days that followed that the defenders were able to dam the River Lezarde at will, using sluices built into the city's defences, and this was to become one of the many obstacles the English would face in their coming assault. Henry set up his headquarters at the crest of the hill, in full view of those watching from behind the walls below, and called his captains to another conference. The King had determined that his campaign would be fought under the strictest code of discipline, chivalry and honour, so that his divine right to have invaded France in the first place could never be called into question because of his subsequent behaviour in the field. He reminded his commanders that every man would be called to account for every breach of those rules, including the treatment of the local civilian population, and he reiterated the protocol for claiming ransom on captive noblemen. When the King had finished his lecture he asked Sir Thomas, as one of the most experienced men in matters of warfare, if he had anything to add. Sir Thomas remembered all too well the chaos he had witnessed in the battles for cities like Edinburgh and the great fortress in Lithuania, and re-emphasised the King's instruction that every Englishman should wear the Cross of Saint George, front and back at all times, lest he be mistaken in the heat of battle for a Frenchman, and run through with an English blade.

Intelligence suggested that the largest French force in the

vicinity was across the estuary at Honfleur, and would therefore face an inland journey, bridge crossing and return march of several days before they could come to the city's aid; crossing by sea was not an option with the English fleet blockading the port. Henry split his force, sending his brother the Duke of Clarence with about one third of the army south to block the road from Rouen, which a relieving army would have to take, and to assault the city from that direction. As he was doing so a company of several hundred French men-at-arms rode into the city by the northern gate, under the command, it would transpire, of the great hero of the defence, Raoul de Gaucourt. They were able to do so unmolested because the great flooded expanse of the river lay between them and the English army. Their reinforcement was to be the only help the city would receive in the coming days of hell.

Terms were offered, and rejected, and so the bombardment of Harfleur commenced. In the years since Sir Thomas had first witnessed the besieging of a city, cannon had been added to the great weapons of destruction available to an attacking army. The English had shipped their own gun stones with them from Southampton, not knowing if such ammunition would be available locally, and now the trebuchets and cannon began their ferocious work, hurling rocks into the stone walls and over into the buildings beyond. The destruction was intense and unrelenting, except in the dark of night while the English rested and the French busied themselves with repair work. Each time the wall was breached, an advance party was sent in to make good the entry point, but each time, after a fierce defence, the invaders were pushed back. Sir Thomas joined in several such raids, fighting toe to toe with the French men-at-arms, wounding and killing several, and stories of his courage became legendary among the English troops. The bitter truth was though, that he had lost the speed and dexterity that had kept him alive in combat so many times in the past and it was only the younger men fighting alongside him and ensuring that he was not overwhelmed, that kept the old warrior from ending his days on the broken walls of a French city. Eventually, Sir Thomas was persuaded by Rufus, and by the other commanders, that discretion should be the better part of valour, and he reluctantly agreed to retire to the hill-top in the role of observer.

It was well into the second week of the siege that sickness had begun to undermine the strength and morale of the attacking force. Rufus had been attending his master Sir Thomas, who was pouring over hastily sketched maps of the local terrain with King Henry and the other commanders, when he was seized with a terrible cramp in his guts and had to rush outside to defecate into a nearby ditch. He tried to finish his bowel movement but found that the spasms continued to double him up in agony long after his body was emptied. He looked down and saw that he had expelled a sickly sludge of almost liquid faeces mixed with blood and mucus which gave off a foul reek, and try as he might, he could not hold his sphincter muscles from continuing to spasm. Many other men were showing the debilitating symptoms and soon the bulk of the army was afflicted by an epidemic of the bloody flux, dreaded decimator of armies fighting away from their home territory. It was widely agreed that local foodstuffs were at fault, particularly the mussels and oysters harvested by the men from local waters, but none of the dietary changes recommended by the army's physicians seemed to have any effect on the devastating march of the sickness through the English ranks.

Meanwhile, Welsh miners had been digging deep, undermining the French defensive walls, and the defenders had countered by digging tunnels of their own to intercept and deter the attempt. When the opposing mining teams met there were vicious underground skirmishes and the knights on both sides began to get involved, chivalric honour being highly prized by emerging victorious from an underground confrontation with a noble enemy. With each passing day, and every hurled gun-stone and breach in the walls, so the city weakened. Occasionally, successful defensive sorties when a number of Englishmen were killed or captured served to prop up morale for a short time, but day by day the spirit of the people within the walls began to break. Henry threatened the harshest treatment of the citizens of the town for having thwarted him for so long, citing Biblical justification for slaughtering them all, but this probably just deferred the day of their surrender for a little longer.

Eventually, the civilian population of the city could take no more and, against the wishes of their commanders Jean d'Estouteville and Raoul de Gaucourt and his remaining men-at-arms, they sued for surrender. Henry sent in Sir Thomas Erpingham, along with two other ambassadors, to discuss and agree terms. The deal that Sir Thomas brokered was very much in line with the chivalrous nature of the battle so far; a cease-fire would be in effect for two days giving the city opportunity to fetch help from whatever source they could, after which, if no relieving army came, Henry would take possession of the city. Sir Thomas had been instructed to offer such seemingly generous terms by King Henry, who was desperate to engage with, and hopefully destroy, the elusive army of the French King, before the strength of his own forces was further decimated by the bloody flux.

No assistance for the beleaguered townsfolk was forthcoming, and on the morning of the third day Henry set himself up on the brow of the hill in full regal splendour, and bade the leaders of the town's defence come to him in humiliation. Having threatened dire consequences for holding out so long, the King then demonstrated considerable restraint and leniency, and in the main treated the inhabitants of Harfleur well; having half a mind perhaps towards the future loyalty of those who he now considered his subjects. A Herculean effort commenced to rebuild all that which had been destroyed and Sir Thomas and the noblemen in his retinue were tasked with much of the organisation and cajoling of the civilian population to begin the work. It seemed likely that Sir

Thomas's immediate future would be to help garrison the town and it was generally assumed that, with the campaigning season now over until the spring, Henry would leave a significant force of men to defend his new possession and return to England by sea, taking those who were afflicted with the bloody flux with him to recuperate with the healthier foodstuffs to be found in England. It therefore came as a surprise and a source of great consternation to his captains, when Henry announced that he would lead his army by road to Calais in a show of strength to the population and of defiance and challenge to the French King. Sir Thomas was just one of many who counselled against such a plan, given the sickness raging among the troops and the likelihood of having to engage with a much stronger force somewhere on route, under timing and circumstances that could be chosen by the enemy, but Henry was set firm on his course, convinced that divine right would see the English through to victory against all odds. Sir Thomas was enraged by the decision, confiding in his servant Rufus Long that he felt his life had been spent as witness to the folly of kings and that he had no intention of ending it in miserable defeat on some field in France. However, in the days that followed, he seemed to regret having spoken out for the safer option and, finding from somewhere within him a trace of the wildness of his youth, successfully sought the King's permission to join the march.

As the month of October passed so the army gathered, a thousand men-at-arms and several thousand archers, plus innumerable civilians. There were horses enough for everyone, and more besides; the sick men who would return to England by sea were to leave their mounts behind and many good horses had been taken with the surrender of the city. It was important anyway that the majority should be mounted; King Henry had set eight days as his target for reaching Calais, a perfectly reasonable objective for mounted troops, and he had given orders that each man would carry provisions for no more than that duration. Almost everyone rode, and took a spare mount on a lead-rein, the extra horse was booty in its own right and would also be eventually used to transport loot home from France to supplement the wages each soldier was contracted to receive.

Rufus Long had not been able to find relief from the crippling symptoms of the bloody flux, and as the army set forth along the road westward, Sir Thomas also began to suffer. The sickness was no respecter of nobility, and many lords, and bishops too were to be incapacitated, or even meet their death on the march, along with the common soldiery. Like many who suffered, Rufus soon gave up trying to stop the painful spasms from forcing a hot trickle of blood-streaked excrement from his anus. He adopted a solution from the more experienced troopers, cutting the seat from his breeches so that the watery stool could run freely down the inside of his thighs and down the horse's flanks as he rode. Rain came down incessantly from leaden skies as all along the column trudged steaming, sweating horses; stinking human faeces and blood mingling with the white foam of their own sweat under the straps and harnesses of the burdens they carried.

The army was soon stretched out for several miles along the coastal road, the ocean to their left and, somewhere to their right or even straight ahead, a great army of Frenchmen. They were occasionally harried by the enemy and several Englishmen were to fall from their horses, a look of surprise on their faces as a cross-bow bolt impaled them. Each time a halt was called, the sick men would dash to the nearest stream or pond to drink water, and fill their containers, the dehydrating effect of the bloody flux being one of the worst of the symptoms of that disease. Men would lay prostrate at the river's edge, slurping all the water their sorry stomach's would hold, while just a few yards upstream, others rinsed out soiled breeches and washed down their horses' flanks, or sat in the shallows, bathing the raw sores and boils where the filthy sludge from within them had rubbed between the skin of their bare buttocks and the sweaty hide of their horses' backs.

For five days the English army made good progress, Henry choosing to ignore and circumvent fortified towns along the route, such as Dieppe. Now only the crossing of the River Somme lay before the Englishmen and Calais, and the men, weakened by disease and growing short of provisions, began to feel their hopes rise once more; confident that they would soon be at rest on safe English soil. At Henry's planned crossing point though, they found a strong force in opposition; the bridge destroyed and all fording points barricaded. Reluctantly,

Henry turned south but by now his path was being shadowed on the opposite riverbank by a much larger force of men. Each potential crossing point was strongly defended and, after several days, Henry advised his commanders that they may have to continue south all the way to the river's source before gaining the eastern bank and heading north once more.

By pure chance, a great bend in the river gave the English army an opportunity to put distance between themselves and their pursuers and at a small village fording point, no more than three horses wide, they began to stream across to form a bridgehead. Soon the bulk of Henry's force was across and once again the men started to think of achieving safety. Then they came to a crossroad and saw the churned up ground where a vast army had gone before them and they knew for certain that they would have to fight their way to Calais after all.

Sir Thomas seemed to be able to cope with the sickness better than most. He drank copiously like all the other sick men, but only wine or weak beer, saying the local water disagreed with him. He stuck strictly to this dubious regimen, even though Rufus bought him fresh water from the streams and ponds whenever they made camp, and gradually, the old warrior's health improved and he began to regain some of the weight he had recently shed. While the bloody flux seemed unable to best him, the damp autumn weather made his back ache miserably, causing him to be unable to fully straighten up and sending shooting pains down the front of both legs and sparking a tingling sensation in his feet. Almost all the

Englishmen's clothing had become sodden and filthy by this time, but Sir Thomas had one item of warm and comfortable apparel remaining which Rufus ensured was cleaned and dried for his master each night, and that was a good grey woollen cloak, which the old man declared he would die, rather than part company with.

Scouting parties were sent out to assess the disposition of the French forces and soon word came back that a great host had gathered into battle formation across their intended route. There seemed to be no path by which the English could skirt this position and so, one by one, each Englishman came to the understanding that he would have to fight for his life, either today or the next. Darkness came quickly and so the confrontation was delayed until the morning, but the French were in no hurry knowing full well that their vastly superior numbers would be decisive the following day. They posted sentries all around the English positions and settled in to await the dawn. Henry had his army drawn up into battle formation and issued strict orders that they should remain in position overnight, maintaining silence so that any sneak attack would be forewarned, before taking lodgings for himself and several of his commanders in a local farmhouse. Rufus had found an old barn attached to the back of the farmhouse building and quickly commandeered it for his master Sir Thomas and the noblemen of his retinue, Sir Walter Goldingham and Hamo Strange who had also been knighted in the field by Henry for conspicuous bravery before the walls of Harfleur. He made up a good fire and they were comfortable enough, certainly more so than the bulk of the Englishmen, cold and wet out upon the field under a downpour of torrential rain. They saw nothing of the King overnight but were summoned before dawn to a final conference before battle would commence. Orders were given by the King and reiterated to ensure full understanding, and then Mass was said and each man prayed that he would conduct himself well and die, if he must, with honour. As the first streaks of light began to lessen the darkness, they walked out among the English positions and prepared for battle.

If you were to believe the stories subsequently told in the taverns around Norwich, you might well think that Sir Thomas Erpingham commanded all the English archers in the battle that followed. Rufus Long always maintained that was only partly true, and that it would have been physically impossible for him to have done so; the archers were drawn up in two main formations on either side of Henry's force of men-at-arms, with further smaller troops interspersed at intervals along the English line, and he had followed as Sir Thomas strode forward to the head of the English ranks and then turned left to join with the archers assembled at that side of the field. He spoke with them at length, and Rufus Long was close enough to hear the exchange, but the archers to the right of the English formation were half a mile away and would not have been able to hear him or follow his orders, so must have been under some other command; at least that was the way Rufus saw things at the time. Rufus had been instructed to stay at the rear with the baggage wagons because of his ongoing illness, but he disobeyed his master's command from the start, staying close behind Sir Thomas throughout the day with his dagger drawn, watching his master's back to ensure the old warrior was not undone by a sneak attack by any Frenchman from behind.

As the dawn light began to lift the veil of night, Rufus could see that the English were arrayed across a narrow field, no more than half a mile wide, with woodland to either side. He noticed that the ground at the centre seemed to have drained off rainwater from the slightly higher ground of the woodland on either side, and from the incline where the English were arrayed. Standing water lay in puddles upon a heavy clay top-soil and he knew that the ground beneath would be treacherous. In his mind he was back on the beach at Calais, Captain Hooper bellowing as men were sucked down into the ground beneath their feet. He saw Sir Thomas standing before the archers' position with his back to the enemy, sharpened defensive stakes already embedded in the ground before the men. Sir Thomas spoke calmly and reassuringly in a voice that seemed quiet, but yet carried to each and every man among them.

'I will not try to teach you your business today. You know the fix we are in and you know your job here; do it well and we may all go home. I know I desire nothing more than that. Have courage within your hearts and trust in God's will to see us through. I will give you one instruction only. Stay on solid ground if you can. The killing ground today will be in the centre. Let the Frenchmen wade through mud to their death.'

With that he turned to face the enemy, now clearly visible in the early morning light. Rufus estimated that the Englishmen were outnumbered by three or four to one, but it was very hard to tell. The French ranks were arrayed across the same half mile stretch of ground between the woodland on either flank, but seemed to entirely fill the space between their men-at-arms in the front rank and the horizon, several hundred yards distant. It seemed that their reinforcements may stretch away to infinity.

Now a game of waiting commenced, neither side wishing to advance first, but King Henry knew that further delay would only weaken the resolve of his men; tired, sick and hungry as most of them were, as well as mortally afraid. After several hours of this stand-off, word finally came down the line to 'up sticks' and advance. Erpingham's archers wrested their stakes from the ground where they had already expended much time and energy embedding them, and moved forward, advancing several hundred yards under the lee of the woodland to their left, then set to again to embed their wooden stakes in a defensive phalanx. The archers on the right-hand side of the field followed suite and the men-at-arms in the centre also began to move forward. This was the signal the French had been waiting for and now their men-at-arms began to advance, heavily armoured knights lumbering into the mud of the field, pressed hard from behind by those in the second rank, who wanted their own chance at glory.

With the enemy finally within long arrow range, Sir Thomas enacted his orders, throwing his baton high into the air with the shout 'Now strike!' and the archers under his direct command loosed a volley which immediately darkened the sky; so many arrows were in flight together. Rufus would never forget the great roar of noise, like the shrieking of a storm wind as the bow strings let loose, and the bodkin-headed arrows flew. By prior command the archers to the right-hand flank waited five heartbeats before launching their own volley and each flank continued to fire alternately, causing the Frenchmen who turned their faces away from the onslaught to find a fresh rain of death coming down upon them from the skies. Those archers positioned within the ranks of the English men-at-arms in the centre held their fire; their role would be to kill men at shorter range as the forward lines closed.

Many of the first arrows bounced harmlessly off armour plate, but some speared horses which reared and panicked at the sudden pain and, careering about, caused chaos in the rear ranks of the French. Now more and more of the enemy's men-at-arms were trying to get forward, unaware that those in the first few ranks were struggling to get through the sodden ground in their heavy equipment. As the two armies closed, the first of the French men-at-arms stumbled and fell forward into the mud. Those immediately behind attempted to form a barrier to allow him to rise but the pressure from behind was too great and further men went down in the melee and were trampled underfoot. With the closer range the bodkin-tipped arrows began to penetrate armour, killing men who fell into the quagmire, dragging others down with them. Still more French knights pushed forward from the rear lines, desperate to take their share of the honours, not knowing that their advance only made the crush worse. Now the archers in the centre of the English lines added their fire-power to the rain of death and then the front ranks of men-at-arms closed with each other and the English were pushed back several yards by sheer weight of numbers alone. Arrows thumped into the Frenchmen from either flank, the closer range now enabling the bodkin-heads to pierce all but the thickest armour plate. Still more of the enemy came and now the numbers of French men-at-arms crowding the field became their own worst enemy. There was no room to move, no space to swing an axe or sword and still they came, forcing men forward to be impaled on English blades, or to be crushed and drowned in the mud, then trampled underfoot.

The English archers' quivers were emptying fast and now the men began to dart forward from their line of defensive stakes, using the bodies of the enemy dead as stepping-stones to keep them out of the quagmire. In twos and threes they sought out lone French men-at-arms who were floundering about in the mud, then smashed them to the ground with their leaden mallets before forcing their victim's steel helmet down into the mud to drown the occupant. As other French knights came to their countryman's rescue, so the archers would dart nimbly back between their defensive stakes while their comrades impaled the would-be rescuers with their remaining arrows.

Rufus stayed close to Sir Thomas as, with the archers' work done, he moved towards the centre of the English line to take his place in battle alongside the King. Henry was not hard to find; a great wall of dead French men-at-arms formed a breakwater between the English King and his attackers; the entire chivalry of France having been focussed on killing or capturing Henry above all other objectives. Sir Thomas fought with the courage and strength of a man half his age, but several times it was the blade of his servant's dagger that stopped him from being overwhelmed. Rufus was aware of a great rushing noise in his ears and a terrible raging thirst. He kept hearing fragments of seemingly contradictory orders and shouted intelligence, sometimes English voices, sometimes French; 'They are through our lines and behind us!', 'Kill all prisoners, without regard to rank!', 'To me Englishmen, to me!', 'Run for Calais, we are done!' all mixed up with the screams of the injured and dying and the hot stink of blood and excrement and the filth of the mud clinging to everything and the cold and dampness everywhere.

Sir Thomas was smashed to his knees by a blow from a war-hammer on his body armour which drove all the breath from his lungs and Rufus leapt in front of him and grappled with an enemy warrior who was trying without success to extricate his weapon from between the corpses of two fellow countrymen where it had become firmly stuck, grasping at the knight's helmet with his left hand until he found the eye slits and then pushing his dagger through into the man's face and twisting the blade until his struggling and screaming ceased. Now Rufus became aware that there was space around him for the first time. Dead men lay everywhere and here and there groups of English soldiers were finishing off prostrate French men-at-arms who had lost their battle with the cloying mud of the field. He caught sight of King Henry surrounded by his own knights, talking in earnest with a number of French heralds who, alongside their English counterparts, had kept watch on the battle from the periphery in order to be able to report an outcome at the end of the day that could not be challenged by either set of protagonists.

Sir Thomas was breathing hard through bloodied nose and mouth, staring into the distance with eyes that had witnessed more than enough horrific wounds and agonised deaths for one lifetime. Rufus held his master's hand as if they had been two children, but could do nothing to ease the great racking sobs which burst forth from the old man's lungs; tears of exhaustion and emotional distress running down his face as he cried for all that he had seen, and all that he had done upon the field of battle that day.

***

Sir Thomas Erpingham had been alerted to the presence of a hooded beggar, living rough in the fields and lanes around the village, by his servants at the manor house. One afternoon he was walking in the field below the church when he came upon Jacob, sitting on a fallen log, drinking a mug of water he had lifted from the stream. Sir Thomas bid the stranger good day and Jacob pulled back his hood and turned to face him. If Sir Thomas had been taken aback by Jacob's disfigurement, he did not show it; he had seen enough of the effects of disease, and the scars left by battle-wounds, to be immune to such things. Deep within him though, there was a sense of recognition that he could not immediately place. 'Have we met, stranger? Do I know you?' asked the lord of the manor.

'My Lord, our paths have been entwined for many years, though I doubt you would ever have been aware of it. My name is Jacob and I was once a leper, but the sickness left me many years ago so you need not fear infection.' Jacob took from the folds of his cloak a purse containing his remaining coins, his mug and tin spoon and his knife, and laid them on the ground at Sir Thomas's feet. 'These are all my possessions. I carry no weapon. It is important you know that, when I tell you that for many years I had been tasked with killing you.'

Sir Thomas looked puzzled; quizzical but not afraid. He had been in too many fights to be frightened of this strange man. Then a recollection from his earliest memory surfaced, and he smiled. 'You? They tell me the story so often, but in reality I cannot remember it myself. Did I really stab you in the leg?'

Now Jacob smiled and felt the old scar behind his knee throb at the memory. 'I have limped ever since.'

Both men sat on the fallen log and Sir Thomas asked Jacob to tell him everything, from even before their encounter on the road south to Norwich with the harvest so many years ago. So Jacob told the story of his life, including all the evil things he had done, and more recently the good things too. He told of the attempt to murder Lady Erpingham in revenge for a beating sustained many years previously, and the subsequent death of the monk Anselmo at Jacob's own hand. Sir Thomas asked just one question, 'What caused you in the end to save one life, by taking another?'

'It was the birds.' replied Jacob.

'The birds?' asked Sir Thomas. So Jacob told him of the dream he had experienced throughout his life of the birds without feet which could never rest, had to fly the whole of their lives, and how finally, as he had watched his master Anselmo ascend the stairway to enact his murderous revenge, Jacob had seen the Erpingham coat of arms on the wall above the fireplace, a white shield surrounded by eight Martlet birds in ceaseless flight, and had known at last his destiny.

***

CHAPTER 15

(In which Sir Thomas Erpingham builds his legacy in Norwich, and lives out his life in peace and prosperity)

I have been known by many names; Jacob Smith, Jacob the Leper, Jacob the Thief, even Jack Honey to the people of this village, but I would wish to be remembered as Jacob of Erpingham and that is how I will sign the last page of my manuscript when it is finally completed.

Do you imagine that my deformities would have made the success of my role as tavern-keeper unlikely? Believe me, there is ugliness aplenty in this world, and few reach adulthood without the marks of pox upon them, or the scars of war, or the healed over abscesses of pestilence survived. People around here have become used to me I suppose and, other than the children who continue to torment me mercilessly, I am as accepted as anyone else who had not actually been born in the village.

What is there left to tell of the life of Sir Thomas Erpingham? You can expect nothing more of war, or travels to foreign lands. This is now a story of quiet living, of the building of a great city and of one man's legacy to the future. First though, it is a story of slow recovery from great trauma.

I will tell it as best I am able, and then I believe I am done.

***

Sir Thomas Erpingham was spared any involvement in the clean-up operation after the battle of Agincourt. Along with many others, injured and sick, he was invalided back to Calais and stayed there in recuperation for several months. He had the ongoing symptoms of the bloody flux together with a back injury that had him doubled up in pain at the slightest movement, and his mind seemed clouded with a great fog; staring into the distance for extended periods, ignoring attempts at conversation and awakening suddenly in the night, screaming in fear. His servant Rufus Long accompanied him of course, though his physical condition was, if anything, even worse. The two men had survived Harfleur, the great march and then Agincourt together, though at significant cost to their physical, mental and emotional wellbeing.

Nevertheless, both men wished to be seen to be made of sturdy stuff and by the early spring of the following year, Sir Thomas was back in his various offices for King Henry, working long hours to try to capitalise diplomatically on the military successes of the previous autumn. Rufus Long watched over him carefully, trying and usually failing to ensure that his master took adequate rest, and ate well. Henry's victory on the field of battle had given him a sense of invincibility and he felt that his confirmation as rightful regent of France should now be no more than a formality. It was older, wiser men such as Sir Thomas who had to counsel caution and patience; the utter defeat of the French at Agincourt had left Henry's enemies militarily weak, but no better enamoured of the prospect of serving him as their king.

One of the key players in the game of diplomacy would be the Duke of Burgundy, and Sir Thomas was given the delicate task of arranging a meeting with the French nobleman, and drafting a treaty which would bring him onside with the plans of the English King. It was Sir Thomas, along with the Earl of Warwick, who rode out to meet with the Duke and his party, welcomed them to Calais, and plied them with good food and drink, and lavish entertainment while the negotiations went on.

This role as ambassador seemed the one to which the nearly sixty-year-old knight was best suited, and Henry was to use Sir Thomas as his chief representative with foreign dignitaries several more times during the next few years, notably when the Emperor Sigismund, ruler of the Germanic states came to visit England, got along famously well with King Henry, and returned to his own kingdom as a Knight of the Garter. People became used to seeing Sir Thomas as chief representative of the King at state occasions; his former role of Steward of the Royal Household had been reconfirmed upon him after Agincourt, and they knew that his opinions and pronouncements could confidently be taken as those of the

King. Sir Thomas was sent to oversee the trial of Henry's old friend, turned traitor, the Lollard John Oldcastle and lobbied unsuccessfully against the verdict that Oldcastle should be hanged and burnt while still living. Sir Thomas felt that his days as king's executioner were long behind him now.

Though Henry remained pleased with Sir Thomas's diplomatic and administrative skills, and liked him very much, he became worried about the old knight's state of mind. The long periods of staring off into space and seemingly ignoring those around him had begun to return, and it was common knowledge that Sir Thomas's sleep was invariably disturbed by waking suddenly, drenched in sweat, screaming aloud and scrabbling to fight off some unseen foe. Henry called the old man to his chamber one afternoon, about two years after the battle which had seemingly damaged Sir Thomas's mind.

'Come, Thomas, my dearest old friend. Tell me what ails you. You have not been your old self since God gave us our great victory.'

Sir Thomas stared out the window at the courtyard below, seemingly lost in thought. Henry wondered for a moment if this was another of the old knight's turns and he was about to shake Sir Thomas gently by the shoulder when he seemed to snap back into the present, from wherever he had been.

'I think I have just seen too much of the death of men, Sire. I feel tired in my mind. I see blood flowing when I close my eyes to rest. I hear the screaming of men that I have killed. I wish nothing more than to serve you, but I fear I am no longer the man I was.'

Tears were in Sir Thomas's eyes and the hero of Agincourt, of Harfleur and of many earlier battles, the winner of countless brave and chivalrous encounters at the lists, found himself weeping openly in front of his liege.

Henry took Sir Thomas in his arms and held the old man tight against his breast.

'Then you shall rest Sir Thomas Erpingham. You shall rest.'

In that way, Sir Thomas found himself once more walking in the fields and lanes around the village of Erpingham. He avoided even the city of Norwich for a while, as the slow, bucolic pace of his home life began to repair his damaged spirit. Rufus was there, as reliable and faithful as ever, as he too took the time to heal himself, although he only carried the burden of physical distress; his mind had remained sound throughout. Sir Thomas indulged his wife's every whim, even suffering, with a resigned shrug, the constant visitations of the ladies of Norfolk to assist Lady Joan with some latest scheme of decoration or fashion, and seemed to enjoy being caught up in the gossiping and tittle-tattle of rural nobility. He spent his days in the fields and the woods around the village, and also walking upon the beach up at the coast at Sheringham village, liking the repetitive sound of the waves crashing down on the shore and sucking sand and pebbles back down into the ocean. He enjoyed the sound of the sea, but had no desire to travel upon it ever again. In the evenings, Sir Thomas often eschewed the formality of taking dinner at the great table in the hall of the manor house with Lady Joan and her guests, preferring to sit quietly with a jug of mead in the tavern run by old Jack Honey, sharing stories of his youth, exaggerating and embellishing his tales along with everyone else.

So the years passed and Sir Thomas became well again in body and in spirit. King Henry missed his wise old counsellor and even arranged ships to fetch Sir Thomas and his retinue to join him in France, but the old man begged leave to remain in permanent retirement from duties of state, and the King reluctantly agreed. One by one, Sir Thomas's titles and offices of state were handed on to younger men, and before long he was able to concentrate the energy that remained to him on matters affecting his home county of Norfolk, and the great city of Norwich.

Whilst Sir Thomas no longer held the lucrative positions of state with their vast incomes that had once been his, he continued to receive the largesse that King Henry lavished on those who had stood beside him in his darkest hours. Money flowed into the Erpingham coffers in seemingly limitless amounts. At one stage Sir Thomas was receiving the income from over thirty manors in the county of Norfolk alone, and it began to become difficult to know exactly what to do with the surfeit of wealth which he found growing in ever greater numbers in the account lists prepared by his banking houses.

When Sir Thomas had departed for France and the campaign that ended on the field of Agincourt, he had left the city of Norwich in a terrible state, the effects of the fire evident everywhere. His friend William Appleyard and others had done much in his absence to repair the damage, but there was a great deal still left to do. So began a long programme of rebuilding, financed predominately by Sir Thomas and a number of other local veterans of the Agincourt campaign.

Many civic and religious houses, including the great church of the Black Friars, which had been under reconstruction at the time of the fire, were raised again from the rubble. Sir Thomas had become a modest man in his behaviour as old age caught up with him, but that did not mean he shied away from self-commemoration in the buildings that he financed. Like all other wealthy and powerful men, he wanted to be remembered once he was gone, and therefore almost every building that he commissioned or financed included somewhere on display within its masonry the Erpingham arms, or his name, or his adopted motto 'Yenk' which nobody else ever understood, and which he had never forgotten since the day that he had fought alongside a troop of archers in Aquitaine as a boy.

The greatest sorrow in Sir Thomas Erpingham's life was that he had been unable to sire children via either of his wives, and so he used a fraction of his vast wealth to commission a beautiful stained glass window in the Austin Friars' priory, just south of the Norwich Cathedral in Tombland. The piece commemorated all those noblemen who had died without having known the joy of fatherhood.

One of the finest buildings that Sir Thomas commissioned

was the great gate that would eventually be known by his name, at the entrance to the Cathedral grounds at the northern end of Tombland. The archway was exquisitely designed, erected and decorated by master stonemason craftsmen, to Sir Thomas's exact specification and was the match even of the beautiful St. Ethelbert's gate at the southern end, which had been built at the expense of the citizenry many years before, as penitence for rioting against the King.

At about this time a pernicious rumour began to circulate in the taverns of the city, that Sir Thomas had been cuckolded while he was away in France by a priest of the Cathedral, had subsequently returned and killed the offending cleric and that the building of the gate was in recompense to the Church for his murderous actions. While Sir Thomas never mentioned the story himself, Rufus Long was quick to denounce it for falsehood, maintaining that people had simply heard the tales from long ago when Sir Thomas and his father Sir John had beaten a monk for attempting to rob them, and turned that old local legend into current gossip.

While the years passed and many of his great building projects came to fruition, Sir Thomas found himself increasingly sought after as a wise old counsellor and peace-maker, being asked to act as judge or mediator in disputes between the nobility of the county. As such he mediated in a long and acrimonious feud between Sir John Howard and Sir Thomas Kerdeston, which at one point had seemed likely to break out into open warfare, and fell out with both the lawyer

William Paston and Bishop Aslake while attempting to find common ground between them both, in a property dispute.

He received the news of the early death of King Henry with great sadness, the bloody flux that Henry had so successfully avoided on his Agincourt campaign finally catching up with him at home, despite the healthful properties of a good English diet. With another Henry now on the throne, a third Lancastrian King, Sir Thomas reflected on the strange chances of life that had seen him survive through the reign of five English monarchs.

Sir Thomas's projects became ever more ambitious as the years progressed. He received a commission to build a ferry or bridge over the River Waveney at St. Olaves on behalf of the King, linking that part of the counties of Norfolk and Suffolk. He expended a small fortune on having scale models of the enterprise built on the table in the great hall, and on artist's impressions of the desired result, but when the day came to travel south to meet with building contractors, he declared that he had taken a chill and did not wish to venture out. Over time the project, like many another, was quietly abandoned.

Sir Thomas's second wife passed away one winter morning, as yet another bout of plague ripped through the population of the village. He seemed to adapt to his second round of widowhood without too much outward expression of grief, and had a stained glass window commissioned for the north aisle of Norwich Cathedral, showing himself kneeling in prayer alongside his coat of arms and military regalia, with both his wives kneeling side by side, looking on from an adjacent panel. The craftsman who designed the piece had the faces of each wife copied from contemporary painted images, but Sir Thomas had them altered before the final version went into production, making each facial image almost identical, so that none could ever say that the beauty of one Joan was greater than the other.

It seemed to Rufus Long in those final years that Sir Thomas spent most of his energies planning for his own death; making complex arrangements within his will regarding the future distribution of his lands and properties among family members, though alas not among direct descendants. Within his instructions were many and various gifts to monasteries, convents and other religious houses and to the poor and destitute of the county. He even paid a considerable fortune to have daily mass sung for himself and his wives in the Cathedral, every day for eternity. His own tomb was designed and built for him in the Cathedral, close by the window glass he had previously installed, its vault already occupied by the mortal remains of both his wives. A kneeling statue of Sir Thomas was commissioned to adorn the tomb and he spent many hours with the stonemasons looking at trial versions, discarding any that he thought made him look too fat, too old, not pious enough. The final version which Sir Thomas felt able to sign off for production had the wise face and long white hair and beard of the elder statesman he had become, and the slender, athletic body of his younger self, when he had been one of the greatest warriors in the land.

Sir Thomas took to walking in the fields around Erpingham village in preference to all other activity, and increasingly he returned to the manor house late at night, or knocked up old Jack Honey for a cup of mead after the midnight hour had passed. Rufus found him one day wandering about in the fields of the Felbrigg estate, north of his own lands. Sir Thomas seemed a little dishevelled and confused, saying that he was on important business for the King and should not be disturbed.

One glorious June day he had been walking along the lane between the village and Jack Honey's tavern when he felt that he might sit down to rest awhile against the bole of an old Oak tree. He watched a pair of Skylarks ascending toward heaven, chirping their joyous song of summer, and thought then that he might close his eyes and sleep for a while. One of the village children found him there several hours later, a little slumped forward but looking comfortable and at peace. The boy poked the old man with a stick to see if he was only sleeping, and then ran like the wind to raise the alarm.

***

The afternoon grows late and now I will hide my papers away for safekeeping while I see to the welfare of my bees, before darkness descends upon the land once more.

***

EPILOGUE

Danny Walker had been 'temping' with a demolition firm for the summer, saving as much money as he could to enable him to spend several months on another archaeological dig with the university team the following year. He had passed his BA Degree in Archaeology two years previously, but had found that paying jobs in his chosen field were few and far between.

The firm had been contracted to demolish, and clear the rubble from, the sites of several pubs in Norwich and the surrounding towns and villages. The pub trade was evidently finished; at least it was in the remote locations outside of the city and town centres, which were still able to draw the weekend and summer evening crowds with heavily discounted drinks, and large outside smoking areas. The only pubs that were flourishing out in the countryside were those which had successfully become 'Gastro' pubs, paying more attention to the food they served than the beer they sold.

Danny was travelling as passenger in the van with Grant Hobbs, the foreman. They were heading for an establishment that had failed to make that transition from alehouse to restaurant successfully; The Beehive, a large Victorian brick monstrosity, on a minor road near the village of Erpingham, which saw very little passing traffic and had, even in its heyday, rarely attracted a full house of customers. It was still only just daylight when they pulled onto the site and saw that the mechanical diggers, shovel tractors and wrecking ball machine were already manned and waiting for the start.

Danny had been detailed to clear away the debris that the big hydraulic shovels and grabs missed, working with a yard-broom, hand shovel and wheelbarrow, and had already made countless trips to the skips by the time the front facade, roof, ground floor ceiling and first floor were down, leaving just the rear wall and the two side walls intact.

He had been on the lookout for finds, particularly when the old floorboards came up, and had pocketed a modest collection of copper and silver coins already, though all the items of real value in the property; the mahogany and brass bar fittings and frosted and stained glass windows and mirrors in particular, had long since been robbed out by the outgoing landlord, or by thieves while the building had lain derelict.

It was getting close to knocking off time for the day when Grant gave orders that the remaining walls should be demolished before they finished, enabling the heavy machinery to be diverted to another job for the following morning; the remaining rubble could then be cleared by hand first thing the next day. The wrecking ball did its work; Danny was mesmerised as always watching its swing and impact, guessing just how much of the structure would fall with each hit.

Finally, with all in ruin, Danny found himself with a few minutes to poke about behind the old wall while Grant conferred with the machine operators about their next contract.

Danny could see that the area behind the old rear wall had never been used for public access. There seemed to be an old storage shed or lean-to type structure which had abutted the brick wall, and he could see a few old rotten wooden crates and bar-stools among the accumulated rubbish of many years. Behind the lean-to was just a jungle of bramble, nettles and Ash saplings which looked completely impenetrable. Danny had developed a keen eye throughout his time working on undergraduate field projects and thought that the old outbuilding structure might even pre-date the pub itself by a couple of hundred years, or so. As he looked closer he thought that one or two parts of the old timber frame might just be even older; one wooden beam in particular looked so ancient that it had twisted itself into a gnarled, distorted shape, probably reminiscent of the living tree it had once been before it had been sawn and hewn into a regular shape fit for building purposes by some unknown journeyman carpenter in antiquity. A great chunk of ancient mortar had broken away along with the Victorian brickwork, revealing the points at which various timber joists had been spliced into one another over time. Between the oldest looking beam and a much newer, though still ancient joist of thick timber which had been inserted at an angle just above it, was now revealed a gap of several inches and Danny reached for the small Mag-Lite torch he always carried in his pocket and used it to peer into the hole.

At first, all he saw was an old bird's, or rat's nest, but looking more closely he observed that the nest had been constructed using pieces of some kind of cloth or paper-like material. Next he saw what looked like the fragmentary remains of some kind of leather item, a tubular container of some sort, each piece dried out and shrivelled but some still lying in situ, retaining the shape of the original item. Danny saw that the gap between the conjoined timbers had formed a miniature cave, several inches wide and about three feet deep; the timber and mortar materials which had accidentally formed this space had effectively kept out the rain and general moisture by using the shelter of, and taking the warmth from, the building they had been attached to, and this had ensured that whatever the item was, it had dried out over a long period of time, rather than rotted away in the damp.

Under the leather fragments, Danny could see what appeared to be layered sheets of some kind of material, which had been rolled up. He reached into the gap to touch the material and a piece of old parchment broke away in his fingers. His heart now pumping with excitement, Danny saw the faintest traces of writing and what appeared to be part of the image of an animal.

Grant had come to find him to say it was time to leave, and Danny explained what he had found, but Grant seemed unimpressed and said that whatever it was it would need to go in the skip first thing the next day. Danny said that he would stay behind to investigate further, and would make his own way home later that evening, but Grant replied that nobody was allowed to remain at the site after he had left, for health and safety and insurance reasons. Reluctantly, Danny accompanied his boss back to Norwich, but a few hours later was heading north again, this time alongside his university professor Max Higgins. They had brought along powerful torches and large flat sealable plastic containers to transfer the find into.

Neither of them would have ordinarily attempted to remove such a find from its original site in such a fashion, but felt they had little choice, given the fate awaiting the piece the following morning. Between them, they managed to remove all the remaining pieces of parchment and leather fragments including the nest, along with some broken pottery fragments and a curious piece of glass which they judged may once have been used for magnification. Much of the rolled document broke up into smaller pieces when moved, but they felt confident at least that with painstaking restoration, the bulk of the document and any legible text it still retained would be recoverable.

In the car on the way home, Danny remembered the first piece he had removed from the find and put in his pocket. He flicked on his little torch and looked at it again. The faint image was definitely that of an animal of some kind. It was inexpertly rendered, and Danny knew for certain that this was no fabulous illuminated manuscript from one of the great medieval Abbeys. The image appeared to be that of a bird in flight.

THE END

16220622R00167

Printed in Great Britain
by Amazon